Sweet

BY

NENE ADAMS

Bella
BOOKS

2015

Bella Books, Inc.
P.O. Box 10543
Tallahassee, FL 32302

First Bella Books Edition 2015

Editor: Ruth Stanley
Cover Designer: Judith Fellows
ISBN: 978-1-59493-470-4

Other Bella Books by Nene Adams

Barking at the Moon
The Midnight Sun

The Mackenzie Cross Series

The Consequence of Murder
Burn All Alike

Dedicated to my Bunny, who isn't chocolate covered,
but sweet as all get out.

Author's Note: "Fondant" used in this story refers to the creamy, soft, sweet, slightly thickened and flavored filling (poured fondant) found in many chocolate bonbons—not the thick sugar paste (rolled fondant) used in cake decorating.

Twill make old women young and fresh, Create new
motions of the flesh. And cause them long for you know
what, If they but taste of chocolate.

—*Don Diego de Vadesforte*

CHAPTER ONE

Ruby Fontaine nestled a dark and deliciously bitter Venezuelan chocolate ganache and pink salt truffle in each small white box, followed by a vanilla bean and stout burnt caramel bonbon. The lids went on next. Tying shocking pink ribbons into neat bows around a hundred boxes took longer. At last, she finished and stepped back from the workbench to admire her handiwork. *Another triumph for the Magic Bean in Summerland, Georgia.*

She enjoyed putting together pretty wedding favors for brides and this order was no exception. Each box held two confections—a small sample of the handmade artisanal chocolates helping cement her reputation as a skilled chocolatier. She packed up the boxes and checked her to-do list. Without a storefront, working out of a rented commercial kitchen meant taking online orders only, but one day, she'd own a real shop.

Time to get started on the goat's milk chocolate fudge.

Moving across the space, Ruby caught her reflection in the steel refrigerator door and paused to poke at her hair. The cotton candy pink had faded and grown out over the last few weeks to reveal dark blond roots. *Orange next time? Ugh, no.* The tint would do no favors for her pale blue eyes, which a former girlfriend had described as the color of anemic cornflowers during their breakup. *I'll stick with pink for now. Better touch up this weekend.* She also decided to change the tiny gold hoop nestled in the curve of her nostril to a silver stud.

She took what she needed from the refrigerator and busied herself at the stove until her cell phone rang. She fished the device from her apron pocket. "Thank you for calling the Magic Bean, how may I help you?"

"Ruby, thank God...It's me. Beatrice. Uh, you know. Bee Brooks."

"I know who you are, Bee."

"I've got a serious emergency on my hands!"

Ruby kept a close eye on the candy thermometer clipped to the side of the heavy saucepan holding the cooking fudge mixture. "What's wrong?" An unwelcome thought struck her. "Is Katie all right?"

"Yes and no." Beatrice sounded frazzled. "I mean yes, Kaitlyn's fine right now. In about two hours, though, my daughter and twenty other kindergartners will be psychologically scarred for life because it's her birthday and I was supposed to order cupcakes for the class and forgot. How the hell could I forget something so important?"

"Bee, calm down and—"

"You don't understand! Chloe Parkinson's mother had a specialty cake made at that fancy bakery—you know the one over on Twelfth Street and Main—and for a solid week, I swear, all Kaitlyn talked about was that damned unicorn carousel cake. So I promised her ballerina princess cupcakes with the frosting and the spun sugar that looks like your hair—"

"Bee, if you'd just let me—"

"Ballerina princesses aren't exactly in, but it was that or some cat farting rainbows, and I forgot, and I'm a very, very bad mother! The worst. Like, the Attila the Hun of mothers. What am I going to do? I screwed up Kaitlyn's birthday—"

"Will you please shut up for two seconds?" Ruby shouted into the phone. Silence fell, but Beatrice didn't hang up in a snit, thank goodness. "Hang on."

She checked the thermometer. *Gosh darn it! Too high.* After rescuing the fudge from outright scorching, she set the pot on a wire rack to cool before she could beat it to the right consistency. Maybe the texture wouldn't turn out grainy.

One crisis down, one to go. She tossed down the potholders, summoned her patience and said more gently, "You're not a bad mother, Bee. I'm sure you've been busy working on that newspaper story you told me about. Katie will forgive you. She's six years old."

She heard Beatrice draw a shaky breath. "Yeah. Okay, yeah, you're right. I panicked. But what am I going to do? Help me, Ruby-Wan, you're my only hope."

"Come over to the kitchen," Ruby said, chuckling. "I'm sure if you show up with anything sugar related, Katie and her friends won't miss the cupcakes."

"I'll be there in ten minutes." Beatrice ended the call.

Sighing, Ruby put her phone away and went to hunt for supplies in her inventory closet. By the time Beatrice swung through the back door, she'd already started assembling treats in individual clear cellophane gift bags set out on two trays.

"You're a godsend, honest." Beatrice grinned and tossed her purse on top of the counter. Her sleek brunette bob swung forward to brush her cheeks when she bent over to examine the bags. "I'd look like a real chump in front of the other moms, to say nothing of Katie's teacher, Mrs. Woods. Every time I drag myself to one of her joyless conferences, I swear the woman's judging me and finding me wanting."

Ruby pressed her lips together to keep from saying, *The situation isn't about you, it's about making Katie happy*, and continued selecting sweets.

Beatrice waved a hand. "Gluten free, I hope. Kids are delicate these days."

"No gluten, no nuts," Ruby replied. "They're getting a couple of goat's milk chocolate mini-bars. Real fruit gummy hearts. You're lucky I made brown rice cereal treats with raspberry marshmallow for a client this morning, so you can have those. I'll make more."

"Sounds yummy. Save one for me."

"You need to stop at the party supply store on your way to the school. Don't make that face, Bee. Buy some favors, like mini boxes of stickers, crayons or colored pencils and little coloring books—enough for each bag. Tie the tops closed with these white ribbons."

"No pink? Katie loves pink."

"White's the only color I've got on hand. And be sure you get Katie a tiara and a sparkly wand. Don't forget."

"Can't you do the shopping? I'm useless at that girly stuff." Beatrice snitched a passion fruit gummy heart. "Mmm, these aren't bad."

"Pay attention. *You* need to go to the party supply store. *I* don't have time." Ruby thought about the ruined pot of fudge that had put her behind schedule and held firm in the face of Beatrice's entreating puppy dog stare.

"Fine. Whatever." Beatrice finally gave in with bad grace. "Stickers, you said?"

"Age appropriate. Crayons and coloring books. Ask a store employee to help you." Ruby stuck an orange-pomegranate lollipop in each bag. "Hang on a second."

She went to a desk crammed in the corner and leaned over to peer at the computer monitor. A few taps on the keyboard brought up a large file. She quickly cut and pasted several blocks of information into a new document, turned on the printer and printed out a copy before returning to Beatrice.

"Here's an ingredients list," she said, handing the copy to her friend. "Give this to Mrs. Woods. She can make sure none of the students with dietary restrictions have allergies or intolerances to any candy in the goodie bags."

Beatrice rolled her eyes, but accepted the sheet of paper.

"Anything special planned for the birthday girl?" Ruby asked, smiling at the mental image of her honorary niece. She'd bought Kaitlyn a child friendly digital camera and planned to bring the present over to Beatrice's house after supper.

"I hadn't really…Would you take her tonight? I'm meeting my informant for an interview and I'll probably run late." Beatrice lowered her voice although they were alone. "I'd rather not miss taking Katie out for some fun, but I'm getting close, Ruby. Real close to something big. There's a lot more going on around here than anybody knows. Trust me. When I file my story, City Hall's going to bust wide open."

Ruby didn't approve, but protesting was futile when Beatrice had a story at stake. She focused on a more immediate concern. "Did you tell Katie you won't be home until late?"

Beatrice averted her gaze. "Would you mind taking her out to eat? Maybe that kids' place she likes with the arcade games and pizza?" she asked, evading the question.

"Sure, but you need to talk to your daughter. I mean what I say, Bee. Don't leave me holding the bag. Katie needs to hear from you why you won't be there."

"Aw, for fuck's sake, do I really have to be the bad guy?"

"You're the mommy, that's your job. Suck it up and deal." Ruby pointed at an empty glass jar on a corner of the workbench. A label on the jar read, *You say it, you pay it.* "You owe me a dollar for the F-bomb."

Beatrice heaved a put-upon sigh, dug in her purse for a wallet and shoved a folded bill through the slit in the metal lid. "Still with the swear jar? God—I mean, gosh darn it to heck." She raised her hands in the air. "Okay, whatever, fine. Party supply store. Buy stuff to amuse rug rats, put into gift bags, apply ribbons. I think I've got the gist. Thanks." She rose up on her toes to lean farther over the counter and brush her lips over Ruby's cheek.

"Here you go. Give Katie a kiss for me." Ruby passed over the cardboard box she'd packed the bags in. "Should I pick up Katie after school too?"

"I'll drop her off at your place. Three thirty work for you?"

"Sure."

Scooping the box under her arm, Beatrice grabbed her purse and hurried through the door, her car keys swinging from her hand.

Ruby threw out the ruined fudge and started working on a new batch. Once she finished, she made more crispy rice treats and whipped up several flavors of her bestselling gourmet marshmallows.

When she checked the website, she saw some out-of-state orders had come in for the Magic Bean's signature Three Little Pigs brittle: bourbon, pecans and morsels of fried pancetta, guanciale and applewood smoked bacon in caramelized sugar. She grinned. *Looks like a BLT for dinner.* She had neither bread, tomato nor lettuce here, but she'd save some of the cooked bacon—another local product, since she preferred buying from small, high-quality producers in the area whenever possible—and take it home tonight.

Of course, that wouldn't stop her from eating a few pieces after the bacon was cooked in the big iron skillet she'd inherited from her grandmother. Who could resist the smell of frying bacon? Cook's privilege, her father called it. Humming, she went to the refrigerator.

A little while later, she finished pouring out the brittle into pans to cool and started packing and sorting boxes for shipment tomorrow. While applying an address label to the final box, she glanced at her watch. Her stomach sank. Three o'clock already. Good grief! She snatched up her to-do list and ticked off items, double-checked shipping and delivery labels, and ensured she had everything organized for the following morning.

Satisfied at last, she locked up and left.

The rented kitchen wasn't far from her apartment building. Pre-rush hour traffic proved mercifully light, but an accident at an intersection had her snarled with other cars moving at a snail's pace for twenty minutes before she could continue at a normal speed.

Finally, she pulled her old Dodge truck into the tenants-only underground garage at her building only to find a lipstick-red, sporty MINI Cooper Coupe parked in her assigned space. A space she paid thirty dollars a month to reserve, no less.

Ruby gripped the steering wheel and stared in disbelief at the MINI. Some inconsiderate so-and-so had stolen her spot!

Hadn't they seen the Reserved sign? She gritted her teeth, despising bad manners almost as much as swearing.

Checking her watch, she realized she was appallingly late. Beatrice and Kaitlyn must be upstairs waiting for her. No time to make a complaint to the management office. No time to sit there and fume either. She banked her frustration and drove forward, intending to swing the truck around and try the visitors' parking lot next door.

A slender, professionally dressed woman came out of the stairwell at the back, catching her attention. Ruby's suspicion flared. She braked and waited to see where the stranger went. Her patience was rewarded when the woman crossed over to the MINI.

Aha!

Now intent on confronting the woman who'd stolen her spot, Ruby got out of her truck, her face flushing when opening the door caused a loud, grating squeal to reverberate off the concrete walls and ceiling. She'd meant to grease that hinge for weeks. Embarrassment added fuel to her annoyance. "Hey!" she called. "That's my parking space!"

The woman turned her head. Loose chestnut curls slithered over the shoulders of her navy blue suit jacket. She was attractive, but her cold gray gaze and sour expression muted some of her beauty. "Give me time to get into my car and I'll leave your precious spot," she said, her impatient tone suggesting she spoke to an idiot.

Ruby's cheeks heated further at the woman's disdain. Common sense urged her to return to her truck. Instead, she put her hands on her hips and stayed right where she stood. "You shouldn't take a space reserved for tenants. There's a visitors' lot next door."

"Really?" The woman jerked open the MINI's door. She paused, her lips drawn up in a snarl. "Just look at all the fucks I don't give." She slid into the driver's seat, slammed the door shut and rolled down the window. "By the way, Miss Manners, you can take your little lecture and shove it," she ranted before starting the MINI's engine.

The car backed up and suddenly peeled out of the garage, leaving behind smoke, skid marks and the reek of scorched rubber.

Ruby waved a hand in front of her face, wrinkling her nose at the stink and the woman's rudeness. The gesture brought her watch in sight. Her stomach dropped. She pushed the confrontation to the back of her mind, scrambled to park her truck and hurried to the elevator on the other side of the garage.

Getting off on the third floor, she stumbled to a halt in the empty corridor. *Where are Bee and Katie?* She walked to her apartment, somewhat relieved. Beatrice must be running late too, in which case her own tardiness would go unnoticed. She went inside to wait.

Another half hour passed with no word from her friend. She began to fret in earnest. When Beatrice continued to ignore her calls, the concern turned to worry.

At four fifteen, the school called to let her know no one had collected Kaitlyn yet. Ruby's worry became full-blown panic.

CHAPTER TWO

Ruby entered the living room feeling like she'd aged five years in the last hour. She flopped down on the sofa, which was covered by a soft, faded crazy quilt her late grandmother had given her. Sitting on the quilt and wrapping the edges around her made her feel as if Meemaw were giving her a hug from heaven. Right now, she needed the comfort.

"When my ovarian alarm clock starts nagging me about having kids, I'm going to remember this day," she muttered, cupping a hand over her eyes and leaning her aching head against the cushion.

On the way from school, Kaitlyn's upset at her mother's unexpected absence had accelerated from mild tantrum to migraine-inducing hysteria. Even a favorite stuffed toy, Morton the Monster, hadn't quelled the storm. At the apartment building, she'd had to carry a squirming, kicking Kaitlyn from the car to the elevator and down the hall while deafened by shrill shrieks. Bribes of pizza, graham crackers, or the most forbidden treat of all—a can of sugary soft drink—were rejected with louder wails.

Finally, out of sheer exhaustion, the tear-stained little girl fell asleep in the bedroom.

Ruby dreaded a possible repeat performance. While not generally given to pitching fits, Kaitlyn's behavior was understandable under the circumstances. *Bee, where are you? Your baby needs you, woman, and so do I. Another couple of hours like that will send me around the bend.*

Her cell phone rang.

She sat up, her heart pounding. *Bee?* Shrugging off the quilt, she grabbed the phone from the wooden trunk that served as a coffee table and answered the call without so much as glancing at Caller ID. "Beatrice Augusta Brooks, where in the world have you been? Katie's cried herself sick and I'm on the verge of a nervous breakdown!"

After a beat of silence, an unfamiliar female voice asked, "Excuse me, am I speaking to Ms. Fontaine? Ms. Ruby Fontaine?"

Ruby blinked. "Yes," she replied hesitantly. "Who's calling?"

"Detective Frances Orsini with the Adult Missing Persons Unit. You called in a nine-one-one report about Beatrice Brooks. I'd like to get more information from you."

"You mean you haven't started looking for her yet?" Ruby made an effort to speak quietly, mindful of the sleeping child. "I called you people hours ago." Well, actually more like two hours, but Kaitlyn's epic fit had made the interim seem like a lifetime.

"I understand, ma'am. We're doing everything we can at this point. What I need you to do is answer a few questions about Ms. Brooks. Any information you give us will help. Can you come to the station now and speak to me?"

"No, I can't," Ruby huffed. "Look, Bee's daughter, Katie, is here with me. She's asleep and I really prefer not to wake her up."

"How old is Ms. Brooks's daughter?"

"Six."

She heard Frances make a thoughtful hum. "I see. In that case, Ms. Fontaine, I'm coming to your apartment. Expect me in about twenty minutes."

Ruby didn't miss the detective's sharpened interest. She wondered what she'd said to provoke the reaction. "I'll be waiting."

After the call ended, her cell phone rang before she could switch it to vibrate. This time, she checked Caller ID: Michael Michelson, Beatrice's editor at the *Central Ledger*. Hoping for good news, she answered, "Hello, Mr. Michelson. Have you heard from Bee?"

"Call me Mike. Sorry, I've got nothing. I sent someone over to her house, but she wasn't there." Michelson sounded concerned. "I left three messages for her, she hasn't gotten back to me yet. It's not like Brooks to flake out and disappear off the map, not with a story on the boil. Did you call the police?"

"Detective Orsini is coming to talk to me."

"Orsini? Why does that name sound familiar? Hang on a sec." Computer keys clicked in the background. He muttered, "Okay...Frances Orsini. Remember the Collins kid who went missing six months ago? Turned out to be a custody dispute and parental kidnapping. Orsini led the investigation that tracked down the dad. She's good at her job."

"I'm glad to hear that."

"Look, I gotta go. If Brooks turns up, let me know."

"Okay, will do. Thanks, Mike." She ended the call, sighed and went to the kitchen for a well-deserved glass of chilled Riesling.

Leaning a hip against the kitchen counter, Ruby sipped the white wine to soothe her nerves and tried to think. The more she considered Beatrice's disappearance, the more bizarre and incomprehensible the situation seemed. So many questions, so few answers. She finished the glass of wine in a gulp and decided to have another.

The ringing doorbell made her put the wine bottle on the counter and hustle to answer the door before the noise woke Kaitlyn.

The woman—*no, make that the Amazon*—in the corridor stood six feet tall in sensible pumps, and wore dark blue trousers and a matching jacket. An amber blouse complemented her warm olive complexion. "Ms. Fontaine, I'm Detective Orsini.

Please call me Frances. We spoke on the phone." She smiled. "I'm sorry we have to meet this way. May I come in?"

Ruby stood aside to let Frances enter. The glossy black ponytail twitched between the tall woman's shoulder blades at each graceful step toward the living room. She'd bet Frances had been a model or an athlete, or both. "Call me Ruby. Have you found out anything?"

Frances removed a decorative pillow from the seat of the armchair next to the sofa and sat down. "It's still early." She pulled a small spiral-bound notebook from her inner jacket pocket and held a ballpoint pen poised over a blank page. Her gaze swept over Ruby and paused. "Interesting hair color."

"Pink suits me better than dishwater blond." Ruby liked the cotton candy-colored stain in her hair and the wild, fluffy, flyaway 'do she spent time carefully cultivating with hairspray in front of the mirror each morning. The color and the style made her happy, even though some people misjudged her. "Problem?"

"I like it." Frances gave her a brief, broader grin. "Let's start with the background. What's your relationship with Ms. Brooks?"

"We're friends," Ruby answered, straightening out the quilt and sitting in the middle of the sofa to leave a cushion's distance between herself and Frances. "We grew up in the same neighborhood and went to school together as kids." For some reason, her nerves got the better of her and she started babbling. "Not college though. Bee got a scholarship to Northwestern University in Chicago. I went to a culinary school in Columbus, then an apprenticeship in Belgium—" She stopped, biting the inside of her cheek.

Frances didn't appear to notice anything wrong. "Ms. Brooks is an investigative reporter for the *Central Ledger*, is that right?" She placidly scribbled notes while they spoke.

"Yes."

"What's your profession?"

"I'm a trained chocolatier and owner of the Magic Bean chocolate and confectionary shop here in town." Ruby made a face. "I mean, I don't have a physical shop. I rent a commercial kitchen. My business is online. That will change in the future."

Frances nodded. "You know, at my brother's wedding last month, the caterer offered the guests these Magic Bean bonbons after dinner. Oh my God, I still remember the white chocolate with green olives." She leaned forward, put an elbow on her knee and pinned Ruby in place with her mischievous brown gaze. "First bite, I almost had the big O right there in front of my mother, my whole family and the priest. It was a religious experience, all right." She winked.

Flustered, Ruby stammered a semicoherent reply.

"All right, moving on…Tell me what happened today," Frances said, leaning back with a neutral expression belied by the slightly upturned corners of her mouth.

Ruby explained Beatrice's visit to her rented kitchen, the forgotten cupcakes, the improvised treat bags. "After she left, Bee went to the party supply store close to Katie's school. She had to buy extra favors for the class, stickers and stuff." A doubt troubled her. She added, "I know she delivered the treat bags to the class because I talked to the teacher when I went to get Katie. But whether the bags contained just candy or if Bee actually bought favors at the party store, I don't know. I didn't ask."

"We'll check." Frances glanced up from her notebook. "Kaitlyn Brooks's school called you when her mother didn't pick her up. Why you? Why not a relative?"

"I'm listed as the emergency contact."

"Right. Now I need to ask, where's Kaitlyn's father?"

"Greg Brooks is across the country in Santa Monica, last I heard." Ruby wished the interview would end. The detective needed to go find Beatrice, not sit in a chair and waste time on trivialities. What did the past matter? "By mutual agreement, their marriage broke up shortly after Katie's birth. He didn't want custody. He never wanted a child in the first place. Bee got pregnant against his wishes." Frances's raised eyebrow spurred her to explain. "Bee loved Greg, but she really wanted to be a mom. Greg had other plans."

"Was the divorce amicable?"

"Absolutely. Greg Brooks isn't a bad guy, although he's not a very good guy either. He's shallow, narcissistic and lazy. He'd never do anything to hurt Bee or Katie. That would take too much effort. He's much more concerned with himself and his good looks to worry about his ex-wife and child."

"Any issues between Ms. Brooks and her ex-husband? Unpaid child support or alimony, that kind of thing?"

"Greg—or I should say, his lawyer—sends the check every month like clockwork. Bee didn't want alimony and even offered to do without child support, but his legal advisors insisted and he agreed. If there were any problems, I'm sure Bee would tell me."

Frances's pen flitted across the page.

Ruby fidgeted while answering the detective's questions, which became disturbingly invasive. Did Beatrice have a habit of excessive drinking or doing drugs, prescription or otherwise? Any financial, personal, or work related worries lately? What about unusual stress? Was Beatrice depressed or seeing a mental health professional for any reason? Had her personality changed in the last few weeks or months? Had she been taking care of herself? Had Beatrice ever talked about or attempted to commit suicide?

"No, no, no!" Ruby burst out, slashing an impatient hand through the air. "For heaven's sake, Bee doesn't have problems like that. And she loves Kaitlyn very, very much. She's a good mother. Ask anybody who knows them. They'll tell you." She stopped, inhaled and exhaled through her nose until tension bled from her shoulders, and went on. "I can't say it often enough: Bee would never, in a million years, walk out on Katie. Never. No matter what. Leaving her baby behind would be totally out of character. Unthinkable."

Frances put away the notebook. "I'm sorry if I upset you."

"You have a job to do. That's fine. I just need you to understand Bee isn't the type to shirk her responsibilities. Besides, she's happy. She loves working for the newspaper. She has friends who love her too. She's not troubled. She's not alone." Ruby swallowed hard. "And Katie needs her mommy. Don't you dare think otherwise."

"I assure you, Ruby, we give every case our full attention." Frances handed over a business card. "My office number, email and cell. If you think of anything we ought to know or if you have contact with Ms. Brooks, don't hesitate to call." A muffled ringtone came from her jacket pocket. She excused herself, stood and walked away a few steps to answer the call, speaking too low for Ruby to overhear.

Ruby got to her feet, scrubbing the palms of her hands on her jeans. She longed to return to the kitchen for a second glass of wine—or to finish the bottle, for that matter—but she didn't want to give Frances the wrong impression. *Better stay put*, she decided, *if I don't want to look like an unreliable lush. This is too important.*

For lack of anything better to do, she studied the tall woman's profile, the aquiline nose, firm chin and generous mouth. She revised her initial impression. Despite the long legs and good looks, Frances couldn't have been a fashion model, not with such a solid body and broad shoulders. Frances could have been an athlete though, she mused. Tennis, maybe, or basketball. No mistaking the grace that made every movement economical and poetic.

Frances returned, a shadow touching her face. "Ruby, do you know what type of car Ms. Brooks drives?"

"A three-year-old Volvo station wagon, silver metallic with black interior. I don't know the license plate number." Uneasiness prickled down Ruby's spine. Her hands clenched around Meemaw's quilt. "Why do you want to know?"

"The vehicle was found abandoned near the airport." Frances's gaze flicked to the closed bedroom door and returned to Ruby so quickly she wondered if she'd been mistaken. The woman went on, "There appears to be blood on the front seat."

Ruby faltered. Her heart fetched an almighty thud. *Bee!* She glanced at the bedroom door, thinking about the little girl asleep in the bed, and prayed the detective was wrong.

CHAPTER THREE

The next morning Ruby stood in tightly wound silence as a social worker carried Kaitlyn from her apartment. Morton the Monster dropped from the six-year-old's grasp.

Ruby darted forward to snatch the almost shapeless stuffed monster off the carpet and push it into Kaitlyn's hand. The green fur was matted and wet with the little girl's tears. "Bye-bye, honey bunny. Be good. Aunt Ruby will see you soon," she whispered.

Kaitlyn stared at her over the social worker's shoulder, blue eyes huge and brimming with tears, face blotched red and white. She had a white-knuckled grip on Morton the Monster. "Bye-bye," she whispered.

The door closed behind the social worker with what seemed like awful finality, breaking Ruby's heart.

Without any legal standing as a parent, designated guardian, or relative, Ruby had been told she wasn't allowed to keep Kaitlyn with her. The child would be placed in emergency foster care for now. She had tried to explain things to Kaitlyn earlier and be reassuring, but wasn't sure she'd been successful. While she knew Frances Orsini had been doing her duty by notifying the Division of Family and Children Services of Kaitlyn's situation, she also cursed the woman's efficiency.

She'd put in a call to Beatrice's divorce lawyer earlier, hoping for advice on persuading the court to grant her temporary custody. When Beatrice returned—not if, she told herself fiercely, but when—they'd sort out any red tape.

At least Frances had given her one piece of good news after their interview yesterday: the blood in Beatrice's abandoned Volvo wasn't a significant amount, just a few drops. A test confirmed the blood was Beatrice's type, but a DNA test wasn't in the cards unless evidence of foul play was found. What the discovery meant, she didn't know. Why the airport? She rejected the obvious conclusion. Beatrice would come home. End of story.

In the meantime, better to keep busy than agonize over what couldn't be helped. Her rent and bills wouldn't pay themselves and she'd been told not to expect an update about Beatrice's case until the investigation uncovered more leads.

Ruby got to her feet, wondering why she felt so cold when she was pretty sure the air conditioner was set to seventy-eight degrees.

Passing the side table on her way to check the thermostat, she noticed a flash of white behind a stack of cookbooks she hadn't had time to read. Suddenly distracted from her mission, she recalled dumping a bunch of mail on top of the books a few days ago. Something must have slid off the pile and she hadn't noticed. She clicked her tongue, annoyed with her carelessness. What if it were a bill or an important notice of some kind?

She drew out an expensive-feeling envelope and checked the return address: *St. Clare Hotel and Resort on Magdalena Island.*

Her breath caught. Thoughts of Beatrice and Kaitlyn subsided to the background. St. Clare, a five-star luxury getaway on a private island off the coast. She'd never been there, of course, but the place was regularly featured in television travel shows and magazine articles. *Times must be tough if St. Clare is sending junk mail.*

She almost dumped the envelope in the trash, but her name and address weren't just a computer-printed sticker. Someone had written the information in the kind of perfect longhand she'd never mastered in grade school. Intrigued, she slit open the envelope and drew out a letter written on heavy white stationery with the hotel's logo centered on top.

Dear Ms. Fontaine:

We are interested in meeting with you to discuss a business opportunity. An appointment has been made on your behalf for an interview with our resident manager and executive pâtissier on Wednesday, June 12, at 1 p.m.

Should you wish to alter the date or time of the appointment, please call 555-7792 Extension 011 no later than Tuesday, June 11, at 5:00 p.m.

Kindly provide six (6) samples of truffles or bonbons showcasing your best and most imaginative work as a chocolatier. Be advised we seek exotic, out of the ordinary flavors with an elegant presentation appealing to our guests' highest expectations.

We have heard good things about your work and look forward to seeing you.

Sincerely,

Delilah Kerrigan, Resident Manager

Severin Valois, Executive Pâtissier

Ruby finished reading the letter, restarted from the top and read the baffling contents a second time. She wasn't interested in giving up the Magic Bean and going to work for someone else, even a luxury hotel, but the letter didn't sound like a job offer. She frowned, tapping the edge of the letter against her lips. Any other time, she'd jump at the chance to visit Magdalena Island, but right now with Beatrice missing, Kaitlyn in foster care and everything else on her plate, she wasn't sure about adding another complication.

Despite her doubts, a spark of excitement kindled.

Everything about the letter screamed money, privilege, exclusivity. She didn't give a hoot if someone had two nickels to rub together or a seven-digit bank account. Wealth didn't impress her, but she couldn't that deny that her high-end chocolates and confectionary business relied on clients with discretionary income and indulgent tastes.

If she wanted to afford a physical shop—preferably on the Grand Strand Boardwalk and Promenade, a real draw for tourists and locals—she needed to increase her profits by reaching more customers. The St. Clare Hotel offer might be a golden opportunity.

She decided to make a call and ask for information. Even with other stressors pressing on her, could it really hurt to find out more?

Sitting on the sofa with her cell phone and the letter, she dialed the number given and got an automated switchboard. After inputting the extension, a recorded pleasant male voice invited her to leave a message for Ms. Kerrigan.

She ended the call without saying a word. *That didn't go as planned.* She gave the cell phone a jaundiced look, but knew who was really to blame. Because of her negligence, she had only until this evening to change or cancel tomorrow's appointment.

Decisions, decisions, decisions. Unable to come to a conclusion, she stood, collected her phone, keys and purse, and let herself out of the apartment, then headed for the garage downstairs. The way she itched on the inside, as though the underside of her skin were filled with cracker crumbs, could only be eased by the familiarity of her work routine.

Ruby stopped at a Jewish deli along the way to pick up an onion bagel with *schmear*. Once she arrived at her rented kitchen, she made a pot of coffee and sat down at her desk to begin the day by checking her website for new orders and printing out the forms. Between bites of bagel, she eyed her apron hanging on its hook by the door. If only she were free to concentrate on cooking instead of all this tedious but necessary paperwork. She sighed.

Promptly at ten o'clock, her part-time delivery driver, Aaron Vargas, arrived to take the day's orders. The gray-haired man glanced over the list she gave him, smoothing his mustache with his thumb. "Sixteen for the mail, the rest local. No problem," he said in his slight Mexican accent. "Post Office and FedEx first, then across town and work my way down. Unless there's a priority I should know about."

"As long as Oakdale Drive gets that Gingerbread Cottage truffle collection before noon, you should be fine," Ruby replied, pushing an errant lock of pink hair out of her eyes and narrowly avoiding poking herself with the ballpoint pen in her hand. "Oh, and here's your check for the week. How's Maria?"

"Doing better, *gracias*. Doc says she can get the cast off her leg in two more weeks. My wife said to thank you for the box of candy you sent. She, her mother and her sisters spent half the afternoon watching *telenovelas* and eating your chocolates. I never heard so much happy clucking from those old hens." Aaron smiled, folded the list and the check, stuck both in his shirt pocket and picked up the large storage cartons containing the packages she'd prepared yesterday. "Okay, I'd better get going. See you tomorrow. Have a good day!"

"You too," she called.

As soon as he left, she double-checked her cell phone. No calls. She went to don her apron. If she spent too long brooding about Beatrice and Kaitlyn, she'd go mad.

She decided to start with a white peach *pâte de fruit*, the filling for a new bonbon she planned to name after Momotarō, the "Peach Boy" of Japanese legend. The peaches she'd bought at the Saturday farmers market were blanched, peeled, pitted and pureed in a blender. She poured the puree into a large saucepan, added measured amounts of freshly squeezed yuzu and ginger juices and sugar, and set the pan on the stove to cook.

The yuzu was new to her, an aromatic Japanese citrus fruit recently cultivated in the area that tasted like a cross between a mandarin orange and a grapefruit. While she carefully stirred the saucepan's bubbling contents—oh so carefully; simmering sugar burns were the worst!—she considered testing a limited collection of Japanese inspired chocolates. Maybe yuzu curd, perhaps a roasted sweet potato with "black" sugar or a shoyu or wasabi caramel.

She glanced at the candy thermometer. Time to add the rest of the ingredients. Getting the peach mixture heated properly without scorching took a while, but once the correct temperature was reached, she only needed to pour the hot gelée into prepared pans and set them out on the counter to cool. *One job down, about a million more to go.*

She kept moving and tried not to think too hard, not to worry too much, not let fear creep around the edges of her increasingly brittle control. Her hands chopped, measured, stirred and molded, but her heart grew heavier and heavier in her chest.

Either Beatrice's attorney called or he didn't. Either Kaitlyn came to stay with her or she didn't. Either the police found Beatrice or—she broke off the thought, put down the spoon she'd been holding and sat down heavily in her desk chair, her head in her hands.

I will not cry...I will not cry...I will not cry. The mantra didn't stop tears from leaking out to wet her palms.

After a while, she raised her head and fumbled a tissue from a box on her desk. She stared at her cell phone. Her gaze wandered to the letter sent by the St. Clare Hotel, which she'd brought to work and propped up on the work counter in front of the knife block. She sat up straight, blew her nose and wiped her face. Beatrice wouldn't want her to worry. Beatrice would tell her to stop blubbering, go to the interview on Magdalena Island and—

The word "interview" brought her internal dialogue to a screeching halt. Hadn't Beatrice said something about a meeting last night... Kaitlyn's birthday dinner... like a quicksilver minnow flashing in the shallows, the slippery memory almost escaped her grasp, but she pinned it down. The light dawned.

Ruby grabbed her cell phone and dialed Michael Michelson at the *Central Ledger*. "Hello, Mike, I need to find out something," she said when he answered. "No, I haven't heard from Bee. Did you know she had an interview last night? Yes, with an informant, a source. Some big story she was working on. Do you know anything about the meeting, like where it was supposed to take place?" She listened to his response, growing more unpleasantly surprised by the moment. "Where? Are you sure?"

She ended the call and sat back in her chair, her palms sweating. According to Mike, the agreed-upon meeting place had been the underground parking garage at her apartment building. He'd told her Beatrice had intended to hook up with the informant right after dropping off Kaitlyn.

She was probably the only person who understood the importance of Mike's information. One incident from that afternoon stood out in her mind. The foul-mouthed, hostile woman in the lipstick-red MINI probably had something to do with Beatrice's disappearance. After all, the woman's presence at exactly the right time in exactly the right place couldn't be a coincidence. She'd known that "b-with-an-itch" was up to no good!

Frances's business card was in her purse. *Time to make another call.*

CHAPTER FOUR

The following morning, Ruby woke abruptly. She blinked at the ceiling, unable to remember much about her dreams and wondering why her heart pounded so fiercely, her whole body seemed to shake with the force of the beats.

She checked the clock on the nightstand and let out a groan. Nine twenty-two a.m. She'd overslept. Throwing back the covers, she sat on the edge of the bed, rubbing the grit from her eyes. She needed to get moving if she didn't want to miss the ferry to the island.

Before leaving the rental kitchen last night, as instructed by the letter, she had picked out six different bonbons for her appointment at the St. Clare Hotel. Now she told the butterflies in her stomach to quit quivering. Either her chocolates were a hit, or she'd waste a few hours of her time in a place she could never afford to stay unless she won the lottery. Either way, a day out of town sounded good.

Thinking about her upcoming interview brought to mind yesterday's events. Frances hadn't been impressed by her assertion that the driver of the sporty red MINI at the apartment building might be involved in Beatrice's disappearance. In fact, the detective hadn't accepted her suspicions at face value. *She believed me when I said I'd met a bad-tempered woman who stole my parking spot; she just didn't think the person I saw had anything to do with Bee. At least she promised to check, so that's something.*

Scowling, Ruby stood, peeled off the T-shirt and panties she'd slept in and tossed the garments on the unmade bed. Her spine crackled when she yawned and stretched. She ran a hand through her pink hair—flat on one side, a tangled mess on the other—and went to the bathroom to shower.

Her frustration was increased by the lack of response from Beatrice's lawyer and her concern about Kaitlyn. She decided to make another call before she left for the harbor. If she still couldn't get an answer from the lawyer, she'd contact the social worker assigned to Kaitlyn's case, though she still preferred to receive legal counsel if possible. The thought of hiring her own lawyer didn't appeal at the moment. She couldn't afford the expense. *That's my desperation plan. Let me try other options first.*

After a shower, Ruby dried off and fixed her pink hair in its usual flyaway style. In the bedroom, she dug out fresh panties, a bra and a white undershirt from a wooden dresser painted with illustrations from *Snow White and the Seven Dwarfs*. Running across the vintage piece in an antique store had inspired her to theme her chocolate business after fairy tales, legends and myths. She patted the top of the dresser fondly, then grimaced at her reflection in the attached beveled mirror and reached for her makeup bag.

Five minutes later, with mascara and eyeliner applied, she rummaged in her closet for a pair of black pants and the white chef's jacket she hadn't worn since her apprenticeship. The jacket fit a little more snugly in the bosom and hips than she remembered, but she needed to present a more professional appearance than a T-shirt.

Hearing the doorbell ring, she went barefoot to answer the door.

Frances stood in the corridor holding two cups from a well-known coffee shop. She handed a cup to Ruby. "Peace offering. I was in the neighborhood and thought I'd drop by for a second. May I come in?"

"Sure, for a few minutes, but I've got an appointment and need to leave soon," Ruby replied coolly, though she took the offered coffee. From the yummy aroma, the barista had added a hazelnut shot. She followed Frances to the living room. "Any news? Are you any closer to finding out what happened to Bee?"

"Too early to tell." Frances sipped her coffee. "At this time, we haven't found any evidence suggesting Ms. Brooks might have been taken against her will."

Her stomach souring with disappointment, Ruby set aside the coffee cup. "Sounds to me like you're quitting already."

"No, we're not quitting." Frances took a step closer and settled a hand on Ruby's shoulder. The weight felt comforting. "We follow up on every lead. I have a feeling you think I'm not taking you seriously about the red MINI's driver. Like I told you on the phone, it's a possibility we'll look into, the same as we're looking into other possibilities."

Ruby took a quick breath, her heart buoyed by a sudden wave of hope. Other possibilities? "What have you found out? Do you have any idea—"

"I can't tell you anything else," Frances cut her off midquestion. "Just trust us to do our best. If you come across any information, call me."

Ruby gazed into Frances's brown eyes. The warmth of the woman's hand seemed to penetrate her to the bone, loosening a little more of her inner tension. Frances stared back at her steadily. She sighed. "Just bring Bee home. That's all I want."

Frances nodded and gave her shoulder another reassuring squeeze.

After the detective left, Ruby called the lawyer's office and left a message. Next, she tried the social worker's phone number. His voice mail was full. *Well, poot. At this rate, I won't see Katie again until she graduates high school.*

She checked her wristwatch. If she didn't leave now, she'd miss the ferry. Gathering her purse and a shocking pink candy box printed with the Magic Bean logo, she walked out of the apartment and took the elevator down to the parking garage.

On the road at last, she rolled down the truck's window and enjoyed her drive to the Grand Strand Boardwalk and Promenade. The distance wasn't too great. Once she got close to the seashore, she breathed in the smells of ocean salt, fish and an ozone freshness that reminded her of a summer storm, though no rain clouds threatened. The sky was a perfect shade of Wedgwood blue, the temperature in the low eighties with enough breeze blowing off the water to keep the heat pleasant.

She left her truck in the multistoried municipal parking garage and continued on foot to the broad, elevated wooden walkway built along the waterfront. The boardwalk was lined with a row of shops and restaurants on one side. On the other stretched the beach and the Atlantic Ocean, a blue-gray sheet disturbed by small, rippling, white-capped waves. Further out, past the distant white shapes of sails and boats, the horizon burned indigo.

She'd arrived just as the shops were opening and there weren't many people out yet. The real crush would start around lunchtime and continue until well in the evening. For now, she enjoyed walking down the quiet boardwalk without the crowds and clutter.

The ferry wasn't due for another twenty minutes, so she took her time peeking into the glass display windows as she went toward the wharf. The high-end businesses here included designer fashions, a couple of art galleries, beach toys, surfing and skateboarding gear, swimwear, jewelry, antiques and "man-tiques," nautical wear, bicycle and roller blade rental and sales, three exclusive boutique hotels, snack vendors and restaurants.

A gaudy white and gold shop decorated with baroque mermaids interested her the most. Ornate gilt letters painted on the window spelled out *Miss Vanita's Finest Chocolates Seaside Emporium*. Ruby snorted. Finest chocolates, indeed! To her knowledge, Vanita McNair bought cheap taffy, fudge and confections wholesale and repackaged them with her own logo—not illegal, just deceptive. Vanita also put on airs, calling herself a trained "chocolate technician" when, in fact, she bet the woman didn't know ganache from gianduja.

Ruby shook off her irritation and continued walking. The instant she had a shop of her own, Vanita McNair had better watch out.

At the end of the boardwalk, she went down a set of weathered wooden steps to the ferry wharf. She could have driven around to the access road and taken her truck to the island, but the day was too nice to skip a stroll in the sunshine, not to mention an opportunity to sneer at Vanita, she admitted to herself. Besides, she could use the exercise.

The Magdalena Island ferry arrived on time. Ruby and a few other foot passengers boarded first, followed by about a half-dozen cars and a motorcycle. She stood on the outside deck at the rail, watching the wharf and the boardwalk grow smaller as the engines churned the blue-gray water to foam and the ferry began its journey.

From her position, she had a good view of the high-rise condominiums spoiling the beach to the north and the emerald-green swath of the country club's golf course toward the west. Further inland, she glimpsed skyscrapers nestled together downtown, steel and glass towers winking bright in the morning sun. Summerland had changed a lot since her childhood, grown up and modernized and become touristy in places, but for the most part, the city still had the small-town feel she cherished.

She moved to the opposite rail to watch the low, humpbacked shape of Magdalena Island swimming into view. In the city's earliest days, the island had been home to the Order of St. Clare, or the Poor Clares, as the nuns were called. If she squinted, she could just make out the scattered stone ruins of the cloister on the hill's summit.

Her gaze shifted to the large hotel sprawled at the base of the hill, an architectural fantasy built in the Spanish Colonial Revival style. The multistoried white structure loomed over the landscape, a gracious Moorish-influenced hacienda on steroids with two square towers at the corners, rows of elongated arched windows on all but the ground floor and a massive glass and ironwork dome rising above a clay tiled roof the color of rust. More tiles covered the roof of a long columned porch that ran almost the full length of the hotel's front.

A nervous chill ran through her. She straightened her spine. *I am a master chocolatier.* No matter what the hotel manager decided, she would never be less than confident in her skills, her palate and her vision.

When the ferry docked at the island's wharf, she disembarked and continued on a paved path lined with tall palm trees through the manicured grounds to the hotel's entrance.

She went inside, paying scant attention to the lobby apart from registering an impression of dizzying space and opulence. At the front desk, she made an inquiry that led her to a door marked Employees Only. She followed the desk clerk's directions to the rather stark administrative offices at the end of a long corridor.

The general manager's office was guarded by a young man seated at a receptionist's desk. "May I help you?" he asked politely, his fingers still tapping on a computer keyboard.

"I'm Ruby Fontaine. I have an appointment with Ms. Kerrigan."

"Please take a seat. I'll let her know you're here."

Ruby sat on the edge of the indicated chair, too jittery to relax despite her brave words to herself on the ferry. She held the chocolate box on her lap. Each passing minute crawled by, the hush broken by the receptionist answering a call on his headset or continuing to work on his computer. She suddenly realized she hadn't eaten any breakfast, only a sip of the coffee Frances had brought. If her stomach growled, the noise would sound as loud as a gunshot in the quiet room. She went hot, then cold at the embarrassing thought.

After what seemed like forever, the receptionist glanced at her. "Ms. Fontaine, Ms. Kerrigan is ready to see you." He stood and opened a door behind his desk.

She went through, summoning a professional smile to her face, and stopped dead in her tracks to stare at the woman in the pale cream business suit who greeted her.

Delilah Kerrigan was the driver of the lipstick-red MINI.

"Ms. Fontaine, it's a pleasure to meet you," Delilah murmured with cool poise, coming around the side of her desk. "I've been looking forward to seeing you today."

Ruby remained frozen, groping for something, anything, to do or say. Her brain scrambled frantically between warring instincts: confront Delilah Kerrigan right now, right this instant, and demand she spill everything she knew about Beatrice, or attempt to find out the information she wanted through more subtle means. While the desire to grab the woman and shake the truth out of her was tempting, subtlety won over brute force as her best option to gather evidence. Clearly, Delilah didn't remember her—a point in her favor.

She shook Delilah's hand, managing to prevent her smile from slipping too much. "Thank you for the opportunity, Ms. Kerrigan."

Delilah gestured to a pair of leather chairs arranged in front of an antique mahogany cabinet on the opposite side of the room. "Let's have a chat." She removed a large brown envelope from her desk and waited until Ruby sat down before claiming the other chair. "Severin Valois, my executive pâtissier—he'll be joining us in a moment—has done his homework about you. He tells me after your graduation from culinary school you apprenticed with Leclerq in Belgium." Her curiosity appeared genuine.

Ruby tried to relax, but her back muscles remained rigid. The woman seemed completely different. She bit her lip against blurting something stupid about a personality transplant and dropped her gaze to the shocking pink chocolate box in her lap. "I have a background in pastry and confectionary and I love working with chocolate. I'm grateful Chef Leclerq allowed me to study under him." She risked a peek at Delilah.

The other day in the underground parking garage, she'd mostly gotten an impression of a slender body, chestnut hair, gray eyes and a snarl. Now she realized Delilah was truly gorgeous, her face strong and striking with the kind of classic, almost flawless bone structure worshipped by cameras. That clear, creamy complexion, which owed nothing to cosmetics, would make most women cry. However, Delilah spoiled the beauty somewhat by wearing her expression like a mask: impenetrable, controlled, almost aloof.

Hard to believe she might have done something bad to Bee, but you never can tell somebody's inside from their outside, Ruby thought.

"We hope to forge a business relationship with you," Delilah said, distracting Ruby from her momentary reverie. "Severin has—ah, here he is now."

The office door opened, admitting a short, squat man whose longish salt-and-pepper hair was held back in a ponytail. His nose was an impressive arched beak in a seamed and weathered face. Powerful shoulders stretched the seams of his chef's jacket, marked on the breast with the hotel logo and a blue embroidered name: Valois. He carried a stack of small plates and a knife. His wrinkles deepened when he grinned.

"Ms. Fontaine, you are so good to come today!" he exclaimed, his English laced with a French accent. "The samples—you have brought them, I hope? *Bien*." Without waiting for an answer, he turned to Delilah. "Did I not tell you? Is not the hair most extraordinary?"

Delilah smiled thinly. "Severin, she just arrived. Don't frighten her away."

He waved his free hand. "Bah." But his black eyes twinkled.

Ruby lifted the chocolate box. "Chef, I have the samples here." Despite her anxiety, she welcomed Severin's presence. Since establishing the Magic Bean, she hadn't had a fellow professional's opinion of her work. She craved an expert critique as much as she dreaded it.

"Then let us begin at once." Severin took the box from her hands and went to the desk. A moment later, he returned with a plate. In the center sat a truffle split in half. He paused and raised his eyebrows at her.

She clasped her hands together to hide any tremors. "My shop is called the Magic Bean and I've named my confections after fairy tales and myths." For the first time, she found herself praying the name and concept weren't as pretentious as they sounded. "This is a Three Wishes truffle—milk chocolate ganache blended with mango purée and a sweet, southwestern Indian thirteen-spice curry powder. The truffle is hand dipped in eighty-five percent extra noir chocolate and sprinkled with Ceylon cinnamon, toasted coconut and black pepper."

Delilah and Severin each picked up a portion. Severin took three bites to finish his half truffle, concentrating with his eyes shut, while Delilah savored a single, dainty bite and returned the rest to the plate. Ruby squelched a desire to scowl. Maybe Delilah wasn't rejecting the truffle, but merely concerned about overindulgence. She found it impossible to breach the woman's composure and read anything significant from her.

Severin turned and walked over to a pretty Art Deco drinks cabinet on the other side of the room. He returned carrying two glasses of water, one of which he handed to Delilah. They both took sips to clear their palates before he went to the desk to prepare another chocolate.

The tasting continued. Severin prepared a bonbon or truffle on a clean plate and he and Delilah sampled the chocolate without any comments. By the time they finished, Ruby was ready to choke on the suspense. She forced herself to sit still in the chair.

"What did I tell you?" Severin said to Delilah with a triumphant air.

Delilah nodded. To Ruby, she said, "Excellent work. Truly exceptional. I have no doubt your chocolates will please guests and our association will be mutually beneficial."

"Perhaps a suggestion, Ms. Fontaine?" Severin put in. "I think a soupçon less of the raw Yucatan honey in your charming Xmulzencab bonbon—the strength of the honey threatens to overpower the vanilla—but otherwise, very good, very good."

Ruby thanked him. "And thank you as well, Ms. Kerrigan," she continued.

Severin took the empty water glasses back to the drinks cabinet and left the office.

Delilah sat in the chair, watching her with hooded gray eyes.

Ruby didn't know exactly what kind of business opportunity was on offer, but she'd passed a crucial test. She was one step closer to getting her foot in the door, one step closer to making her business a success and one step closer to finding out what happened to Beatrice.

Why did she feel more apprehensive than excited?

CHAPTER FIVE

"I have a proposition to offer, Ms. Fontaine." A beam of sunlight poured into the room behind Delilah's head, turning her chestnut hair to bronze. "St. Clare Hotel and Resort would like to offer you a contract to provide us with an exclusive range of handmade artisanal chocolates we'll sell from a new retail shop we're in the process of building in the hotel. You'll find details in the information pack." She tapped a manicured fingernail on the envelope she'd been balancing on her lap. "I'm sure you'll want to consult your attorney, so I've included a basic contract. We can negotiate specifics at a later meeting."

Ruby accepted the envelope. She'd had help from her cousin—Drew Clifton, a business attorney—getting the paperwork together to start the Magic Bean. With any luck, Drew would come through for her again.

Delilah abruptly stood, giving the hem of her jacket a tug. "I'd like to invite you to be my guest this afternoon for lunch, if you have no other plans."

"Oh! Well, uh, actually, Ms. Kerrigan, I'm sorry, really sorry, but I have to work, you know? Business to run, all that good stuff, so, um, thanks, but no thanks. Rain check?"

Ruby had no idea why she turned down the offer. *Idiot!* Lunch might have gotten the formidable Ms. Kerrigan to unbend a little and perhaps let something slip about Beatrice. She blamed her sudden inability to form a coherent thought on Delilah Kerrigan's steely gray gaze—direct, to the purpose and holding the warmth of an Arctic pebble.

"I'm sorry too, Ms. Fontaine. As you say, another time." Delilah strode across the office to her desk. "Please see my receptionist to schedule our next appointment. Would next week be convenient? At that time, I hope you'll have a little something for us to try…but I don't want to get ahead of myself, so I'll say no more. You may bring your attorney if you choose. Thank you for your time."

Heat creeping into her cheeks, Ruby left the room clutching the envelope and feeling as though she'd been dismissed by a stern teacher. Severin had been much friendlier, but she'd expected no less from a fellow chef. She stopped by the receptionist's desk for a new appointment, making a mental note to bribe Drew with a bottle of his favorite bourbon.

After she found her way back to the lobby, she paused. Did she really want to go home yet? Despite what she'd told Delilah, she had taken care of any urgent orders yesterday. She could afford to tour the hotel a little, maybe get a snack before returning to the city.

What if Delilah caught her? She nibbled her bottom lip. Certainly, eating lunch on the property after she'd refused Delilah's offer in a moment of temporary insanity seemed like a faux pas at best. But how often did the general manager wander through the hotel? She weighed the risk versus her demanding appetite and glanced around to orient herself.

In the center of the lobby, four polished, gold crowned, crimson marble pillars soared upward twenty or thirty feet to support the glass and iron dome on the roof. On the pale stone floor below the dome, chairs and sofas radiated out from a round mahogany and steel cocktail bar. An artistically drawn chalkboard advertised a peach cosmotini as the day's special. For a moment, she was tempted, but knew she shouldn't drink on an empty stomach.

She noted the reception counter—a massive, antique mahogany monstrosity carved with nymphs that seemed to have landed straight out of a Victorian gin palace—and the more modest concierge desk. She also saw a golf pro shop, and a sundries shop selling everything from toothpaste to tennis balls. An empty space between the two was swathed in white plastic sheets and barred off with a barricade. *Probably the retail shop Delilah mentioned.*

To her left, a restaurant named Kingfish—most likely seafood. To her right, the Cloisters Grill and a third restaurant, Découverte. The latter opened at six o'clock in the evening, but the others offered lunch service. She decided to try Kingfish.

Although the hostess eyed her excitable pink hair and chef's jacket askance, seating proved no problem. Ruby was whisked to a table with an ocean view and given a menu and a glass of ice water. The prices made her gulp. If she used her lunch money budget for the rest of the week, she could afford an appetizer and a glass of wine.

After placing her order with the attentive waiter, she found herself toying with the envelope she'd gotten from Delilah. Curiosity led her to use the butter knife to open the flap. Inside, she found a sheaf of papers covered in incomprehensible legal gobbledygook. She'd have to wait until Drew did a translation. From the little she gleaned, the hotel wasn't asking her to actually mass-produce the chocolates herself, which came as a relief. Her job would be to develop a selection of exclusive and exotic chocolates. She smiled and sat back in the chair. No problem. She relished the challenge.

The waiter returned with her meal: escabeche of Atlantic mackerel with ruby grapefruit and a wild herb salad. She'd chosen a nice, medium-priced white wine to accompany the dish. To her surprise, the waiter put another dish on the table. She glanced at him. "I'm sorry. I didn't order anything else."

"With the compliments of Chef Pierce, from one professional to another," the waiter said with a smile. "A tasting plate of chilled terrine of salmon with wasabi crumble."

She looked past the waiter to the kitchen door, where a middle-aged man in chef's whites stood. She grinned and gave him a little wave of thanks, which he returned.

While she ate, the waiter returned often, each time bearing a different tasting plate of Chef Pierce's cuisine. She tried roasted cod with a dollop of olive oil and mashed celery root, a marinated scallop paired with a pig's cheek croquette, and crispy squid with charred baby lettuce and a lemony dressing. Everything was delicious. At the end of the meal, the waiter brought a final gift—her bill had been signed off by Pierce.

"Please give the chef my sincerest thanks for a splendid time," she said to the waiter. "Such a treat! I won't soon forget that croquette or his hospitality."

"May I bring you dessert?"

"I'm tempted, but no, thank you. I couldn't eat another bite."

On her way out of Kingfish in a happy daze, Ruby literally ran into the one person she didn't want to see: Delilah Kerrigan. Her guts cramped.

"Ms. Fontaine," Delilah said, her tone freezing. "I trust you enjoyed your lunch."

Ruby was seized by a sudden empathy for the mouse confronting a cobra. "Ah, um, well, you see…yes, you know, Chef Pierce makes some incredibly tasty dishes, doesn't he?" To her horror, a nervous titter burst out of her mouth.

"Yes, he does." Delilah didn't exactly frown, but her expression took on a rigid cast. "I'll see you at our next appointment, I'm sure. Good day."

"Just a second," Ruby blurted, impulsively grabbing the sleeve of Delilah's jacket. The cream-colored material felt expensive and probably cost more than her culinary school tuition. "I'm really sorry. I guess my nerves were so frayed I spoke without thinking when I turned down your very kind invitation. And I got hungry afterward and…" She let her voice trail off, uncertain what else she ought to say. "I'm sorry," she repeated.

After several tense seconds, Delilah's mouth quirked and her manner thawed slightly. "Apology accepted, Ms. Fontaine."

Realizing she still held the jacket sleeve, Ruby let go. When Delilah started to leave, she called to the woman's retreating back, "I meant what I said about the rain check. I'd love to have lunch with you sometime."

Slowly, Delilah turned to regard her with a hint of amusement. "Would you consider dinner with me tomorrow night? Pleasure, not business...I prefer to keep the two separate."

Ruby's mind seized on the most important word: *tomorrow.* A heaven-sent opportunity to make discreet inquiries about Beatrice and find out if Delilah Kerrigan was involved. Who knew what she'd find out? "Yes, works for me."

"Would you prefer somewhere in the city or here in the hotel?"

"How about Découverte? I have a fondness for French cuisine."

"Eight o'clock. I'll make the reservation. Shall we meet there?"

"Sure."

Delilah took her hand in a firm, warm grip. "Then I'll see you tomorrow night. Have a safe trip home."

Ruby watched the woman walk into Kingfish, wondering if she'd just agreed to what might be construed as a date. Maybe. In an alternate universe. If she closed one eye and squinted the other. *Don't be crazy. You just met her and she's as cold as liquid nitrogen.* Delilah probably liked getting to know potential business associates over a meal.

She left the hotel in a much better mood.

On the ferry returning to the city, her cell phone rang. She checked Caller ID and answered the call. "Hello, Detective Orsini. Has something happened?"

"Ms. Fontaine—"

"Ruby, please."

"I've been talking to Ms. Brooks's newspaper editor, Mr. Michelson. He tells me Ms. Brooks's notebook is missing. I was hoping you knew where it might be."

Ruby moved out of the sunshine to a deck chair and sat down. "A notebook...are we talking about a PC? Because she does have a computer at home."

"No, a small spiral-bound book, about three by five inches, navy blue cover, lots of sticky notes, held closed with a rubber band. Ms. Brooks was old-school. She was afraid of hackers and handwrote research notes for stories. Mr. Michelson wasn't sure if she kept the notebook at home or on her person. He searched her desk at work. We didn't find it in the Volvo. I hoped you might be able to help."

"I'm sorry, I've never seen Bee with a notebook, she never mentioned one to me. I'm afraid I really can't help."

Frances's sigh gusted over the phone. "Well, it was a long shot."

"Have you asked Kaitlyn?" Ruby offered.

"Do you think she'd understand the question?"

"She might. Katie's pretty observant for a six-year-old. Oh, and Bee mentioned a safe deposit box to me once. I think at First Federal or maybe the paper's credit union."

Frances sounded a bit enervated. "That's very helpful, Ruby. Thanks."

"Wait, before you go...do you think the exposé Bee was working on has anything to do with the way she dropped out of sight? Is that why you're looking for the notebook?" Ruby pulled the phone from her ear when she received no answer, just several seconds of silence. The call hadn't ended, so she replaced the phone and cleared her throat. "Hello? Detective, are you still there?"

"Think very carefully about what you're going to say to me next," Frances finally replied, her voice an octave deeper and quivering under some kind of strain. "This is very important—*what* exposé?"

Ruby faltered, her mouth dropping open. How could the detective not know? Hadn't Mike Michelson—she broke off the thought as her temper flared. That so-and-so hadn't said a word to the police about Beatrice's story. Protecting the newspaper's scoop, no doubt. Well, she'd have some sharp words for him next time they spoke.

"I don't know many details," she admitted. "Hardly anything at all. Bee could be secretive that way. Maybe the story has something to do with politics. Last I spoke to her—the day she disappeared—she said the story would, I quote, 'break City Hall wide open.'"

Frances fell silent again. At last, she said, "Ruby, I'd like to talk to you. Can you meet me somewhere for coffee? My treat."

Part of Ruby giggled like a schoolgirl at the thought of snagging not one, but two "dates" in a single day. Her more practical side quickly brought her back to reality. These weren't social meetings. To behave otherwise was stupid. She sobered. "Do you know Alfonso's on the boardwalk?"

"Yes. Can you make it in an hour?"

"Not a problem."

Ruby ended the call. She remained in the deck chair for the rest of the journey, staring at the cityscape, the clouds, the gulls, the water and the blue-gray waves bashing the beach, wondering when and why her love life had gotten as pathetic as sugar-free chocolate.

CHAPTER SIX

Ruby managed to reach Alfonso's only five minutes late. "Sorry," she said, sliding into the chair next to Frances and setting her purse on the floor between her feet.

"I'm just glad you made it," Frances replied, pushing aside the muffin she'd been picking apart. "What can I get you?"

Still full from lunch, Ruby checked the chalkboard menu hanging on the whitewashed brick wall behind the counter. "A latté, please."

"One latté, coming up." Frances rose and went to the counter. She returned in a few minutes, resumed her seat and slid a coffee cup to Ruby.

"Thanks." Ruby glanced at Frances over the rim of her raised coffee cup. "Muffin not to your taste?" she asked after taking a sip. *Mmm...I needed some caffeine.*

"Kind of dry, actually." Frances gave Ruby a direct look, her espresso-dark gaze intense. "I need you to be straight with me... are you and Ms. Brooks lovers?"

Ruby almost choked on a mouthful of milky coffee. After recovering from a coughing fit, she glared. "That's rude, Detective."

Frances winced. "My apologies. I didn't mean—" Appearing as flustered as Ruby felt, she ran a hand over her black hair, smoothing strands that had escaped from the ponytail gathered at the crown of her head. "Let me start over. You and Ms. Brooks are very close."

"We're good friends. I told you, we've known each other a long time, remember? Since childhood. And what makes you think either of us might be lesbian, anyway?"

"Are you? Is she?"

"Why does it matter?"

Frances's mouth thinned. "A police investigation tends to bring up secrets, Ruby. Things people might prefer to keep hidden. I take no pleasure in making you uncomfortable, but it's my job to ask questions. Why does it matter if she's lesbian? Because if she is, she flies under the radar. She's a private individual who's never betrayed herself as far as I can tell. Self-concealment can be dangerous. People have killed and been killed over secrets and you know it." She sipped black coffee before continuing, "If you and she are lovers, I'm not here to judge. The information may be relevant to my case, that's all. I thought I'd do you the courtesy of asking the question to your face instead of nosing around your friends, family and associates. I'm not looking to out you. I can be discreet."

"Bee is straight. I'm not. She and I are friends, never lovers," Ruby stated flatly, beginning to dislike Frances. "She's like a sister to me. You know, just because I love women doesn't mean I want to jump in the sack with every female in sight."

"Neither do I." Frances waited until Ruby stopped spitting coffee and spluttering to add, "Thank you for your honesty," and passed her a handful of paper napkins.

Ruby mopped up the table. "You're mean."

"I'm sorry."

"No, you're not."

"You got me." Frances raised both hands in a gesture of surrender. Sunlight from the window gleamed on the thick silver ring she wore on her thumb. "At least at this point I can rule out a couple of theories, which saves me time." She toyed with her coffee cup. "I checked into Delilah Kerrigan, by the way. The owner of the red MINI you saw in the garage."

Ruby leaned forward, damp napkins forgotten. "What did you find out?"

"I'm only telling you this much because I don't want you to do anything…well, anything you might regret later." Frances mimicked Ruby's posture. "Ms. Kerrigan is clean. She has no connection whatsoever to Beatrice Brooks. Zip. Zilch. Nada. As far as we can tell, your friend never met Ms. Kerrigan. Their lives never intersected."

"But I saw her—"

"I know you did, but you did not see Ms. Brooks speak to Ms. Kerrigan, meet with her, or get into her car."

Ruby knew Frances was right, but she persisted anyway. "Then what was Ms. Kerrigan doing in the garage? She doesn't live in my building."

"It's not my business to care and it's not yours either." Frances made a shushing motion when Ruby would have spoken. "I appreciate everything you tell me. You're welcome to call me anytime."

"I hear a 'but' coming," Ruby muttered, downing what was left of her latté and shoving the wad of used napkins into the empty cup.

Frances's smile gave her the appearance of a Renaissance Madonna, but her firm tone was at odds with the serene expression. "Don't expect me to chase after every slim possibility, coincidence, or gut feeling you have. I deal in facts. If I decide a fact is relevant, I'll investigate." She covered Ruby's hand with hers. "I understand you miss your friend and you're worried about her. Both she and I need you to keep it together, okay? Don't jump at shadows or waste your strength reaching for nonexistent straws."

"Got it." Ruby drew away her hand with great reluctance. Frances's touch soothed her, as did the woman's confidence.

Somehow, she knew Frances would find Beatrice if it were at all possible. "Did you find Bee's notebook?" she asked to change the subject.

"We're still looking. Do you remember anything else she might have told you?"

"She mentioned the story to me in passing as the reason she needed me to babysit Kaitlyn for the evening. I didn't ask for details." Ruby paused when a group of chatty teenagers entered the coffee shop. She waited for them to find seats before she went on. "Do you think—" The question stuck in her throat. "Do you think Bee's okay?"

"There's no reason to believe otherwise," Frances replied.

Ruby noticed the detective hadn't really answered her question, but she supposed empty promises wouldn't do the families and friends of missing persons any favors. "I'm sorry I wasted your time with Ms. Kerrigan." She sighed. "I feel helpless and I hate it."

"I understand." Frances finished her coffee. "Promise me you won't run off and start investigating on your own. Don't interrogate anyone. This isn't a made-for-TV movie."

"Promise." Ruby kept her fingers crossed under the table. Delilah Kerrigan might have a clean record and no obvious connection to Beatrice, but she remained suspicious of the woman. Poking her nose around the hotel and keeping her eyes open couldn't possibly hurt, not when she had legitimate business there anyway.

"Don't forget you're not alone. A lot of people care about Ms. Brooks, even her ex-husband." Frances almost knocked her cup off the table when Ruby squawked.

"You haven't told that man about Bee and Katie!" she started to yell, only lowering her voice to a more reasonable volume when she realized most of the shop's customers and employees were staring at her. "Why would you call him?" she asked in a furious whisper.

"You told me Greg Brooks wasn't a bad guy."

"I also told you he wasn't a good guy."

"He's Kaitlyn Brooks's father."

"Greg is Katie's sperm donor," Ruby retorted. "He's so far removed from his daughter's life, Bee might as well have done the deed with a turkey baster."

"Greg Brooks has a legal right to know about his daughter." Frances took Ruby's hands in a firm grip, not letting go when she tried to pull free. "I called the Santa Monica PD. Apart from speeding tickets and a few noise complaints from neighbors, he has no criminal record. His divorce from Beatrice Brooks was amicable. At her insistence, he retains some parental rights, though apparently he's chosen not to exercise them. His finances are stable, he pays child support on time and his personal life passes scrutiny. Brooks's lawyer even provided us with his alibi before we had a chance to ask, which checked out. He's not a suspect in his ex-wife's disappearance. So what haven't you told me, Ruby?"

The way Frances's gaze searched hers made Ruby realize the detective suspected her of concealing information. Something terrible, perhaps. She hastened to explain. "Like I said before, Greg isn't a monster. He's not violent or abusive. The best way I can describe him is careless. He's a beautiful, selfish, careless butterfly of a man who never grew up and shouldn't be allowed to take Katie. Two seconds after the excitement wears off, he'll be bored and move on to the next thing that catches his attention. Katie won't be physically neglected. He'll make sure her needs are met, but he'll starve her emotionally."

Frances nodded and released her hands. "I'm sorry. What's done is done. The social worker contacted him yesterday and he has an appearance in family court soon."

"Have you spoken to Greg yourself?"

"Yes, this morning before he caught a flight out here. He said he plans to request temporary custody of Kaitlyn until her mother returns home."

Ruby drew a deep breath. Nothing she could do would prevent Greg from taking Kaitlyn with him to California, just as she'd been unable to stop the social worker from removing the little girl from her apartment. Impotent anger unspooled in her gut, most of it directed at Beatrice. By not making a power of attorney and giving Kaitlyn's guardianship to someone she trusted, Beatrice had left her daughter to the court's mercy and Greg's whims. He'd give Kaitlyn—or pay someone else to give her, sparing himself the effort—everything she might want and very little of what she actually needed, like discipline and unconditional love. Guilt washed over her a second later. How could she be angry with her best friend, who might be in danger? Might be hurt? Her heart ached.

"Maybe he's changed," Frances said, clearly a peace offering.

Leopards and spots, Ruby thought, but she nodded, unwilling to argue.

"Will you be okay? I'd stay longer," Frances said, giving her an apologetic look, "but I'll be late if I don't get back to the office."

"I'm...I'm disappointed and upset, but I'm not the brooding type. You're right. Katie will be fine with her father and it won't be for long, just until Beatrice comes home. Thanks for the latté." Ruby stood and collected her purse, afraid to glance at Frances in case the woman noticed her wet eyes. "If you hear anything—"

"I'll call."

Ruby left Alfonso's and hurried to the parking lot, half blinded by tears.

CHAPTER SEVEN

The next afternoon, Drew Clifton sat at the desk in the corner of her rented kitchen examining the St. Clare Hotel contract. Ruby didn't want to distract her cousin with questions, so she focused on making a batch of wild huckleberry cordial chocolates according to a new recipe she was developing to take advantage of this year's bumper crop.

The berries, bought from a foraging group, had been soaking in a homemade huckleberry cordial she had created weeks ago using crushed berries, honey and vodka. While Drew worked, she coated a bonbon mold with a layer of tempered dark chocolate and popped it in the freezer to set. Once the mold was ready, she added her special huckleberry fondant and a couple of the soaked berries to each cylindrical cavity. More tempered chocolate was piped on top to seal the bonbons, the excess scraped off, and the mold returned to the freezer. She had time to wipe down the table and clean the kitchen before retrieving the mold, gently tapping out the bonbons and arranging them in a storage container.

Drew cleared his throat. "You in a good place to take a break?"

"Yes," Ruby replied, turning to give him her attention. "Let's hear the news."

"Looks like a generous offer to me, but you be the judge." He blinked mild blue eyes at her and folded his hands over the paunch filling out the front of his button-down shirt. "Basically, you're being hired to create a line of twelve exclusive artisanal chocolates. If that sells successfully, you'll be asked to make seasonal chocolates as well. The hotel will produce the chocolates in-house according to your recipes. You'll be part of a management team providing oversight and final product decisions. Their marketing department will handle presentation and promotion—stuff like boxes, logos, advertising. The corporation's offering excellent compensation." He named a figure that made her eyes stretch.

"Holy cow," she breathed, sitting down on a stool before her knees buckled.

Drew chuckled. "Maybe I should renegotiate our deal," he teased, glancing at the bottle of Maker's Mark she'd given him as payment for his help.

She shook her head and laughed weakly. "Nope. You're stuck. But I'll consider upgrading your annual Christmas bottle."

"This is big, Ruby. A really big opportunity for you." He rubbed his hands together and gave her a gleeful grin. "You'll earn a nice fat fee, plus licensing each quarter once the product is in production. Maybe you should consider talking to a financial manager."

"I didn't win the lottery."

"No, you did better. A damned sight better."

"Oh, Drew, you know the drill. Swear jar, please."

He dug in his pants pocket for a dollar bill and shoved it into the glass jar on the counter. "I'm taking that out of your birthday present budget," he griped good-naturedly.

Ruby ignored him for a moment. Her dream was closer than ever. A physical shop on the boardwalk seemed within her grasp. She stared at the stove, hardly able to think through her excitement and apprehension. Creating twelve signature chocolates represented quite a challenge. How could she manage to satisfy the hotel—and, by extension, Delilah Kerrigan—and keep her current business afloat at the same time?

"If you want my advice," Drew said, breaking into her thoughts, "you won't sign the deal or talk to anybody from the hotel until we meet with their legal team. I've marked a few places in the contract we can discuss before the meeting. Don't be scared of negotiating, Ruby. These types expect some give and take."

"Ms. Kerrigan has invited me to dinner—pleasure, she says, not business."

He grunted and rose from the chair. "Could be a tactic, might be sincere. You decide, but don't agree to anything business-related and for God's sake, sign nothing. I'll swing by your place on the day of our negotiations so we can go in together." He picked up the bourbon bottle and leaned down to give her a peck on the cheek before walking out the back door.

"Thanks," Ruby called before the door swung shut.

She got up from the stool. Nothing short of a natural disaster or act of God would prevent her from grabbing this chance with both hands. However, she couldn't afford to let her established business falter. Could she do both? She decided she'd have to try.

Gathering her purse and a shocking pink box containing a twelve-piece assortment of chocolates she'd named Bella Venezia after an Italian fairy tale, she left the shop and drove home to prepare for her dinner with Delilah Kerrigan.

A little over two hours later, Ruby stood in the lobby of the St. Clare Hotel. Wall sconces and chandeliers cast a golden glow over the marble and wood. The space seemed empty to the point of echoing. Although the restaurants and central bar appeared busy, only a skeleton staff manned the reception counter. The golf pro shop was closed, the windows dark. A lone employee was wiping down the glass counters in the sundries shop.

"Good evening, Ms. Fontaine," Delilah said from behind her.

Ruby turned and stared, wide-eyed. Delilah's fitted black sheath dress and pearl collar made her glad she'd decided to wear her fancier Indian print palazzo pants and a matching cerise, beaded knit top instead of her only business suit—a drab gray jacket and pencil skirt that didn't flatter her at all and made her feel like a corporate sausage.

Recovering her composure, Ruby licked her dry lips and replied, "Good evening, Ms. Kerrigan. I brought you a little something." She offered the Magic Bean box, which Delilah took with a spark of interest in her cool, beautiful face.

"I'm sure they're delicious. Thank you." Delilah gestured to the entrance of Découverte. "Are you ready to be seated? Or would you prefer a drink at the bar first?"

Her nerves thought a drink sounded like a good idea, but at the same time, her brain informed her that guzzling alcohol was the very worst idea in the world. She took the safe option. "Whichever you prefer. I'm ready if you are."

Delilah preceded Ruby into the restaurant, giving her an opportunity to admire the way the woman's upswept chestnut curls accentuated the slender neck encircled by strands of lustrous pearls. She also couldn't help noticing the delicious sway of Delilah's hips and buttocks, emphasized by clinging black satin. Realizing her thoughts had strayed into forbidden territory, she told herself to stop. She was here to eat dinner with a potential employer who was *not* on the menu.

They were seated at a good table away from the kitchen. Instead of menus, serving staff brought glasses of white wine and delicate cheese soufflés to start.

Ruby tasted the soufflé, so light and creamy the forkful disappeared on her tongue almost like a cheesy vapor. "That's seriously delicious," she murmured.

Delilah hadn't touched her soufflé. She set the chocolate box on the table and leaned back in her chair, the wineglass in her hand. As a waiter whisked away the pink box, she said, "You're something of a mystery."

"Am I?" Ruby let her surprise show. "In what way?"

"On paper, you seem fairly conventional. Cooking school after high school, apprenticeship in Belgium, opening a web shop on your return to the States. You make a superior product and have begun marketing in a small way. A gradual buildup of your reputation, slow and steady." Delilah took a sip of wine. "But your hair and the nose piercing tell another story. Unconventional. Wild. Something of a rebel."

Ruby deliberately took another bite of soufflé and drank several swallows of wine before replying. "Maybe I'm fashionable. Pink's a very 'in' color these days." She touched the little diamond stud nestled in the curve of her nostril—a graduation gift from her mother. "And as far as piercings go, this one's pretty tame."

"If we insisted you lose the stud and dye your hair a less eccentric color, make your appearance more mainstream, would you be willing?" Delilah's gray gaze held a challenge. "After all, you'll be representing the hotel. We have a certain image to maintain."

Not a business dinner, only pleasure, my eye! Well, Ms. Kerrigan, if you insist on bringing up a corporate topic, I'll go along. Ruby didn't need to consider the woman's question. She would rather give up the opportunity than kowtow to other people's definitions of normal. "My appearance has nothing to do with my skill as a chocolatier. You don't make confectionery with your hair."

Delilah watched her from across the table. An elegant brow arched. "True." She let several tense seconds tick past and finally added, "I appreciate your honesty."

Servers cleared the soufflés and brought citrus marinated salmon with vodka jelly.

Ruby toyed with the salmon, waiting for the ax to fall. Surely she'd blown her chance. She didn't regret taking a stand for herself, but she could have spoken a bit softer, perhaps not been so blunt. She ate the vodka jelly absently, appreciating the lemony acidity in passing, and finally tried the salmon. The dish might have been exquisite, but the strain she was under prevented her from appreciating the nuances.

As if testing Ruby's patience—or taking perverse delight in torturing her—Delilah said nothing further regarding the hotel, merely made innocuous remarks as their dinner progressed from salmon to roast duck with confit shallots and port jus. The food smelled incredible and looked beautiful, but Ruby's stress made dinner almost impossible to enjoy.

Finally, the meal ended. Servers cleared the table. Ruby refused the dessert menu.

A waiter returned the Magic Bean chocolate box to Delilah. She glanced at Ruby with the tiniest smile. "Do you mind?"

"No, of course not." Ruby's heart thumped.

Delilah opened the box and made a show of choosing a bonbon. "This one." She held a white chocolate square between her thumb and forefinger.

"I call it Meladoro," Ruby answered through the knot in her throat. "Golden apple. A caramel apple ganache with a layer of crispy feuilletine."

Delilah popped the bonbon into her mouth and chewed. Her tone remained businesslike despite her obvious enjoyment when she asked, "How did you achieve such a strong, natural taste of apples?"

"Apple cider reduced to a syrupy consistency and an apple puree cooked down with caramelized sugar. A shot of green apple schnapps helps too."

"Conformity stifles creativity. I'm glad you won't be pushed into trying to become something you're not, Ms. Fontaine, because what I've seen of you so far, I like very much."

To cover her flush of embarrassment and relief, Ruby murmured "Thanks" and pretended to wipe her mouth with her napkin.

"Would you care to see something of the hotel?" Delilah offered, her manner thawing. She scrawled her signature on the bill presented by the hostess.

"A tour would be nice." Ruby checked her watch. The last ferry left Magdalena Island around midnight. She had plenty of time to dawdle.

Delilah stood and addressed the waiter. "Please ask Andre to take the chocolate box to my room." To Ruby, she continued, "Come with me, Ms. Fontaine. There are few things I enjoy more than showing off my baby."

Ruby smiled and allowed another waiter to pull out her chair.

CHAPTER EIGHT

Ruby had seen pictures of the St. Clare Hotel and Resort but never considered staying there. The prices were out of her league, even for a weekend, and the resort activities were wasted on her anyway. Golf was a mystery. Tennis left her cold. Biking bored her to tears. Sailing was okay, she supposed, just not a hobby she knew much about.

Nevertheless, she'd always admired the hotel's magnificent architecture and the sense of history. She had also been impressed by the luxury, but never given a thought to how much work it took to maintain such a high level of service.

As she followed Delilah to a discreet, keycard-access service elevator and rode down a level below the ground floor, she began to realize that behind the hotel's opulent exterior lay a vast, hidden world most guests never saw. Huge storage areas, locker rooms, an employee cafeteria open twenty-four hours, a labyrinthine network of pipes and ceiling ducts, and another maze of beige carpeted, fluorescent lit hallways leading to offices—everything needed by an army of staff to ensure the five-star hotel ran like clockwork.

"Operating a hotel requires preparation and organization," Delilah told her. "We map out every aspect of guest services to the finest degree."

In the Housekeeping department, for example, corkboards on a wall held pinned photographs of each type of room or suite for housekeepers to use as reference guides on how every little detail should be handled during daily cleaning. Printed explanations such as, "Position pen straight across center of message pad. Message pad placed one-half inch from phone" made Ruby think hotel housekeeping must be an obsessive-compulsive's dream job.

An official management notice on hotel letterhead stuck in a prominent place on a corkboard caught her eye. "To take immediate effect for all employees: please do not mention the alleged 'haunting' or 'ghosts' in regard to the hotel when speaking to guests or fellow employees of St. Clare Hotel and Resort. If guests wish more information on Magdalena Island legends, direct them to the Gift Shop in the lobby, where books are available."

"I didn't know the island was haunted," Ruby said, her curiosity sparked.

Delilah glanced at the notice. "Staff members can be terrible gossips. We've had good employees quit because they were frightened by ghost stories." She sighed. "These things happen in waves. We'll have a surge of supposed sightings or other so-called activity, then the excitement will die down and there'll be nothing for months. It's just mass hysteria, people working themselves up over nothing."

"I take it there's a wave right now."

"We believe one's getting started. Some of our staff goes up the hill during their lunch or dinner breaks when the weather's nice. Management staff has heard mutterings the last couple of days about strange noises."

"What do you think it is?"

Delilah shrugged. "Probably just the wind," she said with a dismissive sniff. "The old ruins have cracks and crevices that make noise when the wind blows off the ocean."

Ruby forgot about the notice as the tour continued. Most of what she learned went in one ear and out the other, but the hotel's food preparation area made her jaw drop.

"We're striving to get as close to zero kitchen waste as possible," Delilah said proudly, gesturing at the industrial-sized cooking equipment.

The place resembled a small-scale factory. Even at this time of night, chefs were hard at work trimming and breaking down sides of beef, whole poultry, pigs and fish. Bushels of vegetables were cleaned and chopped. Another set of chefs labored over pots and pans, or shaped bread dough into loaves or rolls and manned ovens. As far as Ruby was concerned, the steamy atmosphere held too many conflicting scents to be appetizing.

"You've got a very impressive operation here," she commented.

"We make our own stocks and sauces, artisan breads, pastries, cakes, desserts…everything possible. Severin oversees the entire pâtisserie department. Should you accept our offer, you'll be working with him." Delilah turned to gaze at her directly, looking as though she expected an answer to an unspoken question.

Ruby didn't take the bait. She smiled. "A definite perk if I agree to your offer, Ms. Kerrigan. I'll let you know at our next business meeting."

Delilah took the failure of her ploy in stride. She spun around on her black, high-heeled pumps and click-clacked across the floor. "Our waste management department sorts through the hotel's garbage every day. Food scraps are sent to a local pig farm, for example. In exchange, the farmer provides us with excellent quality organic pork at a very low cost."

"What about other garbage?"

"We recycle what we can, including donating older linens, towels and blankets to homeless and women's shelters. And you'd be surprised what guests discard. We always find quite a few personal items like dentures, car keys, credit cards, wallets, glasses, jewelry, guns, sex toys, prescription medicine bottles, sometimes illegal drugs. Even a prosthetic eye once."

"Unbelievable." Shaking her head, Ruby followed Delilah to the elevator.

They exited on the penthouse floor.

"The best view on the island, apart from the hill," Delilah promised, taking Ruby to the end of the corridor and a French door. After she swiped her ID card through a keypad and entered a four-digit code, the door locks clicked open.

Ruby stepped through and onto a balcony. She halted at the curved, ornate iron railing.

Magdalena Island's hill lay behind and a little west of the hotel, the summit crowned by the ruins of the Poor Clares' cloister. From her position on the balcony, she could also make out a golf course, red clay tennis courts, an Olympic-sized pool and a fanciful gazebo apparently constructed of stiffened white lace. Bright moonlight spilled over the small, crescent-shaped beach and the boats docked at the hotel's private marina, and meandered over the water, connecting the island to the mainland by a milky, flowing ribbon.

"You weren't kidding about the view." Ruby tried to take in everything at once.

Delilah shifted closer, coming to stand right behind her. "As I told you, some people think the cloister is haunted. In the past, we've had to ask trespassers to leave, so-called ghost hunters who've heard the legend that the spirits of two nuns can be seen at night, walking among the stones. Sometimes, they say, the nuns whisper to each other."

Ruby shuddered a little, unsure if her reaction was due to the story or Delilah's proximity. Did the woman have no respect for personal space? "Whisper what?"

"Who knows?" Delilah paused. When she spoke again, her voice was pitched an octave lower, her lips almost touching Ruby's ear and creating a shivery buzz. "I heard the nuns were lovers who died together."

"What happened to them?"

"They were caught making love by a visiting priest and burned at the stake."

Ruby stared up at the broken, scattered stones that were once a sanctuary for women of faith. "That's sad."

"Perhaps." Delilah moved closer, her breath puffing warm on Ruby's neck. "Perhaps not. According to the story, the lovers' ashes were still glowing hot when lightning struck the cloister, killed the priest and destroyed the building. Divine retribution."

"Small comfort to the dead nuns." Ruby rested her hands on top of the railing, trying to focus on the landscape, not the woman standing behind her.

"Is there no romance in your soul?" Delilah mocked.

Ruby turned around and gasped. Delilah stood far too close. Close enough for their knees to brush, in fact. If she took a deep breath, their breasts would touch too. She'd rarely been more aware of another woman's heat. Warmth poured off Delilah in dizzying waves.

The railing dug into her back as Ruby stood still, intoxicated by Delilah's gleaming gray eyes and the way the moonlight traced the sculpted planes of the woman's face, lending an ethereal touch to an already stunning beauty. For once, Delilah's expression was radiant rather than cold. Her breath caught. Her gaze strayed to Delilah's mouth, the red lips barely parted. Anticipation shivered through her.

Delilah chuckled, breaking the spell. She stepped away. "Shall we return downstairs?"

Her face hot, Ruby croaked a reply and followed Delilah off the balcony and into the hotel. In the elevator, neither of them spoke, but she had a sneaking suspicion Delilah might be silently laughing at her. By the time they exited to the lobby, she'd decided to ignore their moment on the balcony as though it had never happened.

Delilah stiffened and put a hand on Ruby's arm. "Stay here." She strode across the lobby, arrowing toward a man in a business suit who had just exited a guest elevator.

Ruby stared at the man, dredging her memory. Although she didn't know him right off the bat—middle-aged, balding, running a bit to fat, good suit, loud tie—he seemed vaguely familiar. She just couldn't put a name to his face.

Delilah clearly knew him. She confronted the man without pause. They were too far away for Ruby to overhear their conversation, but whatever the man said made Delilah pale and try to turn away. The man grabbed her wrist and yanked her around to face him.

Ruby began walking over. Slow anger ignited in the pit of her belly. "Is everything okay here?" she asked loudly as she drew closer, ensuring she could be heard by everyone in the lobby. The more witnesses, the better. She didn't think he'd do something monumentally stupid like take a swing at her, but stranger things had happened. "Ms. Kerrigan, is there a problem? Should I ask someone to call Security?"

"No." Delilah gave the man a basilisk stare. "No problem at all."

The man released his grip. "You remember what I said." He pointed a thick finger in Delilah's face. "Don't get any cute ideas."

"Hey, that's no way to treat a lady." Ruby pushed his hand aside and stood firm. "You should mind your manners."

"You should mind your own business," the man said, giving her a glare as cold and hard as freezer burned *gelato*. An instant later, he straightened his tie and made for the front doors. "Don't test me," he said over his shoulder to Delilah. "I know where you live."

Delilah stood looking after him, her nostrils flared. She took deep, measured breaths, the color returning to her face bit by bit.

Ruby picked up Delilah's hand and examined the wrist. The skin was darkening with bruises already. "Let's put some ice on that to help with the swelling."

Delilah pressed her lips together. Her gray gaze became frostier. "I don't need your help or your advice," she said in a clipped tone. Whatever sweetness she'd held in her expression earlier was gone, replaced by her usual icy mask. "Good night and goodbye, Ms. Fontaine." She walked away without another word.

"You're welcome," Ruby muttered to Delilah's retreating back. Her conscience made her sigh and hasten to catch up. "Please," she said, walking backward in front of Delilah, forcing the woman to stop and listen to her. "At least sit down and have a drink with me. A nightcap. Then I'll leave, I promise. What'll it be?"

Delilah reversed direction and got as far as a black leather sofa half-hidden behind an exquisite Japanese screen and a potted palm. She sat and crossed her legs, glaring at the screen as if attempting to set it on fire with the heat of her gaze. "Gin and tonic."

Ruby went to the bar and ordered the drinks from the bartender. After a moment, she returned to the seating area.

Delilah took the offered glass, sipped and nodded. "Thank you."

"Want to tell me what that unpleasantness was about?" Ruby sat on the opposite end of the sofa and tried her own gin and tonic. The crisp bite cleared her palate and her head.

"No," Delilah replied flatly.

"You know, I'm sure I've seen that man somewhere before…" Ruby let her voice trail off and raised her eyebrows.

Delilah ignored the opportunity to fill in the conversational blank. She continued drinking with grim determination until only ice cubes and a mangled lime wedge rattled in the glass. "Thank you for coming this evening," she said in a monotone.

Ruby stood hastily when Delilah got to her feet. "Are you okay?"

"Good night, Ms. Fontaine." Delilah set down her glass on a nearby side table. "Your concern is noted. Hadn't you better catch the last ferry home?"

"Who was that guy?" Ruby persisted. "What did he want? Why—" *Why did you let him manhandle you? What did he say that upset you so much?* And one more: *why didn't you kiss me on the balcony?* The questions stuck in her throat, refusing to be asked because common sense told her poking a lioness with a sore paw wouldn't get her anything except grief. "Why did he hurt you like that?" she concluded, troubled by the scene she'd witnessed.

Delilah shook her head and left.

After watching Delilah walk across the lobby and disappear through the Employees Only door, Ruby left the hotel, headed for the wharf and home.

CHAPTER NINE

The next couple of days went by in a blur as Ruby worked hard to fulfill orders for her Magic Bean business while trying to develop signature flavors for the St. Clare Hotel.

The meeting to negotiate her contract went fine, she thought, removing a saucepan of pomegranate jam from the stove. Delilah Kerrigan hadn't made an appearance at the meeting, but her lawyer had clearly received instructions. Drew and the hotel's lawyer spent time hashing out the details before she signed and initialed the contract. Committing herself to the new endeavor was taking a very scary step into the unknown, but she had faith in herself and her skills. If she didn't succeed, it wouldn't be for lack of trying.

Ruby tasted the jam, careful not to burn her lip. The sweetness level was good. She wanted to pair the jam with a homemade roasted peanut butter spread. The combination should work with milk chocolate and she'd garnish the bonbons with pink Himalayan salt to give some contrast. She poured the jam into a bowl and left it to cool on the counter while she continued with other tasks.

Three abrupt bangs on the kitchen's back door made her jump. She wasn't expecting anyone. Perhaps Aaron had been unable to deliver a package? Wiping her hands on her apron, she went to the door and opened it.

Nobody there.

Her gaze was drawn to an object on the ground—a prepaid cell phone, the kind available for sale at convenience stores. She glanced around and picked up the device. Except for her truck, the rear parking lot was empty.

When the phone vibrated a few seconds later, she shrugged and answered, "Hello?"

A text message appeared on the screen. *B Brooks is alive.*

Her heart froze in her chest. Horrified, she stared at the phone.

Tell the paper $3 million or she won't be. No cops. No feds. Understand?

Slowly, she typed, *Yes.*

Instructions later. Keep this phone.

The sender ended the call.

Shaking, Ruby returned to the kitchen and sat down at her desk. The phone dropped from her nerveless hand onto a stack of inventory forms. Beatrice had been kidnapped. Her friend was in danger. Not theoretical danger, not some vague and shadowy peril, but an actual threat made by criminals who would carry it out if she didn't comply with their demands.

She used her own cell phone to call Mike Michelson at the *Central Ledger.* He heard the story and asked few questions. His matter-of-fact attitude calmed her. At his insistence, she locked up the kitchen, got into her truck and drove to the newspaper's downtown office, a hundred-fifty-year-old dinosaur built when the Federal architectural style was in vogue.

Michelson worked on the fourth floor. Ruby took the elevator from the marble-clad lobby and was shown straight into his glass-walled office by a receptionist. She was instantly struck by the smells of strong coffee and cigarettes despite the Thank You For Not Smoking sign stuck to the nicotine-stained wall.

A man with a dark brown crew cut stood when she entered, revealing a ketchup stain on his white shirt. His tanned face creased in concern. "Ruby, come in. Brooks talks about you so often, I feel like I know you already. Please sit down. How are you holding up?"

Ruby sank into a chair opposite his desk, eyeing the stack of newspaper copies in front of her that seemed on the verge of sliding onto the floor. "I'm scared," she admitted after waving away his offer of coffee. "I don't know what to do."

"I've informed the paper's CEO. He's calling an emergency meeting of the board. Did you bring the burner phone? The phone the kidnapper gave you."

She set the phone on his desk next to the computer keyboard and a chipped red mug declaring "World's Biggest Asshole Award 1997."

Michelson's sharp blue gaze examined the device, but he didn't touch it. He finally grunted and sat back in his swivel chair, the one piece of furniture in the office that appeared modern. "I'm sure the police will want to dust the phone for fingerprints and check for other evidence, so we'll leave it where it lies until they get here."

"Police?" The betrayal left Ruby breathless. She could have strangled the man. "I told you, the person who texted me said no police or they'd kill Bee."

"Kidnapping is a serious crime, not some minor story I can sit on a few days. I had to call in a report as soon as you told me."

"I hope you don't get Bee killed," Ruby snapped. Realizing her anger was misplaced, she apologized. "Okay, I get that you believe you acted for the best. I'm sorry. I'm just so worried about Bee. I didn't mean to take it out on you."

Michelson nodded. "You're under a lot of stress." He paused. "To be honest, I can't figure out the kidnapper's angle. The paper isn't going to do nothing and get a reporter killed—forget about doing the right thing, ethics don't come into it, just that Bee's death would be a PR nightmare from the board's perspective— but three million dollars is a lot of cash money. So I have to ask: why Brooks? Why not a TV anchorman or someone with more public visibility who works for an institution that hasn't taken a lot of financial hits in the last ten, fifteen years? And Brooks hasn't got a spare penny as far as I know. Is her family rich?"

Ruby had been considering the matter during the drive downtown in the moments when she wasn't sick with dread. "Her family isn't wealthy, but her ex-husband is loaded."

Michelson looked thoughtful. "That's right. Greg Brooks is a trust fund baby."

"What I don't get is why the kidnappers contacted me. I have no pull with Greg."

"Perhaps Brooks gave them your information. She trusts you."

"Maybe." Ruby tensed when the door opened to admit Frances Orsini and a man with a boxer's thick build crammed into a suit. Frances introduced him as Detective Anderson.

After Ruby told her story, Anderson donned latex gloves, took the burner phone, delicately removed the SIM card—an amazing feat considering his meaty hands—and switched it with another phone's card. The burner phone went into an evidence bag, presumably for fingerprinting. He handed the new cell phone to her. "Next time the kidnapper gets in touch, we'll record the call and trace the signal." His voice had a nasal quality, likely due to his flattened nose. "Ask for proof of life when the kidnapper calls."

Ruby didn't like what she heard. "Proof of what?"

"Video, photographic or verbal proof that Beatrice Brooks is alive right now," Anderson explained. "We need to know. Ask if he'll put Ms. Brooks on the phone to talk to you. That would be best. You can identify her voice, I assume?"

"Yes, but why would...I mean, why... Oh no. No, no, no." She didn't want to think about Beatrice being dead. Horrible visions jolted through her head: Beatrice strangled, Beatrice stabbed, Beatrice staring at her with dead eyes while blood trickled from the bullet hole in the middle of her forehead...

Frances spoke from the corner of the room, pulling Ruby back from the nightmares. "In a public disappearance—and in this case, we've put bulletins out, local TV station and radio news broadcasts, a newspaper story courtesy of Mr. Michelson—it's not unknown for some scumbag opportunist to fake a ransom demand, so tell the caller you must have proof of life. If the call's genuine and you do talk to Ms. Brooks, ask if she's okay, but don't ask for her location or any specifics because the caller will be listening."

Ruby sucked in a breath and nodded, thankful for Frances's timely reassurance. She had to have faith that Beatrice would come out of this ordeal alive and return home. Any other alternative was unbearable. "I can do that." The cramp in her chest eased.

Anderson's cell phone rang. The bull-necked man pulled the phone from his pocket—the device looked tiny in his hand— and answered the call, turning his broad back on her.

Ruby stood and joined Frances next to a bank of old-fashioned wooden file cabinets. "Do you work kidnappings too?" she asked quietly, gazing up at the taller woman.

Frances's black ponytail swayed from side to side when she shook her head. "No, but Beatrice Brooks the missing person was my case. Beatrice Brooks the kidnapping victim isn't my case, but I'm here as a courtesy because my captain and Anderson's are on a departmental cooperation kick. Besides, I wanted to see how you were doing."

"I've been better."

"Anderson's a good guy. He knows what to do. Trust him."

"Oh, I think he knows his business. I just don't trust myself." Ruby waved the phone she'd been given through the air. "I mean, what if I say something wrong? What if I do something wrong? What if—" Fear clenched her throat shut, leaving her without words.

Frances put an arm around Ruby's shoulders and gave her a brief hug. "You'll be fine. Just follow the kidnapper's directions and don't get creative. If you have questions or concerns, talk to Anderson. Or you can call on me and I'll do what I can to help."

Ruby reluctantly let go when Frances ended the embrace. She wouldn't have protested a longer hug—the woman was soft and solid in the right places and smelled like oranges and white flowers—but her budding attraction's timing couldn't have been worse. "I still don't like it, but I'll do whatever it takes to get Bee back safely."

Anderson's call ended. He turned his head to talk to her. "Ms. Fontaine, we prefer you remain in your apartment until the kidnappers make contact. An officer will be assigned to stay with you."

She didn't like the idea of a stranger hanging out in her apartment, but there wasn't another choice. "I don't have a second bedroom, they'll have to stay on the couch if they spend the night," she said, feeling an irrational need to explain her lack of preparedness for guests. She blamed the twinge of shame on her mother, who'd always deemed hospitality one of the more important skills all Southern ladies should cultivate.

"Are you okay to drive home?" Frances interrupted her thoughts.

"I'm fine, thanks. And thank you for reminding me that Bee...that she's probably fine too. I needed to hear that." Without waiting for a reply, Ruby cleared her throat and raised her voice. "Can I go now, Detective Anderson?"

Anderson and Michelson were talking. When she asked her question, the detective glanced over his shoulder, gave her a short nod and returned to his conversation.

Frances made a shooing gesture accompanied by a small smile.

After leaving the newspaper building, Ruby drove to her apartment in an uncertain, uneasy mood. When she parked her truck in the underground garage, she recalled Delilah Kerrigan's rude temper tantrum with a faint chuckle despite her concerns about Beatrice. Now that she'd met Delilah under much less strained circumstances, the woman seemed nothing like the vicious, sharp-tongued harpy who'd shouted at her that day.

In the elevator on the way up to her floor, Ruby heard the cell phone ring.

The text message read: *$3 million cash in 2 days. Cumberland Ave bus terminal. Put money in backpack & leave in locker 21. No cops. No feds or bitch dies.*

She ignored the elevator ding and the opening doors to text back: *Need proof of life.*

Money or B Brooks is dead, came the reply.

Proof of life or no $$$, she typed doggedly.

The elevator doors slid shut.

In response to her demand, the caller began texting a torrent of abuse and threats with many misspellings, abbreviations and exclamation points. She almost dropped the phone. Soon, her shock faded. She glared at the screen. Was the caller so juvenile he had to bang on his chest and make a big noise to prove himself to her? The person texting seemed less like a criminal and more like an adolescent boy trying to intimidate her with nasty language.

"You'd owe so much money to my swear jar if you were here," she remarked at a particularly foul comment. She stabbed at the keypad with her thumbs. *Proof of life.*

Her own cell phone rang. She freed a hand to answer the call, keeping her gaze on the kidnapper's phone. "Hello?"

"Ms. Fontaine, we've tracked the call to an Internet café. Units are responding," Anderson said. "Are you still in communication with the suspect?"

"Yes."

"Good. Keep them on the line if you can."

She dropped her cell phone back into her purse to concentrate on the other phone. To every bubble of profanity that popped up on the screen, she responded with, *Proof of life.* Rather than deter the suspect, he continued spouting insults and abuse.

The elevator jolted, moving down to the below ground level. She paid scant attention to the people entering from the parking garage and pressing buttons for various floors. Wedging herself into a corner, her gaze remained fixed on the phone she held.

At last, the texting cut off midbluster. She tried to goad the caller into responding, but nothing happened. The screen remained frighteningly blank. Had she done the right thing? she wondered, staring at the blank screen. Or had she doomed Beatrice?

The elevator car emptied. The doors closed.

Her cell phone rang. "Do you have him?" she gasped.

"Yes," Anderson confirmed. "We've arrested a suspect. You did good, Ms. Fontaine. Go ahead and go home."

"What about Bee? Do you know where she is? Is she okay?" Ruby's pulse raced.

"There's nothing else I can tell you right now. We'll take things from here. Go home."

He ended the call without so much as a good-bye, leaving her frustrated, fearful and wishing she could reach down into the phone, wrap her hands around Anderson's throat and shake him until his teeth rattled.

Instead of fretting about the impossible, she snorted, dropped the cell phone into her purse and jabbed a finger at the elevator button for her apartment's floor.

CHAPTER TEN

Later the same evening, Ruby sat in her living room nursing a glass of sauvignon blanc from one of her favorite wineries. The grassy, gooseberry notes rolled over her palate, but from the little enjoyment she took from the experience, she might as well have been drinking grape juice laced with cat pee.

The apartment was quiet. Too quiet to settle her fretfulness.

After the evening news hadn't mentioned anything about the kidnapper's capture, she had called Anderson's number at the police station and was told rather curtly by the detective that the case was still under investigation and he couldn't give her any details. She hadn't dared make a second call to him, but she'd dialed Frances's number twice and gotten voice mail both times. Her initial pins-and-needles suspense had dulled over the hours to a constant, niggling distraction.

Her doorbell rang. She put down the wineglass to answer the door.

Frances Orsini stood in the corridor, looking well put together in a tobacco brown jacket and pants paired with a scarlet blouse that matched her lipstick. "May I come in?"

Ruby tried to smile in welcome, but her facial muscles seemed paralyzed and the best she could manage was a grimace. She stood aside and closed the door behind Frances. "Please tell me what happened," she pleaded, following the tall woman into the living room. "I've been going crazy worrying. Did you find Bee? Is she okay?"

"First of all, the man arrested at the Internet café isn't a kidnapper," Frances replied, taking a seat on the sofa and crossing one long leg over the other.

"Are you sure?" Disappointment as bitter as unsweetened chocolate curdled inside her. She sagged down on the sofa and reached for her wineglass.

"Terence Prewitt has a criminal record—petty theft and check fraud, mostly—but he's not a kidnapper. Turns out the *Central Ledger*'s story on Beatrice Brooks's disappearance mentioned you by name as a family friend. Prewitt saw the story as a way to make some easy money by faking a ransom demand, so he looked you up on the Internet and got your address from your company website."

Ruby drank a big swig of wine. Belatedly recalling her manners, she raised the half-empty glass and an eyebrow at Frances, who shook her head. *More wine for me, then. After the day I've had, I'm going to need the rest of the bottle if I want to sleep.* "He had nothing to do with Bee?" she asked, replacing the glass on the coffee table.

"I'm afraid not. Anderson did a thorough check. Terence Prewitt has no connection to Ms. Brooks." Frances gave her a sympathetic glance. "Since Ms. Brooks's disappearance was on the news, we're getting lots of tips on the hotline, but we have to weed through them. Some people genuinely want to help. Others tell lies to get their fifteen minutes of fame, or they're just plain delusional. A small percentage are blatant opportunists taking advantage of someone else's fear and grief to extort money from them."

"That's sick."

"I can't disagree."

Silence fell between them. The intricate stitching on Frances's caramel leather knee-length boots—a style Ruby had always wished she could pull off but didn't suit her shorter legs—caught her attention. Her gaze lifted, following the lines of the strong legs encased in form-fitting pants. Realizing she'd let her thoughts stray in an idle moment, she hauled herself back to the matter at hand. "What do we do now?"

"We keep the investigation open. We check leads. We do everything we can to bring Beatrice Brooks home safe."

"Okay, well, thanks for coming by to let me know."

Frances patted Ruby's hand. "No problem." She sniffed the air. "Are you cooking?"

"Yes, ah, just a second, let me go check the oven." Ruby hurried to the kitchen.

Needing something to do with her hands after she had come home earlier, she'd decided to make a batch of orange cinnamon rolls. Culinary school had taught her that kneading dough was a great stress reliever, taking her away from her problems for a short while and stretching her muscles. The two dozen rolls would score major points with her neighbors when she shared the bounty of buttery dough spiraled around a moist cinnamon and pecan filling scented with orange zest.

She opened the oven door, allowing a gust of hot sugar-and-spice-scented air to escape, and tested the golden brown rolls for doneness. Satisfied, she removed both pans, setting them on racks to cool so she could apply a drizzle of sweet orange icing later.

"Oh God." Frances's awed voice came from the doorway. The woman gestured with both hands, her brown eyes alight with humor. "You make divine chocolates and now you bake cinnamon rolls. If you can cook a homemade pizza as good as my *nonna*, I'll get down on one knee and propose right now."

Ruby set aside the pot holders. "I make a mean pizza base," she said playfully. "Roman style, stone baked, really thin and crispy."

"You are such a temptress." Frances stepped further into the kitchen. She had shed her jacket. Her scarlet blouse's neckline dipped in front, revealing the surprisingly delicate wings of her collarbones under the olive-toned skin. In the hollow of her throat nestled a small cross hanging from a gold chain. "Get thee behind me."

"Would the devil top a pizza with slices of buffalo mozzarella?"

"Probably not. *Mozzarella di bufala* is too heavenly. What else goes on your pizza? No, don't tell me. My heart can't take it."

"Parmigiano-Reggiano shavings and roasted cherry tomatoes."

"This is like pornography for Italians. You know that, right?"

Ruby smiled, enjoying herself for the first time in days. "When the pizza's out of the oven, I sprinkle torn basil leaves over it. Is that a sin?" she added, feigning innocence.

Frances came to a halt right in front of Ruby, the corners of her mouth twitching. "A deadly one. Stop. Just stop, I'm begging you, or I swear, I won't be able to control myself." She plucked at the front of her blouse. "Is it hot in here or is it just me?"

Leaning as close as she dared, Ruby whispered, "Sometimes right before serving the pizza, I scatter the top with a handful of arugula leaves tossed with garlic olive oil."

"You are terrible." Frances suddenly gave her the wickedest, filthiest grin imaginable. "But you can toss my salad anytime."

Ruby couldn't help giggling at the joke and Frances's mugging. Every time her hilarity started to run down, Frances's sniggering set her off again. After a few minutes, the laughter finally died to occasional hiccups. Despite the ache in her ribs, she felt good, as if a cloud had lifted and the sun had come out on a gloomy day.

Breathless, she dashed away involuntary tears with the back of her hand and found herself staring into Frances's lovely face. All at once, every trace of her humor vanished, replaced by a rush of emotions too complex to sort out. She found herself staring at the generous, gleaming curve of Frances's mouth. A question flitted through her mind: would Frances taste like cherries if she stood on tiptoe and kissed the gloss off those shining lips?

Common sense asserted itself. Was she insane? She'd met Frances just days ago. Besides, why on earth would the beautiful woman want her? She had no illusions about her appearance—she stood five-foot-five in her bare feet and was heavy-breasted, heavy-hipped and about a dozen éclairs shy of pudgy. Frances was tall, fit and athletic, a real Amazon. They couldn't be further apart in the looks department if they came from different planets.

Besides, she'd felt a pull of attraction toward Delilah Kerrigan that night on the balcony at the hotel. Not that her chances there were any better—Delilah wasn't even gay as far as she knew—but she had no time in her life to deal with complications. *Better take a step back and exert some self-control before I make a fool of myself.*

"Anyway, that's how I make a pizza," Ruby said lamely. She turned around and moved to the counter to fuss with the pans of hot cinnamon rolls, willing her heart to stop beating so fast.

Frances stayed put. "Sounds amazing. Well, I've got to head back to work." She sounded as awkward as Ruby felt. "Um…I didn't offend you, right?"

"No, not at all," Ruby hastened to say, keeping her back to Frances in case she accidentally betrayed her moment of madness. *You will not make the situation worse*, she ordered herself. *Frances isn't interested in you, just your cooking.*

"Okay, then. See you around. I can let myself out."

"Sure. Thanks for coming. Bye."

Ruby heard Frances leave the kitchen. A few seconds later the front door opened and closed. The apartment's atmosphere immediately changed, losing some of its warmth.

So did she.

CHAPTER ELEVEN

The following week, Ruby packed the sample bonbons she'd prepared for the St. Clare Hotel. Despite her jitters, she was prepared to receive criticism and outright rejection if a bonbon didn't make the grade. After the evaluation, she'd have a better idea whether she was headed in the right direction and how much work remained to be done.

Arriving at the beach, she parked her truck in the municipal garage. The Grand Strand Boardwalk and Promenade was beginning to stir. Maintenance workers wearing neon orange safety vests were pushing wheeled trash bins around and picking up windblown rubbish. Other workers were changing bulbs in the turn-of-the-century wrought iron streetlamps that marched in an ordered row on the ocean side of the boardwalk.

The ferry was ten minutes late, but she'd allowed extra time. Once on board and on the way over the water, she sat in a deck chair, her thoughts as turbulent as the white, foamy wake churned up by the ferry's passage. Would Severin and more importantly, Delilah, like her samples? Had she made the right choices?

When the ferry arrived at the island, she disembarked and walked to the hotel. She had to dodge five bicycle riders in Spandex shorts and shirts who came racing around the building and swept toward the path leading to the hill. In the busy lobby, she made her way to the Employees Only door and through the corridors to the administrative offices area.

On the way to Delilah's office, she spotted a familiar short, barrel-chested figure in chef's whites walking out of a room ahead of her. "Chef Valois!" she called.

Severin turned around. He clearly hadn't shaved that morning—silvery stubble bristled on his cheeks, chin and throat. "Ah, my dear Ms. Fontaine with the excitable hair," he cried in delight, clapping his hands together. "You are well, I hope?"

"Please call me Ruby. I'm doing fine, Chef," Ruby lied. Between her business, her obligation to the hotel and worrying about the lack of progress in finding Beatrice, she hadn't slept much. "I brought samples of proposed flavors for you and Ms. Kerrigan to try."

"Ms. Kerrigan has meetings all day. Bah. So tiresome." He gave her a Gallic shrug—lower lip pouted and eyebrows, shoulders and hands raised simultaneously. "*Alors là*. What can be done? You are here. Let us go where I may taste your chocolates in peace."

Ruby had assumed Delilah would participate. She'd even taken the time yesterday to buy a professional outfit: a flattering, tailored pair of pants in charcoal gray worn with a robin's egg-blue blouse and dark gray pumps. Looking her best had nothing to do with impressing Delilah on a personal level, she'd told her reflection in the mirror that morning. A business-like appearance proved she was taking her work for the hotel seriously.

Fighting a pang of disappointment, she held the chocolate box tighter to her chest and asked, "Where do you want to do this?"

"Follow me." He led her to an office tucked beside the kitchens area.

Ruby went inside. The décor was spare—a simple wooden desk with a computer and phone, a couple of chairs and a bookcase crammed with cookbooks and awards. The pastry department was visible through a large rectangular window in the wall to the left of the door.

Severin indicated she should sit down opposite the desk. After settling himself in his chair, he poured a glass of water from a carafe and removed a napkin, a notebook and a ballpoint pen from a drawer. His black gaze held an expectant look.

Ruby put the bright pink box on the desk. She licked her lips. Her mouth had gone dry. "I suggest we use only a seventy percent or better Madagascar criollo," she said, naming the rarest cacao bean variety. "The flavor profile of the chocolate is rich and dark with subtle essences, and it has a good mouthfeel and a clean finish."

"Agreed," Severin remarked, making a note. "Go on."

"Dark chocolate. Perhaps a little milk for variety. No white except for embellishments on the bonbons."

"Why?"

"To give a slightly more sophisticated, adult edge to the final product. At least, that was my thinking. Was I wrong?"

"We will see."

Anxiety ran cold through her veins. Self-confidence in her skills didn't exempt her from nervousness at being judged by a chef with an expert palate. Severin's opinion mattered to her a great deal. "Okay, here we go." She took a breath and lifted the box's lid. Inside lay one dozen chocolates—two each of the six new flavors she'd prepared. "The first bonbon has a filling made to taste like traditional Mexican café *de olla*."

He accepted the offered bonbon. The tempered chocolate enrobing the filling made a crisp snap when he bit into it. After a moment to allow the bite to melt in his mouth, he said, "Coffee, cinnamon, coffee liquor, a soupçon of smoke." He raised his eyebrows at her.

"In Mexico, sometimes the coffee is made over a wood fire."

"Ah, *bien*, a most pleasant touch. And the sweetness has molasses notes that remind me of *sucre cassonade*. You know it, yes? Unrefined cane sugar."

"Yes, Chef. I used *piloncillo*, a dark brown, unrefined cane sugar."

He discarded the remains of the bonbon on the napkin and drank from the glass of water, his Adam's apple working as he swallowed. When he finished, he picked up his pen to scrawl over the notebook page, writing several sentences Ruby couldn't read upside-down. "Let us have the next," he said, setting down the pen.

One by one, Ruby went through the bonbons she'd created. Severin tasted, asked questions and wrote in his notebook. His expression remained thoughtful and somewhat friendly, but otherwise impossible to read. She couldn't tell if he was delighted or disgusted. By the time he sampled the last of the six bonbon flavors and took his time scribbling notes, the tension was stretched as tight as piano wires.

"All your chocolates are good," Severin said at last, ending her agony. "Two are exceptional: the kabocha squash and the strawberry. The rest...*comme ci, comme ça.*" He wobbled his hand back and forth. "Good, as I say, but not good enough for our project. You have an extraordinary talent, *petite*. You can do better. Remember, each bonbon should be a work of art and a seduction of the senses."

"Yes, Chef."

"Perhaps in the future, you will concentrate more on creating a single exceptional bonbon rather than a half-dozen which are only excellent." He smiled. "I will confess, the kabocha bonbon is my favorite. *Délicieux*! The hint of maple, the chestnuts, the kabocha puree with bourbon are perfectly balanced. A lovely bite." He smacked his lips. "I may steal the idea for my pastry menu," he added with a wink.

Ruby blew out a relieved breath. Two out of six wasn't bad for a maiden effort. She paid attention while he gave his critiques, pointing out which bonbons needed work and which concepts should be nixed.

As Severin wound down, his office door opened and Delilah swept inside, her face flushed. "I can't believe Avery had the nerve to treat Maria Herrera that way, scaring her half to death with those stupid ghost stories—oh, I'm sorry," she said, glancing from him to Ruby and back again. "I didn't know you were engaged."

Severin waved off the apology and gave Delilah a look interpreted by Ruby as: *We'll talk about your problem later.*

Ruby decided to pretend she hadn't heard Delilah's outburst, although the brief glimpse of the woman's temper reminded her of their accidental encounter in her apartment building's parking garage on the day Beatrice disappeared.

Since the fake ransom demand debacle, she hadn't really done much on her missing friend's behalf. Her conscience prickled. She studied Delilah, wishing she knew for sure if a connection existed to Beatrice that the police simply hadn't discovered. *I don't know who to trust. Delilah might be a criminal, but she doesn't look like one.*

Delilah wore a black-and-white houndstooth dress cinched in at the waist with a shiny patent leather belt—very chic and stylish—that drew the eye to her slender figure. Ruby's gaze moved to the faded bruise on Delilah's wrist, hardly more than a yellow stain on skin almost hidden under a silver wrist cuff set with moonstones the color of the woman's eyes.

Who was the ill-mannered stranger who'd assaulted Delilah in the hotel lobby a week or so ago? She hadn't had time to discover the man's identity. The recollection led to another— her moment with Delilah on the balcony prior to the unpleasant scene. Almost against her will, her mind lingered over the moonlight on the water, the cloister ruins on the hill, the warmth she'd felt when she and Delilah stood so close together...

"Hello, Ms. Kerrigan," she said, thrusting aside the unsteady feeling in her stomach to focus on her purpose—confirming or ruling out Delilah as a suspect. "How are you today?"

Delilah flicked a glance at her. "Fine," she said coolly.

"We're taste testing sample bonbons," Ruby continued undaunted, cutting Delilah some slack. *Maybe a little sugar will sweeten her mood.* "Would you like to try one?"

"No." Delilah paused and took a deep breath. Her shoulders went back, her spine straightened. She gave Ruby an apologetic smile. "I appreciate the offer, but no, thank you," she added. "I'm sure Severin has done an evaluation and I trust his judgment."

"But you must try this one," Severin said, standing and coming around the desk. He reached into the box and brought out a dark chocolate square topped by a crystallized rose petal. "Go on. Trust me."

Delilah started to shake her head. At Severin's insistence, she accepted the bonbon and took a bite. A noise came from her throat.

Alarm shot through Ruby. Was Delilah choking? She rose from her seat, trying to remember a long-ago first aid class.

"Strawberries, rosebuds, meringues and wine," Severin said, touching Delilah's free hand. "What does the taste remind you of?"

"Summer in the park in Paris," Delilah said after a moment. A faint, rueful smile ghosted over her face. She turned to Ruby. "How did you achieve the flavor and texture?"

"A Marc de Champagne ganache and a whipped strawberry-rose cream studded with crushed vanilla meringues, freeze-dried strawberries and rose petals," Ruby answered, her concern fading. She sat back in her chair.

"I'm pleased our partnership is starting off so well." For the first time since Delilah entered the office, she seemed to relax. She leaned a hip against the edge of Severin's desk. "Where did you come up with the idea of using meringues in the bonbon?"

Having been handed an opening on a platter, so to speak, Ruby didn't waste the opportunity. "A friend, Beatrice Brooks, is crazy about strawberry and rose macarons." The falsehood almost stuck in her throat. Beatrice loathed macarons and would rather eat the refrigerated chocolate chip cookie dough sold in tubes at the grocery store.

When she finished speaking, she watched closely for the tiniest hint of guilt or self-consciousness her mention of Beatrice's name might cause, but Delilah just nodded. "Your friend has good taste."

Either she's an awesome poker player or she really has no idea, Ruby thought. *Well, it can't hurt to do a little more prying.* "By the way, do you know Beatrice's work, Ms. Kerrigan? She's an investigative reporter at the *Central Ledger*."

Frowning, Delilah glanced down as though gathering her thoughts. "Didn't Ms. Brooks write a piece last year about a sweatshop exploiting Korean immigrants?" At Ruby's nod, she went on, "I recall her now. Do you know her very well?"

"We've been best friends a long time. Bee recently went missing," Ruby continued. "It's been on the news."

"I'm very sorry," Delilah said, raising her head to show an expression of genuine sympathy. "I hope Ms. Brooks returns home soon."

Ruby couldn't detect a single false note in Delilah. She didn't like to think of herself as one of those people who clung to a cherished delusion despite evidence to the contrary. Perhaps she'd been mistaken and her clash with Delilah in the garage was just a coincidence as Frances Orsini had suggested. No, not perhaps. She was wrong, period. *Mama always says I'm more stubborn than Balaam's ass.* Thank goodness she hadn't made a fool of herself.

Severin stood. "Pardon, ladies, I must go and see to the desserts on tonight's menus. Ruby, we will have another meeting soon…shall we say, next Wednesday?"

"Yes, Chef, that works for me." Ruby got to her feet and took a step toward the door to follow Severin out, only to be stopped by Delilah's voice.

"I have some time between meetings. If you can spare an hour or so, I'd like to discuss the proposal Marketing has come up with for the brand. I have some mock-ups in my office." Delilah was half-seated on the desk. The way her body leaned slightly backward, her weight supported on her hands, appeared almost flirtatious. The posture pulled up the hem of the houndstooth check dress a little higher, showing even more of her shapely legs.

Ruby didn't trust herself to read Delilah. She'd been wrong about the woman's connection to Beatrice. Thank goodness she hadn't embarrassed herself by making an accusation. No doubt she was wrong here, too, and Delilah's pose meant nothing.

She accepted the invitation and followed Delilah through the corridors.

CHAPTER TWELVE

Noting the receptionist wasn't on duty when she passed by, Ruby walked across the threshold of Delilah's office and stopped so abruptly, she almost fell over. Her breath caught on the name jolted out of her, turning the single syllable into a gargled cough.

The man standing by Delilah's desk gave her a limpid look from beneath absurdly long lashes. "Ruby. Nice to see you, I guess."

"Greg," she choked. What was Beatrice's ex-husband doing here? She'd assumed he would take Kaitlyn back to California after the court granted him temporary custody. She studied him, comparing her memories of the man to the unexpected reality.

Greg Brooks remained thin and somewhat boyish—as sinuous, slinky and supple as a snake, or so Ruby had thought the first time Beatrice introduced him to her. He'd upgraded his wardrobe since she saw him last, from jeans and a polo shirt to a tailored dark blue suit and Italian shoes. Clearly, his trust fund was in no danger of running out.

On sheer good looks alone, she'd still rate him nine-point-five out of ten. Greg was inhumanly beautiful, like a fine statue or a painting by a master. Skin touched with gold, striking green eyes, platinum hair in a stylish faux-hawk and cheekbones sharp enough to shave chocolate. Too bad he wasn't capable of loving anyone more than he loved himself.

"How can I assist you, Mr. Brooks?" Delilah's calm expression suggested unexpected and unannounced visitors in her office were a regular occurrence. She moved to her desk and sat down, giving him her full attention.

The receptionist barged into the office, almost colliding with Ruby in his mad dash. He halted, his head swiveling from Greg to Delilah. "I am so, so sorry, Ms. Kerrigan," he babbled breathlessly. "There was a problem with the printer in housekeeping and Caroline needed a hand. I was gone five minutes tops—"

"Everything's fine, Kyle, thank you." Delilah waited for the flustered receptionist to leave and close the door behind him before she glanced at Greg, who smirked.

"Sorry, I don't like to wait," he said, waving an airy hand and not looking the least apologetic. "When I have a problem, I skip the minions and go straight to the top."

To Ruby's surprise, Delilah nodded like Greg's attitude sounded reasonable. "Of course. I'm here to help any way I can, Mr. Brooks. What can I do for you?"

"When I made the reservation, I asked for two adjoining suites. Instead, you people gave me two suites down the hall from each other. I mean, really, it's a simple request."

"Please accept my apologies for the inconvenience," Delilah said in her unruffled way. She began to type on her keyboard while checking the monitor. "Let me see what I can do to accommodate you. One moment, please."

Ruby took a few steps closer to Greg, needing to ask the question burning in her heart. "Where's Kaitlyn?"

He shrugged without glancing at her. "The kid's fine. She's with her nanny."

"In California?"

"No, she's here in the hotel and I'm kind of busy over here. Can you wait?"

Ruby opened her mouth to insist he let her see Kaitlyn right this minute, but Delilah broke in, "Mr. Brooks, there are two adjoining suites on the tenth floor overlooking the golf course; would that work for you? Or I have a penthouse suite available or a three-bedroom cottage with a view of the ocean and the marina."

"Adjoining suites are fine." Greg stood in an elegant slouch, his hands buried in his pants pockets. His lips pursed. "Next, I need a half dozen bottles of premium rainwater in my suite at all times. And I want a new toilet seat every day."

"I'll instruct housekeeping to take care of it. Have you any other requests?"

"An egg white omelet and black coffee for breakfast at eight sharp. And fresh flowers in my suite daily. I'm partial to orchids."

Delilah continued typing, no doubt sending notes to the right departments. "I'll see to it, Mr. Brooks. Does your daughter have any special requirements?"

Greg stared, clearly taken aback. "I have no idea about the kid. Ask the nanny. She's the expert. I pay the woman to keep track of that stuff. So, Ms. Kerrigan, are we done here? No more screwups? Good. I've got a spa treatment scheduled in ten minutes." He turned and sauntered toward the door.

"Hey, what about Katie?" Ruby blurted, lunging and latching on to his arm.

He paused to speak to her with ill-concealed impatience. "Talk to the nanny, for God's sake. Leave me out of it." He shook off her hand when she tried to speak. "Look, I know you never liked me, but you're my ex-wife's best friend, so if you want to see the kid, knock yourself out. Just don't expect me to get involved. I've got my own life going on and I've been inconvenienced enough, don't you think?"

Delilah's office wasn't the best place for this conversation, but Ruby couldn't remain silent. "Greg, why did you even take your daughter if she's such an inconvenience?"

"You think I'd let the kid get shoved into foster care? Hell no. Abandonment wouldn't be good for my image. A lot of my friends have children and I'd be *persona non grata* in certain circles."

"I'd have taken care of her."

He shook his head, his green eyes glittering as he surveyed her up and down. "No."

Ruby's fists clenched. She lowered her voice, aware of Delilah seated behind the desk within earshot. "Is it because I'm a lesbian?"

"No. That'd be kind of hot if you weren't so...you know." He wrinkled his nose and gestured at her generous curves, ignoring her indignant glare. "I'm sure you mean well, but my lawyer told me if Bee wanted you to have custody, she'd have filed the right paperwork. Since she didn't, that means she stuck me with the kid on purpose. Sneaky bitch."

Ruby clamped down on her temper. She didn't know how to refute his statement when Beatrice's carelessness had landed them in this mess in the first place.

"I don't really care if you hang out with the kid," Greg went on, "or take her out shopping, or have a tea party, or whatever butters your muffin. Like I said, get with the nanny, do your own thing with the kid, leave me out of it, okay? I'm a busy guy and—"

"Kaitlyn," Ruby gritted.

"What?"

"Your daughter's name is Kaitlyn or Katie. Not 'the kid.'"

He snorted. "Whatever."

"May I walk you to the spa, Mr. Brooks? We'll pick up your new keycards on the way," Delilah said, smoothly inserting herself into the conversation. She joined them near the door. "And Ms. Fontaine, I'll be right back. Don't go anywhere." She escorted Greg out of the office, throwing Ruby an unreadable look over her shoulder as she went.

Ruby stood still and controlled her breathing, her hands clenching and unclenching. Slowly, her ruffled feelings subsided enough to give her some perspective.

Greg Brooks was selfish and horrible, but he wasn't a monster. She couldn't condemn him for indifference when he'd made his wishes clear to Beatrice at the beginning of their relationship—at least, that's what she'd been told. While she didn't approve of his attitude, at least he was willing to provide care for Kaitlyn in Beatrice's absence.

She blew out a breath and tried to relax the tightness in her shoulders. Getting angry with Greg for being himself was as useless as railing at bad weather.

Her gaze fell on Delilah's desk—neat and well organized, every item placed just so, utterly unlike the chaos of her own workstation. With a jolt, she realized she hadn't asked Greg where to find Kaitlyn and the nanny, and Delilah hadn't mentioned any suite numbers.

She eyed the computer. Delilah hadn't logged out. If she peeked at the arrangements made for Greg's stay, what could it hurt? She went around the desk to look at the monitor, only to gasp and snap upright when the office door opened.

"You didn't tell me you knew Greg Brooks," Delilah said, entering the room. She halted, her gray eyes narrowing. "Can I help you find something?" The sharp edge of sarcasm in the question was unmistakable.

"I'm sorry," Ruby murmured, mortified. "I was just looking up the suite number so I can see Katie's nanny."

Delilah's frosty glare thawed a bit. "Mind telling me what's going on?"

"Beatrice Brooks—my missing friend, the reporter, we were just talking about her—is Greg's ex-wife and Kaitlyn is their daughter."

"I see. I didn't make the connection. Brooks isn't an uncommon surname. Let me get that information for you." Delilah moved to her desk, where she gave Ruby the suite number and then paused, her fingertips trailing across the front of a colorful presentation folder. "I have a proposition for you. I need to attend a fund-raising dinner and charity auction tonight at the railroad museum," she continued, raising her hand to smooth a chestnut curl behind her ear. "This is short notice, but would you like to go to the event with me as my plus-one?"

Initially, the question skidded off Ruby's mind without leaving much of an impression. Her thoughts were busy forming different approaches to use with Kaitlyn's nanny depending on the woman's friendliness and cooperation, or lack thereof. *Can't expect any help from Greg if the nanny turns down my very reasonable suggestion of a day out with Kaitlyn to the aquarium, maybe a sleepover, and—wait, what?*

Somewhat shocked, she replayed what Delilah had said to her. "Did you just ask me out on a date?" she asked after a slight hesitation, ready to backtrack and apologize if she'd misinterpreted the situation.

"Yes," Delilah said, gazing at her steadily, an eyebrow arched in anticipation. "To a charity auction and dinner tonight. I'm sorry for the late notice. Things have been a little hectic around the hotel and the event slipped my mind."

"Oh." Ruby forced herself to smile, uncertain whether or not to accept.

Dating her boss couldn't be a good idea…except Delilah wasn't technically her employer. As a freelancer, she had a contract with the hotel's owners, not the general manager. And Delilah was very attractive and had been flirting with her—*not my imagination, thank goodness.* The only other consideration was Frances Orsini, the gorgeous Amazon who definitely sparked an interest, but Frances wasn't here, probably wasn't available and, more importantly, would never ask her out on a date in the first place.

She finally made a decision to keep things with Delilah casual, no expectations, no drama. They were both mature adults. The worst that could happen was a rubber chicken dinner, an awkward evening and maybe a little embarrassment that would pass in time. And the best… She cleared her throat, her cheeks burning when a fantasy image of a naked Delilah popped unbidden into her head. *Don't go there, fool,* she told herself sternly. *Stay cool.* "Sure, sounds like fun. When and where?"

"I'll pick you up at your apartment at six, if you don't mind."

"Great. How should I dress?"

"It's not a black-tie affair. Just choose something nice, like you'd wear to a cocktail party or a night out on the town." A gleam shone in Delilah's eyes. Her lips curled in a smug, self-satisfied little smile that reminded Ruby of a cat with helpless prey trapped under its paw. "An outfit you'd wear to impress a date. In this case, that would be me."

Ruby flushed brighter and made some feeble reply about "putting on the Ritz for all her dates" that broadened Delilah's smile.

At that moment, she also caught a hint of nervousness beneath Delilah's usual chilly mask and realized the woman had worried she wouldn't accept. The idea seemed ludicrous, yet even the suggestion gave her a warm, melting feeling. Most of the time, Delilah appeared smart, controlled and in charge, so it was endearing that even such a confident woman got the jitters when asking someone out on a date.

She left holding the presentation folder under her arm—mock-ups for the chocolate brand from the hotel's Marketing Department—with her attention half on the coming meeting with Kaitlyn's nanny and half on the evening to come with Delilah.

CHAPTER THIRTEEN

Later that night, Ruby checked her appearance in the mirror, pursing her lips at her reflection. She'd reapplied pink stain to her hair in the shower, giving the flyaway, gravity-defying locks a deeper cotton candy hue. The color flattered her pale complexion, the result of too many hours spent working indoors. Perhaps business would calm down and let her enjoy a day at the beach—good for a suntan, but bad for her bank account at the moment. *Maybe not the best idea. I'd rather be fish belly white and pay the bills than tanned and broke.*

The delicate silver nose ring hugging the curve of her nostril was matched by a pair of dangling silver hoop earrings swinging jauntily with each movement of her head. Satisfied with the effect, she reached for the mascara tube on the sink.

Her makeup was dramatic: lots of black mascara contrasting with her pale blue eyes, pearly pink shadow, lipstick several shades more intense than her hair. The silver lamé dress she'd chosen sent the right message, even if the skirt was a little shorter than she normally wore and the neckline dipped low enough to make her glad she'd invested in a good push-up bra. In her opinion, the outfit said, "We might hook up if our chemistry sparks and if not, that's okay," rather than "Bow-chicka-wow-wow." She had the balance right.

The doorbell rang, breaking into her musings.

Her heart pumping in anticipation, Ruby went to answer the door, but the caller was Frances Orsini instead of her date. "Hello, Detective. I wasn't expecting a visit."

Frances's friendly expression soured. "Am I interrupting something?" Her dark gaze traveled upward from Ruby's pink pumps, wandering over the black lace tights and the sparkling dress that ended midthigh, and lingered on the bold plumpness of her décolletage.

"I'm going out soon on a date," Ruby explained, smoothing her dress self-consciously. "Did you want to talk about Beatrice? Is there any news?"

"Not exactly. We're pursuing a possible lead. Can I come in?" Frances didn't wait for Ruby to stand aside, but brushed past her into the apartment.

Ruby bit back a startled exclamation and followed her unexpected visitor to the living room. "Is something wrong?"

"No." Frances held a PC tablet in her hand. "I need to ask you a couple of questions, it won't take long." Flipping open the tablet and tapping the screen to activate some program, she showed Ruby six photographs. "Do you recognize any of these guys?"

Leaning in to study the photos, Ruby pointed at the man in the center of the second row—balding, middle-aged, a little tubby around the middle. She wouldn't forget that jerk in a hurry, given his abusiveness toward Delilah and herself. "I saw him once at the St. Clare Hotel," she said, recalling his hostile manner.

"Okay. Anybody else?"

"Sorry, no."

"Are you sure?"

"I'm positive; I don't recognize anyone else." Ruby folded her arms across her chest, feeling defensive in the face of

Frances's skeptical tone. "I've seen that man in the hotel lobby speaking to Ms. Kerrigan, the general manager. I don't know his name. Who is he?"

"Okay, let's talk about the man you identified," Frances said with strained patience. "This is City Councilman Harrison Lovett, he owns the—"

As soon as the tall woman said the name, a memory surfaced in Ruby's mind: the man posing with two bikini-clad blond beauties against a backdrop of automobiles. She nodded. No wonder she hadn't put the grinning, friendly car dealer together with the rude stranger in the hotel. "Yes, the 'You'll Lovett' used car dealerships. I've seen his ads on TV."

"Right. Now look at these other men. Does anyone else seem familiar to you?"

Ruby obediently scrutinized the photos. She shrugged. "No. Why?"

"Look carefully."

"Who are they?"

"Frank Marion and Eugene Burley, Lovett's business associates." Frances closed the tablet cover. "What was Councilman Lovett doing when you saw him at the hotel?" She loomed taller, her gaze intent. "And when did this happen?"

"What does all this have to do with Beatrice?" Ruby countered, somewhat annoyed and unwilling to get Delilah involved. "Before we continue with the third degree, I'd appreciate an answer." She summoned her most stubborn chin tilt and resolved not to say another word unless the matter involved her missing friend.

Frances gave her a hard look, but finally opened the tablet again and indicated another photo—a thin, wiry, scruffy dark-haired man. "Red Iverson, Councilman Lovett's hatchet man. We have a witness placing him with Ms. Brooks a few hours before her disappearance. I can't really say anything more," she put in when Ruby drew breath to pepper her with a dozen or so questions clamoring to be voiced. "Are you sure you didn't see him in the hotel?"

"I didn't see anyone else that day, only Councilman Lovett," Ruby repeated, wishing she knew what Frances was after. "Lovett seemed out of sorts. Not as friendly as his TV ads make him out to be. He and Ms. Kerrigan had…well, not exactly a fight."

"What happened?" Frances's features seemed to sharpen with eagerness.

"I don't know. I overheard only part of the conversation. Lovett told her, 'Remember what I said,' and 'Don't test me.' He also grabbed her wrist hard enough to leave a bruise."

"What was Ms. Kerrigan's reaction?"

"She was understandably upset."

"Did Ms. Kerrigan say anything to you?"

"Other than to mind my own business? No."

Frances closed the tablet and put a hand on Ruby's bare upper arm. Frowning down at her, she said, "If Iverson or Lovett contacts you, call me. Promise?"

"Do you think they're involved with Bee?" Ruby shivered—partly because of Beatrice and partly because Frances's comforting grip seemed hot enough to scorch, touching her skin with fire. She reminded herself she had a date with a different woman and to stop lusting after someone else. Delilah deserved her full attention.

"It's a connection and an avenue we're pursuing, but it may be nothing. No need to panic. Just call me." Frances released Ruby's arm and turned to go, her glossy black ponytail swinging. She paused at the door and glanced over the shoulder of her linen jacket, her face blank. Some undecipherable but strong emotion burned in her eyes. "Have fun on your date tonight." She sounded unhappy.

Ruby hoped Frances's attitude had nothing to do with Beatrice's case. She summoned a smile and a goodbye wave as the door closed behind the departing woman.

What could Councilman Lovett and/or Red Iverson have to do with Beatrice's disappearance? The most obvious answer had to do with the newspaper story. Were they part of the secret exposé Beatrice had talked so little about? As sources or subjects? Too many unknowns whirling in her head made her clench her teeth until her jaw ached.

Sitting on the sofa, she used her phone to look up Frank Marion and Eugene Burley on the Internet. She learned both men were in the construction business and suspected of having ties to organized crime. In fact, Marion had been indicted for illegal alcohol manufacturing and distribution last year when a former employee blew the whistle on a cache of moonshine and a still at one of his building sites, but the witness changed his story and the case fell through. While she wasn't surprised to learn a politician like Lovett had connections to the new Dixie Mafia, the knowledge didn't bolster her faith in government.

The doorbell's chime sealed her resolve to have a good time and not worry about things she couldn't change. She opened the door to find Delilah standing in the hallway, appearing utterly edible in a midnight-blue strapless cocktail dress fitted to her body. Sequins shimmered on the tight bodice, sparkling brighter where they caught the light.

"Ruby, you look beautiful." Delilah's smile crinkled the corners of her gray eyes, their stormy color deepened and warmed by pleasure. "Are you ready to go?"

"Let me grab my purse." Ruby resisted the impulse to check herself in the mirror one last time. She snatched a pink leather clutch from the table by the door and headed out of the apartment to join Delilah walking down the hall to the elevator.

Inside the elevator, Ruby caught the subtle fragrance of Delilah's perfume: clean citrus and warm spices with a ghostly hint of honey and florals, like the tobacco in the *shisha* water pipe she'd sampled once in a Cairo café during a vacation in Egypt when she was younger. She studied Delilah's wavering reflection in the metal doors. The woman's evening makeup, heavy on the eyeliner, smoky shadow and sheer red lipstick, gave her an exotic and sexy appearance that suited the delicious scent.

The parking garage was quiet when they exited the elevator. She and Delilah went outside to the visitors' lot, where a Lincoln Town Car was parked. The sleek black luxury ride seemed out of place among the Volkswagens, Hondas and oversized SUVs.

Ruby was relieved she wouldn't have to shoehorn herself into Delilah's MINI. Briefly, she considered making a quip about not stealing a resident's parking space this time, but kept her mouth shut. Delilah didn't know she'd seen her epic meltdown on the day Beatrice disappeared. Revealing the information now might be a real date-killer. *Let tonight just be about tonight and nothing else. Tomorrow can take care of itself.*

She settled into the Town Car's passenger seat for the trip downtown and stared out the window while Delilah drove to the historic district.

Night had fallen over Summerland, but the streets were never dark. Lighted windows, streetlamps and signs created smears of color on the windshield. As they came closer to the historic district, the buildings changed from modern construction to more graceful eighteenth and nineteenth century architecture. Ruby knew the area housed mainly law offices rubbing shoulders with art galleries and antique shops, a famous two-hundred-year-old coffeehouse and a couple of museums, including their destination—the railroad museum.

"Are you all right?" Delilah asked, giving her a sidelong glance. "You're very quiet."

Ruby roused herself. "I'm sorry. I have some stuff on my mind."

Delilah brought the Town Car to a smooth halt at a traffic light. "Want to talk about it?"

"Not at the moment." Ruby sought a way to draw the subject away from her. "You've been to Paris?" she asked. "You mentioned a picnic in Paris when you tasted my strawberry-rose bonbon. I just…I wondered," she concluded lamely.

"I lived in Paris a while ago," Delilah answered, setting the car in motion when the light turned green. She stared steadily out the windshield while she spoke. "After college, I worked in a boutique hotel in the Bastille district. The owners were great, they taught me a lot." The play of shadow and light over her profile cast her cheekbones in high relief. "Josette—Severin Valois's stepniece, who later became my lover—was studying art history at the Sorbonne. We met at the Petite Palais. I was drawn to her the first time I saw her shouting abuse at some poor man in front of a Fragonard. Josette really stood out from the crowd. She had flaming red hair and a loud voice and she wasn't afraid of anything or anybody. At the time, I wanted her like nothing else I'd ever wanted in my life, like I was stranded in a desert and she was the drink of water I needed to save my life."

Sounds like love, Ruby thought. Was Delilah still hung up on her French lover? "I'm curious...why are you telling me all this?" For all Delilah knew, she might be taking a huge risk revealing so much of herself to someone she didn't really know.

"Because I want no misunderstandings with you. I don't advertise the fact that I'm gay, but I'm not in the closet either. And in case I wasn't clear before, we're on a date." Delilah's gaze met Ruby's in the rearview mirror. "Shall I continue?"

"Please do."

"Josette found me sufficiently unusual—an American girl as green as the grass. She moved into my room at the hotel, where she stained the sheets with spilled wine and burned holes in the pillowcases with these foul cigarettes she chain-smoked. In the summer, we'd buy strawberries, bread and cheese and a bottle of cheap Bordeaux, then have a picnic on the *Esplanade des Invalides*." Delilah sighed. "The lime trees, the grassy lawns, the amazing blue color of the sky...we were young and everything was perfect. Just like your bonbon."

Ruby felt a pang at the pensive note in Delilah's voice. "Are you and Josette—" She broke off. "I'm sorry, it's none of my business."

Delilah waved a hand. An oversized aquamarine ring on her index finger shone like a chunk of sea ice. "What Josette and I had together was pure passion and very little else. Like I said, we were young. Eventually, we grew apart, we fought a lot, she found someone else, end of story. No regrets. I moved back to America and buried myself in work. When I took over the St. Clare a few years ago, I hired Severin as my executive pastry chef." She smiled. "He was very supportive when Josette and I broke up, but apart from that, his work is very good."

"He has an amazing palate," Ruby agreed, bracing her shoes against the floor when the Town Car made a tight turn down a one-way street.

Silence fell, broken when Delilah said quietly, "I hope you don't think I'm prying—and if you don't want to talk, just say so—but I've been curious since you mentioned knowing Beatrice Brooks. How did you two meet?"

"Bee and her mom moved next door to my family when she and I were five years old. I can't say we bonded right off the bat. I hit her with a wooden block and she bit me on the thumb." Ruby smiled. "We were in the same class at school and I guess we grew to love each other like sisters." Unshed tears suddenly burned. She glanced up, blinking to prevent ruining her makeup with tears. "I miss Bee. We've never been out of touch except when we were at different colleges and even then we called each other every week. I'm her daughter's unofficial aunt. Now Bee's missing and I'm worried. No, more than that. I'm terrified."

"What do the police say?"

"I saw the detective in charge, Frances Orsini, right before you came to pick me up. As usual, they're 'pursuing leads.' No details. No new developments that I can tell."

"Do you think the detective is spinning her wheels?"

"I hope not."

Delilah frowned. "The detective isn't taking your friend's disappearance seriously?"

Ruby blew out a breath. "I'm sure Detective Orsini is doing her best, there's just not a lot to go on. They did find Bee's car. There was blood on the seat, but not much."

"Her blood?"

"Who knows? They won't do a DNA test, but the detective said it's consistent with Bee's blood type. Apart from that, there hasn't been very much progress."

Delilah reached over and patted Ruby's knee. "I'm sorry."

"Me too." Ruby opened her purse and groped for a tissue. *So much for not being a downer.* Carefully patting the tissue under her eyes, she made an effort to put her emotions in check and focus on the evening. "Aren't we almost there?"

"We're here." Delilah slowed the car and turned in to a parking lot filled with luxury cars: Mercedes, BMW, Lexus, Cadillac, even a vintage Rolls Royce.

Ruby peered at the brightly lit railroad museum's main building, a wedding cake confection of white stone that used to serve as the city's main terminal. The Antebellum heritage site, an important part of the city's past with its historic outbuildings, working steam locomotive, exhibits and garden, was a favorite spot for upscale weddings and parties.

"Dinner in the Roundhouse and an auction afterward." Delilah eased the Town Car into a parking space and killed the engine. She shifted in her seat. "I have to do some schmoozing for the hotel during the cocktail hour, but I promise I won't neglect you."

"I understand." Ruby had figured the date would be part business, part pleasure, and had brought Magic Bean business cards in her purse just in case.

Delilah opened the driver's side door and slid out of the car. She leaned back inside to say, "I want you to know you're not alone. If there's anything I can do to help you or Ms. Brooks, anything you need, or if you want to talk, I'm here. You don't need an appointment."

The sincerity and concern in the woman's beautiful face touched Ruby. She took another moment to compose herself before she got out and joined Delilah, walking side-by-side to the museum's entrance, where light and music spilled out the open door.

CHAPTER FOURTEEN

The cocktail hour took place in the largest exhibit room, containing locomotive models, railroad art and a beautifully restored, first class Pullman car in all its elaborate, excessive, gilded and swagged nineteenth century glory.

Groups of men and women in evening dress clustered together chatting while tuxedo-clad waitstaff circulated the room carrying trays of appetizers and drinks. Checking the guests and their finery, Ruby recognized some of Summerland's and the surrounding cities' wealthiest, most powerful, most famous and/or most fashionable citizens, including prominent politicians and a few sports figures. She clutched Delilah's arm and tried not to gape.

Delilah plucked a martini glass from a waiter's tray and handed it to her. "Will you be okay on your own for a little while? I'll come and get you before dinner in about..." She checked a clock on the wall. "A half hour. And the rest of the night is ours." She leaned in closer, her perfume as intoxicating as the promising heat in her smoky gray eyes, and licked her lips.

"You know, I have a room in a nice hotel on Magdalena Island. If you like, I can promise you a very good time and breakfast in the morning. Or we could go to your place instead." Her fingertips grazed Ruby's collarbone, leaving goose bumps in their wake. "I'd love to wake up in your bed and see if that pink hair gets any wilder."

Struck dumb by a surge of blatant desire, Ruby nodded. She watched Delilah move off into the crowd and took a sip of the red liquid in her glass. The flavor startled her. Pineapple juice, vodka and crème de framboise—an unusual combination. She caught herself speculating whether crème de cassis might work better in the mix and laughed. *A new world record, Chef: from the bedroom to the kitchen in zero-point-oh-two seconds!*

She spent the next half hour listening to the live band and sampling appetizers. She first tried a mini grilled cheese brioche served with a tiny cup of warm tomato and mascarpone soup. Emboldened by the quality of the catering, she skipped the blinis with caviar and nabbed a bite-sized pulled pork sandwich from a passing waitress, followed by a piece of lobster flatbread, a Wagyu slider and a small crostini with gorgonzola and fresh figs. At that point, she'd worked herself further into the room, made a handful of promising new contacts, including the caterer, and finished her drink.

A perky brunette waiter recommended the museum's signature cocktail, the Roundhouse Tonic. Intrigued, Ruby asked for the drink at the bar. The drink, made with fresh basil, dill, cucumber and lemon verbena combined with chilled gin and tonic, refreshed her palate. She finished the glass and ordered another from the bartender while vowing to make this one last. *You are not getting sloppy drunk on the first date, girl.*

Between the stellar appetizers, the music, the conversations and the alcohol, she managed to distract herself from lustful thoughts about Delilah. Even so, every now and then, like an inconvenient tap on the shoulder, an image of Delilah naked in bed would pop into her head, leaving her blushing and taking a sip of the cold drink in her hand.

Someone bumped into her, making the Roundhouse Tonic slop over the rim of her glass. She turned around, glad the cocktail was colorless so her dress wouldn't stain, and realized she'd been nudged from behind by City Councilman Harrison Lovett.

"Well, now, ain't you a treat," Lovett boomed. "Do excuse me, honey. I'm not in the habit of making pretty girls spill their drinks. Waste of damned good alcohol, you know." He grinned and chuckled, radiating good humor.

Ruby could hardly believe this was the same man who'd been so nasty to Delilah. *But since he's a politician and a car salesman, I guess he's got to be a decent actor too.* Lovett might be running to fat and have more dark hair on the backs of his pudgy hands than the top of his head, but he was still handsome and oozed twinkle-eyed charm—no doubt the reason he'd risen from used car dealerships owner to local politician in the first place.

She mumbled a reply to his apology, unwilling to stick around given the way he'd lost his temper and shown such an abrasive side at the hotel in the past. She made to leave, but he moved adroitly to prevent her escape.

"Not so fast, honey. I know we've met before," Lovett said, making a show of furrowing his brow in concentration. "I'd never forget that hair. Hang on while I solve this riddle." His loud voice attracted the attention of the guests around them. Noticing his audience, he pressed two fingers to his brow and struck a pose. "Folks, gather 'round, don't be shy. It's time for ol' Harry to play the guessing game and see if I can recall this little lady's name. Let's pray me and her have crossed paths someplace my wife would approve, 'cause Eugenie will kill me if my business with this gorgeous specimen of femininity involved dollar bills and an aluminum pole." His broad wink got snickers from the mostly male onlookers.

Her face flaming, Ruby tried to edge away.

"Oh, honey, don't be mad," Lovett cajoled, taking her upper arm in a firm grip. "It's a compliment. The way you look, all hot and bothered with those big melons and that sparkly dress, you could make your fortune in any club in town."

Ruby considered throwing the dregs of her cocktail in his face.

"There you are!" Delilah called, pushing through the crowd. She gave Lovett a bare nod before turning to Ruby. "I've been looking for you. I'm sorry I had to abandon you on our first date. We should find our table now, don't you think?"

Ruby sighed with relief when Delilah wrapped a hand possessively around her wrist.

Lovett scowled. A microsecond later, he returned to his former affability, but this time the smile didn't reach his hazel eyes. He ignored Delilah and spoke to Ruby, dropping her arm. "Honey, had you told me you were one of them queers…my hand to God, I wouldn't have teased you. I sure didn't mean no harm. Forgive a foolish man his trespasses?"

Trapped by the expectant people around them, Ruby could only stammer an acceptance and let Delilah tow her out of the crush. As soon as they were clear, she plunked her cocktail glass on a passing waiter's tray. A glance at Delilah's pale, set expression made her heart plummet. *Oh no, I've ruined everything already.* "I'm sorry. I didn't—"

"Harry Lovett is a foul man," Delilah gritted, her expression thunderous. She stopped and pressed Ruby into a secluded area behind a scale model of a train exhibited in a glass case. "Don't let him come near you ever again."

Ruby's mouth went dry at the sharpness of the gray eyes boring into hers. "Maybe tonight wasn't a good idea," she mumbled.

Instantly, Delilah backed off. "My apologies," she said, her shoulders stiff, her manner dropping into a familiar cold formality that made Ruby ache inside.

"No, no, I didn't mean it that way." Ruby tasted acid and wished she'd skipped the gorgonzola crostini. "Listen, he bumped into me and turned the whole stupid thing into a stage show. To be honest, I wouldn't voluntarily have anything to do with that man, but everybody was staring and I didn't want to make a public fuss."

Delilah shot Lovett a venomous glare when he passed by with a group of men and a few women headed toward the dining area. She refocused her attention on Ruby. "Just avoid him. He's dangerous, more dangerous than you know."

The statement struck Ruby as incongruous. Although she'd seen him lose his temper, Lovett didn't appear very threatening. Sexist, yes. Misogynistic? Almost certainly. Vicious? Maybe. She wanted to ask questions, but didn't get a chance.

"We don't want to be late for dinner." Delilah offered her an arm. "Shall we?"

Ruby waited to speak again until they were seated at a table in the Roundhouse—a nineteenth century circular structure made of weathered brick where locomotives had been serviced in the past. Yellowed glass roof panels were supported by crisscrossing iron ceiling beams strung with white fairy lights. Crystal chandeliers hung above their heads, shedding a mellow glow. She put the napkin in her lap and ventured, "How do you know Mr. Lovett?"

"I've done business with him," Delilah replied shortly. She drank a swallow of ice water and pinched the bridge of her nose. "Lovett is on the city council. He's petty, full of himself and, as you found out, not above sexual harassment. He also recommends my hotel to his associates and business partners. Thanks to Lovett, we've booked numerous lucrative corporate functions, company retreats and conferences. The man's an ill-mannered pig, but my job requires me to put up with him." She sounded biting and bitter.

"What about me? I work for the hotel."

Delilah opened her mouth and closed it when a waitress returned to take their orders. She remained silent until they were alone. "You won't have any contact with Lovett in your capacity as a contract worker."

"And in my capacity as your date?" Ruby asked. A server arrived to slide a plate of braised short ribs on the table in front of her. She thanked the young man with a polite smile while thinking, *I hope the whole date isn't a washout. I'd hate to think I messed up our night out on account of that son-of-a-biscuit-eater Lovett.*

"If you feel he's acting—" Delilah accepted her roasted flounder from the server with a nod and stopped speaking to search for a word "—inappropriately toward you, or if he makes you feel uncomfortable, I want you to walk away. There won't be any fallout."

Greatly daring, Ruby covered Delilah's hand with hers. "Thanks. Is Lovett often unpleasant with you? Abusive? Like that night in the hotel lobby when he hurt your wrist," she clarified. They'd been cozy together in the Town Car on the way to the museum, but her expectation of further confidences went unfulfilled.

"I really can't say," Delilah answered, pulling her hand free without haste. She took a bite of flounder, signaling an end to the conversation.

Ruby sighed and picked up her knife and fork.

The braised short ribs were tender and delicious, served with a port reduction over creamy polenta and braised kale. She accepted a glass of red wine—a wonderfully tannic Rioja Cune Imperial with plum, tobacco and licorice notes—poured by the waiter and tried to enjoy her meal in the face of Delilah's stony silence.

The band had moved to the Roundhouse to play swing standards from Count Basie to Benny Goodman and Glenn Miller. A dark-skinned man in a white tie and tails and a thin Latina woman in a floor-length, black sequined dress crooned along with "A String of Pearls." Ruby's mood lifted a little when the band segued into "April in Paris." She glanced across the table, reminded of Delilah's story in the car.

Light from candles on the tables and the crystal chandeliers shimmered over Delilah's skin, gilding the delicate wings of her collarbones exposed by her strapless midnight-blue dress and glittering on the aquamarine studs in her earlobes. Tonight, the woman's gray eyes seemed almost the color of the ocean before summer storm clouds rolled over the beach.

Ruby forgot the food, forgot the wine, forgot everything except giving herself permission to drink in Delilah, the beautiful oval face, the slope of the cheekbones, the mouth—so voluptuous and inviting now that the lips were relaxed instead of compressed into a tight line. She watched Delilah's tongue sneak out to lick a drop of sauce from the fork. The innocent yet provocative gesture set off a low, slow throb of desire in her belly.

As though acting in response to the scrutiny, Delilah finished her wine in a few swallows, set the empty glass on the table, tossed her napkin next to her plate and gave Ruby her full attention for the first time since they'd sat down for dinner. "Have you been to the railroad museum before?"

Her concentration shattered, Ruby attempted to focus on Delilah's question. "Uh, no, but some of the weddings held here have given out my chocolates as favors."

"Then you've never seen the Pullman car. The restoration work is amazing. You shouldn't miss it." Delilah paused. "Did you want dessert?"

"Not really." After working with chocolate for years, Ruby didn't have much of a sweet tooth. She stood and followed Delilah's lead out of the Roundhouse.

The exhibit room was deserted and quiet. Delilah went straight to the Pullman car, pulling Ruby along with her. The exterior was painted a distinctive dark green. Old-fashioned swirling letters spelled a name in gold: *Elberta*. A set of metal steps led to the interior.

Ruby let Delilah precede her inside.

The ceiling was lit by bulbs, but it didn't take much imagination to conjure flicking gaslight on the burgundy damask papered walls. Individual seats upholstered in plush velvet matched the swagged green drapes dripping gold fringe at the long windows. Ruby noted a small mahogany bar with a brass rail sitting at one end of the car flanked by a pair of brass spittoons and a fern in a Chinese blue-and-white pot. Everything was first-class and overly rich in the high Victorian style—too fussy for her taste, but the height of luxury at the time.

Delilah walked to the bar, her high-heeled shoes making little noise on the burgundy carpet. "What do you think?" she asked, her lips twitching into a small smile.

Ruby didn't want to disparage Delilah's opinion. "Nice."

"Nice?" Delilah chuckled, shaking her head. "I wasn't talking about the décor." Her voice dropped lower, almost a purr. She cocked a hip and ran both hands down her sides, molding the form-fitting dress even tighter to her body. "I meant me."

Caught by the challenge in Delilah's gaze, Ruby moved closer, one step at a time. Arousal pulsed between her legs. Rising heat flushed her skin from scalp to toes. "Shouldn't we take this somewhere more private?"

Delilah's lipstick had worn off, leaving her mouth coral pink, her lips full and soft. She crooked a finger in a "come here" gesture. "How about an appetizer? Just a taste."

Unable and unwilling to resist, Ruby closed the distance between them, her heart thudding. The moment their lips touched, her bones turned to water and her flesh to flames. Her eyes closed. Delilah's perfume rose around her, dizzyingly sweet. She reeled.

Delilah deepened the kiss. Ruby trembled. Hands slid into her hair, holding her head still while a soft tongue traced her mouth from corner to corner. Teeth nipped her lower lip. Her skin felt thinner, her senses keener, as if her nerves had risen to the surface in response to her desire. She melted against Delilah, yearning to touch the body close to hers.

Ruby broke away gasping and dazed when she heard voices outside the Pullman car. Dinner must be over. People were headed toward the auction room.

"Let's go," Delilah whispered in her ear, the two words so ripe with promise, Ruby shivered.

"The auction?" she asked with difficulty, her chest heaving as she struggled for breath.

Delilah stared at her, gray eyes smoldering like ashes over banked embers. "What about the auction?" She took Ruby's face between her hands. "I don't want to wait. Do you?"

Unable to speak, Ruby nodded and closed her eyes when Delilah leaned forward to brush light kisses over her cheeks, eyelids and the tip of her nose.

"Then like I said—let's go," Delilah whispered against Ruby's lips.

Ruby could only nod again, helpless against the fire in her blood.

CHAPTER FIFTEEN

Rather than travel all the way out to Magdalena Island and the hotel, Ruby suggested they return to her apartment. Delilah agreed.

The drive seemed to take forever, yet the Town Car pulled into the underground parking garage far sooner than Ruby expected. She tumbled out of the passenger side, somewhat giddy and breathless, to wait for Delilah and walk to the elevator with her.

The elevator doors slid shut behind them. The slight jolt as the car started to rise sent her bumping into Delilah, who caught her around the waist and devoured her lips in a brutal kiss. She moaned, anticipation becoming fevered participation in a stroke of Delilah's velvet tongue. She yielded to the pressure as tingling warmth spread through her, tightening her stomach with need.

Delilah pressed against Ruby, the hot hands moving to her thighs. Goose bumps rose on her skin at the insistent touch molding their bodies together until she couldn't tell where Delilah ended and she began.

Lost in the kiss, Ruby was barely aware of a chime signaling the elevator doors opening. When Delilah pulled away, a wordless sound of protest tore from her throat.

"Where are your keys?" Delilah asked, gripping her wrist and almost stumbling with her down the hallway toward the apartment door.

Ruby fumbled with her purse's clasp and thrust her hand inside. At last, groping among the miscellaneous contents produced her key ring. By some miracle, she managed to get the right key into the lock on the first try. *Thank goodness!* She threw open the door. Delilah staggered with her across the threshold, bumping the door closed with a hip as soon as they entered the dark apartment.

The faintest light filtered through the windows from the building across the street, but only enough to distinguish the vague shapes of furniture. In the shadows, the sequins on Delilah's dress shimmered subtly, but even blind, Ruby could have found the woman by her scent. The exotic perfume reached inside her head and tripped a switch, making her want to rip off Delilah's dress and lick her all over, glutting on a feast of that glorious body.

Ruby guided Delilah to the bedroom without tripping over or crashing into anything. "I'll put on the lamp." She kicked off her shoes into a corner of the room and tossed her clutch on the dresser, then crossed to the nightstand by the bed.

Suddenly, Delilah's arms circled her from behind. Warm, soft lips pressed against the back of her neck, followed by a sharp sting of teeth soothed by a tongue.

Trembling, Ruby flicked on the lamp and tried to turn, but Delilah prevented the movement. Her dress's zipper was dragged down and the two halves of the garment pulled apart. Delilah kissed her bare shoulders, fiery kisses igniting urgency deep within her as the scorching mouth moved over her bared flesh.

She arched her back and groaned in frustration, desperate to see and touch Delilah, who huffed a chuckle against her skin when she squirmed. More kisses drifted over her throat, her jawbone, her cheek. She needed more.

"Relax, we'll get there." Delilah's fingertips glided up the groove of Ruby's spine.

Encouraged by a nudge, Ruby managed to wriggle out of her dress and send the garment sliding to the carpet to form a silver lamé puddle around her feet. She'd worn a matching bra and panties set, pretty white lace she kept for special occasions. Delilah unhooked the bra clasp and slipped the straps down her arms. She shifted to release her heavy breasts from the satin cups and let the bra fall to join the dress.

Delilah palmed her breast, the pad of a thumb stroking the firming nipple. Each caress was sweet torture, seeming to tug an invisible string connecting her swollen peak to the core of warm, liquid pleasure flowing through her.

Ruby had to remind herself to breathe. She sucked in air, her other breast aching with neglect. Her knees nearly buckled. *The bed.* She twisted out of Delilah's grip and hastily bent over to fold back the floral print coverlet. Impatient to pick up where she left off, she spun around to find that Delilah had already shed her clothes.

Her lust swelled higher, as heady as wine. Ruby stared at the naked woman, her gaze rising from lean calves and thighs to hips and the slight, endearingly feminine swell of belly, the indentation of the small waist, the beauty of the modest breasts tipped with palest pink. A runner's body, different than her fuller curves. Exciting. "Gorgeous," she whispered.

Delilah's cheeks were flushed, her gray eyes brilliant. Her hair had come unfastened from its pins. Chestnut curls framed her face and hung past her shoulders. "So are you." She stared at Ruby hungrily, her mouth shiny and red.

Ruby shoved off her panties and fell back on the sheets, wanton and wanting.

Delilah crawled up onto the bed to pepper kisses over her breastbone, shoulders and neck—ticklish kisses like teasing butterfly brushes. When Ruby hissed at the feather-light touches, Delilah used the tip of an agile tongue to trace swirls and patterns over the underside of her arm, the crease of her elbow and the pale blue veins at her wrist. Each finger received the same treatment.

Ruby wiggled her hips, hoping to encourage Delilah and that wicked tongue to pay attention to other, needier parts of her body. She groaned, feeling open and exposed—almost overexposed. Raw and tender in her most secret places. A whine escaped her throat.

Delilah rose up on an elbow and leaned over. A mass of chestnut hair fell forward to act as a veil, obscuring the woman's face. The curling ends grazed Ruby's skin, prickling for a second before cool air blew across her nipple. She dug her nails into the cotton sheets, a blaze of desire spiking when a hot mouth latched onto the puckered flesh.

The delicious friction conspired to drive Ruby crazy. She cried out, balanced on the thinnest edge of pleasure and pain, unable to stand one more moment, yet certain she'd die if Delilah stopped. Finally, when she'd been reduced to a mewling, quivering mess, Delilah released her nipple and moved lower, planting devouring kisses on her belly and biting at her thighs while shifting on the bed. Fingertips suddenly pushed between the folds of her sex, straight to the soaking place where she ached most, followed by a tongue.

Her choked gasp turned into ragged breathing. She melted into the mattress, boneless and mindless. At the same time, her muscles clenched on wave after wave of shocking pleasure. Yellow and crimson sparks flew behind her closed eyelids. Her body burned, an uncontrollable inferno blazing from her center outward, flaring fiercest in the center, where she knew nothing except the cresting wave of fire she chased. Flames leaped under her skin. Lost, she panted and moaned, her hips working on the fingers and tongue filling her, caressing her inside to draw out exquisite sensations that stoked her pleasure higher and higher.

Powerful ecstasy finally crashed through her. Her body shattered. She came, shuddering again and again, riding the inferno until she fell back, utterly consumed.

* * *

Sometime later, Ruby was jarred awake by the thud of something hitting the dresser across the room and the sound of fiercely whispered curses. She squinted at the surrounding darkness, just able to make out a shadowy figure standing near the dresser. "Delilah?" she asked, reaching for the lamp on the nightstand beside the bed.

The light switched on, revealing Delilah wearing a strapless bra and panties, her knee bent, cherishing her bare foot with one hand while holding her midnight-blue cocktail dress with the other. "I stubbed my toe, damn it."

Ruby decided to ignore the profanity. "Where are you going at—" she checked the alarm clock "—four in the morning?"

"My night manager called," Delilah explained, giving her foot a final rub before slipping on her shoes and yanking her dress over her head. "Sorry, I didn't mean to wake you." She glanced at Ruby. Dark mascara was smeared under her eyes. Even looking thoroughly debauched, her curls hanging in tangles around a sleep-creased face, she was beautiful. "I'm needed at the hotel. Emergency. Sorry."

Swallowing her disappointment at losing the prospect of morning cuddles, Ruby sat up and pushed off the covers. Was Delilah manufacturing an excuse to ditch her? Studying the woman's chagrined expression, she didn't think so. "Come here. I'll zip you up."

"Thanks." Delilah walked to the bed, twisting her hair into a messy knot to allow Ruby access to the dress's side zipper. "I owe you breakfast."

"All done." Ruby smoothed a crumple in the skirt's fabric, reluctant to let Delilah go. "When can I collect your debt? I'm partial to French toast with blueberries."

"Whenever you like." Delilah leaned down to look at her, their faces inches apart. "I can't apologize enough. I need to take care of this problem as soon as possible. Believe me, I wouldn't leave you alone if it wasn't necessary."

Ruby nodded and took the woman's baby smooth mouth in a kiss. Not as searing as last night, but sweet and lingering. The lips clung to hers. A combination of tenderness and temptation welled inside her heart. She longed to tumble Delilah back into the comfortable sheets and hold her close, bury her fingers in the thick chestnut hair, burrow against the satiny skin and bask in warmth and lingering traces of sweet perfume and female musk until a decent hour of the morning.

After permitting herself a long, delicious moment, Ruby ended the kiss and eased away to murmur, "I know. It's okay." Sighing, she rested their foreheads together. "Give me a minute. I'll get dressed and run you over to the ferry in my truck."

Regret shone in Delilah's eyes. "My Town Car's here and the ferry will be waiting for me at the wharf." She gently pulled out of Ruby's grip. "I've got to go."

"Is there anything I can do to help?" If there was a chance of remaining in Delilah's company a little longer, she'd take it.

"No. I'll…I'll see you later, I promise." Delilah turned in a swirl of dark blue satin and glittering sequins and hurried out of the bedroom.

Restless and unaccountably bereft, Ruby sat on the edge of the bed, running her hands through her snarled hair. She waited to hear the front door click shut before she got out of bed and walked through her empty apartment to the kitchen to make coffee. Part of her wondered what kind of emergency would drag a hotel's general manager out of bed at such an hour.

The rest of her already missed Delilah.

CHAPTER SIXTEEN

Using a sharp knife, Ruby cut through the dark chocolate bonbon on the work counter and studied the layers of bright apricot marmalade sandwiched between smooth, pale green pistachio and cardamom cream. The presentation looked good. She tasted a piece, letting the chocolate melt on her tongue and the flavors spread over her palate.

Tasty, but not spectacular enough for the St. Clare. She considered what might be lacking. The pistachio cream was yummy, the cardamom lending a touch of earthy spice. The apricot marmalade, on the other hand…she grimaced. On its own, delicious. But the sweet marmalade didn't fit the rest of the bonbon. She needed to start over.

Her eyes lit on the storage cabinet. As she walked over to search for inspiration, her thoughts turned to last night and her date with Delilah. Or rather, the aftermath of the date, falling into bed hot and eager for each other, and the way Delilah had rushed out of her apartment in the middle of the night because of an emergency at the St. Clare Hotel.

Delilah hadn't returned her call after she'd left a message this morning. Ruby was torn between keeping her pride intact—not wanting to seem desperately clingy—and concern at the lack of contact. She hadn't seen any mention on the news about the hotel or the island and figured whatever had happened concerned some internal matter.

She stood in front of the storeroom shelves, worrying her bottom lip between her teeth and trying to decide what to do. Eventually, she came to the conclusion that her best bet would be to finish the bonbon experiment and use the test batch as a perfect excuse to head out to Magdalena Island to see Delilah and make sure the woman was okay.

Surveying a shelf, she suddenly recalled a recent trip to a new Chinese supermarket catering to the growing immigrant population from China and South Korea. Curiosity had prompted her to buy a small, dark bottle of pandan extract made from the leaf of the screwpine, indigenous to Southeast Asia. Pandan was a common flavoring in Chinese baked goods, especially the green chiffon cakes for sale in the store's bakery. Some called it the "vanilla of the East," though the stuff neither smelled nor looked anything like vanilla.

Ruby unscrewed the cap and sniffed. The first aroma to hit her was grassy, almost flowery, followed by nuttiness and a citrus undertone. Unusual but interesting, just as she remembered. Roasted pistachios would suit, but something was still missing. The combination lacked punch. Lemongrass or Meyer lemons could be a solution. She quickly gathered ingredients and returned to the kitchen, her mind now focused on the task ahead.

She spent the next several hours working, not only on the components of the new bonbon, but packing orders from the Magic Bean website, updating her inventory and bookkeeping records, and organizing her notes on the hotel's marketing materials for the new chocolates line. She also surfed the Internet to get more information about the university's marine education center and aquarium, where she planned to take Kaitlyn tomorrow.

After a while, she checked the bonbons. The molded chocolate shells had set, so she tested one. The pandan cream combined with a layer of Meyer lemon and roasted pistachio caramel created a very decadent, pleasurable gratification—the "feel good" sensation akin to love and sex, which in turn reminded her of Delilah. She smiled.

Her watch read four thirty p.m. She decided to end her workday early and take the ferry to the island. Severin Valois might be busy overseeing preparations for the dinner services in the hotel's restaurants, but she felt certain Delilah would make time for her.

Ruby entertained a pleasant fantasy of a romantic, candlelight supper with Delilah while she put the finished bonbons into one of her company's signature hot pink candy boxes and got ready to leave. She wiped down counters, put away supplies, packed orders for tomorrow's deliveries and stored the apricot marmalade and pistachio cream in containers in the refrigerator to be recycled into other sweet creations tomorrow. When she was done, she took a last look around the spotless kitchen and nodded to herself, satisfied.

Buoyed by happiness at the thought of seeing Delilah soon, she left the kitchen, locking the door behind her, and fairly floated across the parking lot to her old Dodge truck.

She made excellent time in the pre-rush hour traffic, but had to park on an upper floor in the municipal parking garage since the other levels were still full of cars. Although she didn't dawdle on the walk down the busy boardwalk and the weathered wooden steps to the wharf, she arrived just seconds before the Magdalena Island ferry was about to pull away. With the long, deep blast of the boat's whistle ringing in her ears, she jumped onto the deck, the candy box and her purse clutched under her arm.

Today, the ocean seemed to reflect her good mood, Ruby thought, standing at the rail. The water was dark blue and as smooth as glass, a perfect mirror for the sun. The salt in the air, the piping seabirds gliding through the sky, the sharp prow throwing back curling white waves as the ferry sliced through the water… *Absolutely perfect.* Too bad she had to meet Delilah at the hotel instead of the beach. An image of Delilah showing off that runner's body in a minuscule bikini made her tingle.

The ferry finally docked at the island. Ruby disembarked, stepping aside for a few passengers coming aboard for the return trip to the mainland. She paused on the way to the hotel to look at the hill and the convent ruins. Perhaps one day she'd climb to the top and listen for the ghostly voices of the nuns who had died for love.

On reaching the hotel lobby, she let herself through the Employees Only door and headed straight to the administrative area and Delilah's office. The receptionist—Kyle, she recalled—sat behind his desk.

Kyle glanced up, smiled and said into his phone headset, "One moment, please." Covering the headset's mouthpiece with his hand, he greeted Ruby, "Good afternoon, Ms. Fontaine. Ms. Kerrigan isn't in right now, but she'll be back soon. Do you want to wait?"

"Thanks."

She moved into Delilah's office, closing the door behind her, and settled into a chair. The box of sample bonbons went on a nearby table. Lifting her oversized purse into her lap, she removed the notes on the marketing materials she'd printed earlier and laid them next to the candy box. A moment's consideration had her also rooting around the bottom of her purse for a roll of breath mints. *Better be kissably sweet just in case.* The mints were ancient, an impulse buy at the checkout counter she didn't recall making, and dissolved to artificially sweetened crumbs in her mouth.

Options for another date occupied her for a time. Dinner and a movie sounded too conventional. She'd read about a special event in a couple of weeks: an evening "crawl" among the boardwalk's dining establishments where participants ate a special course at one restaurant before moving on to the next. Tickets were still available. Delilah would probably like sampling the different cuisines and wines. And later, after the good food and good conversation, she'd invite Delilah back to her place for a very special dessert.

A thrill of excitement gripped her.

Twenty minutes passed. Ruby began to fidget. She stood and paced across the room, coming to a halt in front of Delilah's desk. The sight brought a flush to her cheeks when she recalled being caught by Delilah red-handed, so to speak, attempting to sneak a peek at the computer to get the number of the suite where Kaitlyn and her nanny were staying.

She noticed a desk drawer partially open. The carelessness bothered her, at odds with the otherwise meticulous state of Delilah's office. She tried to ignore the anomaly by returning to the chair and reading through her notes, but like a persistent itch, the wrongness kept nibbling at her resolve and wrecking her concentration.

Finally, she stood. There couldn't be any objection to closing a desk drawer, she told herself, paying no attention to the little inner voice reminding her how embarrassed she'd been the last time she got caught. Good grief, she wasn't stealing company secrets or committing industrial espionage. In fact, she was doing Delilah a favor.

With her justifications marshaled, Ruby stepped over to the desk. She reached for the drawer and froze when she glimpsed an object inside that she'd never actually seen, but knew from Frances Orsini's description: a spiral-bound notebook, three by five inches, the pages bulging and bristling with colorful sticky notes, the navy blue cover held closed by a rubber band. *Bee's missing notebook. What's it doing in here—oh.*

Her heart sank to her toes.

So many emotions flooded through her at once, she felt as though she were drowning. Her head throbbed. Her pulse boomed in her ears. She couldn't breathe. Nausea rose in a choking wave of bitterness. She didn't know how long she remained paralyzed, her mind screaming. Anger—at Delilah and at herself for being such a gullible fool—won in the end.

I never should have trusted Delilah. Never. The day I saw her in my building's parking garage, I knew she was up to no good. Ruby picked up the notebook and shoved the drawer closed. *We made love. She held me while we slept. And all that time—* She couldn't bear to think any longer. After retrieving her purse, she left the office, paying no attention to Kyle's "wait a minute" hand gestures as she marched past his desk.

Cold fury carried her through the lobby, out the door and down the paved path to the wharf. While waiting for the next scheduled ferry, she pulled out her cell phone and dialed a number. A sob knifed loose, but her eyes stayed dry. "It's Ruby," she said when Frances Orsini answered. She gripped the phone so tightly, her fingers ached. "I found Bee's notebook. I'm on Magdalena Island now, but I'll meet you in a couple of hours on the boardwalk. Alfonso's."

She wouldn't answer any of Frances's questions. She couldn't. Her chest was hollow and her tongue had turned to stone. She stabbed a button to end the call and stood there with her heart in a million pieces, listening to the piercing cries of seagulls wheeling overhead, until the ferry finally came into sight churning across the bright blue water.

CHAPTER SEVENTEEN

"Tell me again where you found Beatrice Brooks's notebook." Frances nodded at the troublesome little book lying on the table between them at Alfonso's, the coffee shop on the Grand Strand Promenade and Boardwalk where she and Ruby had met once.

Ruby lifted her coffee cup and paused. "In an open desk drawer in the private office of Delilah Kerrigan, general manager of the St. Clare Hotel and Resort on Magdalena Island," she replied wearily. "Do I really have to go over the whole thing? I told you what I know." The hot latté scorched her mouth when she took a drink. She welcomed the pain, hoping it might help overcome the agony in her heart and mind.

Frances made a negative noise in the back of her throat. "No, that's okay. I'll read through the notebook, see if there's anything that might give us more information on Ms. Brooks." She frowned. "Are you okay? You look kind of pale."

"I'm fine. I've been busy with work." Ruby finished her latté and banged the empty cup into the saucer harder than she intended. She winced at the loud clatter. "Sorry. When are you going to question Ms. Kerrigan?"

"You know I can't discuss details with you, but I promise I will follow up and let you know as soon as I can." Frances leaned forward, her eyes as dark and warm as the black coffee in the cup in front of her. "At the beginning of the investigation, you brought Ms. Kerrigan to my attention."

Ruby nodded, keeping her anger and grief off her face with difficulty. Her voice only wavered a little. "That's right." The latté churned in her stomach. "I told you I saw Ms. Kerrigan in the parking garage of my apartment building on the same day Bee disappeared. Since Ms. Kerrigan doesn't live in my building, it seemed odd."

"And I checked her out. There was no connection."

"So you said. Now there is."

Frances hunched her broad shoulders, creasing her brown leather jacket, but didn't say anything for a long moment. "We'll pursue every viable lead in the investigation, don't worry," she finally replied, meeting Ruby's sharp glance with bland, clear-eyed directness.

"That's not evasive at all," Ruby complained.

"It's the literal truth. Hey, I have an idea." Frances reached across the table to take Ruby's hand in hers. The calluses on her palm and fingers felt slightly rough. "Sounds like we've both been working our butts off and need a break. Let's go out and do something fun together. A movie, maybe. Dinner. I don't know. What's your pleasure?"

Ruby considered rejecting the offer outright, but changed her mind. A renewed surge of self-irritation prickled. Why shouldn't she go out with Frances, who'd treated her honestly and never pretended to be…what? She hesitated, unable to say she and Delilah were friends. Lovers? Yes, she conceded, but only once. In her apartment. Last night.

A tingling spark of arousal bloomed as her traitorous body responded to the memory. Regret added a note more bitter than raw cacao nibs. She ordered herself to shove the messy episode with Delilah to the back of her mind. Eventually, she'd have to make an excuse about why she no longer wanted an intimate relationship. Now, she wanted to forget.

Shoring up her brittle feelings, Ruby looked at Frances—strong featured, solid, built on heroic lines, thousand-watt smile Frances who stared back at her with anticipation. "There's a restaurant crawl on the boardwalk in a couple of weeks. Does that work for you?"

Frances looked relieved. "Great. That's…that's great." She grinned and shook her head, laughing a little. "Wow. I haven't felt that nervous asking for a date in a long time."

"I'd better head home," Ruby said, picking up her purse and standing. She wasn't in the mood for socializing. She needed time to get over her depression and sort out how to deal with Delilah's betrayal. "Will you…I know you can't give me a lot of information, but could you at least tell me if you find anything relevant in Bee's notebook?" She had leafed through the pages on the ferry, but Beatrice's scrawl and use of code names muddled the context, making comprehension difficult at best. Maybe the police or Beatrice's editor at the newspaper would have better luck.

"I'll see what I can do." Frances also stood, pushed in her chair and collected the notebook. "You could ask Mr. Brooks to share information. He's pretty well updated."

"I'd sooner crawl through flaming dog poop." Ruby curled her upper lip when Frances choked on a guffaw. "That man's a pill."

"Don't hold back," Frances wheezed between giggles. "Tell me how you really feel."

Ruby shrugged. "Greg and I don't share the same priorities." She waited until Frances's laughter died down before moving outside with the woman.

Streetlamps held back the dusk painting the ocean and sky in broad strokes of lavender, salmon pink and a shade of blue just a touch lighter than indigo. A dim moon glimmered above, silvery in the dying sunlight, but the stars weren't out yet except Venus, the evening star, glittering like a tiny diamond on the horizon. Ruby walked along the boardwalk with Frances next to her, sticking to the ocean side, where the sound of the surf drowned out the murmurings of diners at the outdoor restaurant tables and the instrumental music piped over public address system speakers attached to the storefront façades.

She looked over the wooden railing at the beach below, where a few couples and single people waded in the shallow water. The romantic setting ignited a strange longing. For an unguarded instant, she wished Delilah was there, sharing the moment with her.

She imagined Delilah's smile, the little crinkle at the corner of the mouth, the pink lips turned red from kissing. Her mind's eye conjured Delilah as she had looked last night, sprawled on the bed with that cool, untouchable mask stripped away to reveal passion and a heated wantonness as bare as the naked body writhing in the cotton sheets. *Beautiful. So beautiful.* She sighed and thrust the image aside. No sense crying over seized chocolate. She'd do better to focus on the present, not the past. Her bruised feelings would heal in time.

When Frances halted, Ruby turned her head to find the last person on Earth she wanted to see standing right in front of her: Delilah Kerrigan, with her face wreathed in an affectionate smile, appearing relaxed and a bit tired. *Speak of the Devil.* She quailed internally, wishing she had more time before the confrontation she knew was coming.

"Kyle said you came by the office," Delilah told Ruby after a puzzled glance at Frances. "I'm sorry I was out. What was supposed to be a phone conference turned into an emergency meeting with a supplier in town." She leaned closer, clearly intending a kiss.

Ruby twisted to avoid the attempt. At Delilah's frown, she tried to smooth things over. No need to make Frances a witness to their personal business. "Hi," she said as normally as she could manage. "Did you taste the new bonbon yet? I left a box on the table in your office. I'm trying out pandan as a flavor with pistachio and lemon caramel. Very interesting."

Delilah shook her head. "Not yet. Severin and I have a meeting tomorrow, we'll discuss it then." Once again, her gaze darted toward Frances. "Who's your friend?"

"Detective Frances Orsini," Frances said, stepping forward with her hand extended. "Adult Missing Persons. May I ask you a couple of questions, Ms. Kerrigan?"

"Oh, I'm sure she doesn't have time for that," Ruby interrupted, realizing Beatrice's notebook was plainly visible clamped under Frances's arm. Dread weighed heavy in her stomach. *Not now. Oh, please, not now.* Her silent pleas went unanswered.

As if prompted by a malign star, Delilah's glance zeroed in on the notebook. She paled, a muscle working in her jaw. At last, her bewildered gaze flicked to Ruby. In a split second, understanding mixed with pain and anger blazed in her eyes. Her mouth twisted.

Ruby wanted to cry out when Delilah's mask slammed into place, cloaking the affection with familiar, hateful coldness. *Delilah fooled you first,* she reminded herself. *The woman lied to you all this time and probably helped whoever kidnapped Bee.* Yet she couldn't help a pang of guilt at the betrayal she'd seen in Delilah's expression before the mask hid every emotion but disdain.

After a final icy glare at Ruby, Delilah turned to face Frances, every movement precise. "How may I help you, Detective?"

"I thought you might be able to identify the owner." Frances held out the notebook. A breath of salty ocean wind fluttered the rainbow of sticky notes poking out from the pages.

Ruby really regretted finding Beatrice's notebook in Delilah's office, but she couldn't help hoping for answers about her missing friend.

Chestnut curls blew forward, veiling Delilah's face. She scraped back her hair and gave Ruby another contemptuous glance before replying, "I have no idea."

The bald-faced lie hit Ruby like a slap. Any guilt she harbored was replaced by indignation. "I found that notebook in your desk drawer!"

"Ms. Fontaine is mistaken," Delilah replied to Frances, her expression and voice impassive. "I've never seen that book before."

When Ruby would have challenged the falsehood further, Frances broke in. Her eyes narrowed. Her gaze shifted between them. "Ms. Kerrigan, are you sure?"

"Positive."

"The notebook belongs to a missing journalist, Beatrice Brooks."

"I'm sorry. I wish I could help, Detective, but I don't know anything."

Ruby had to speak up. "That," she said succinctly, "is not the truth and you know it."

Frances put a restraining hand on Ruby's forearm. "It's okay." She returned her attention to Delilah. "Do you know Beatrice Brooks?"

"I've seen her byline in the newspaper." Delilah's reply sounded far too airy for Ruby's liking. "And Ms. Fontaine claims she's a friend. Other than that, I know virtually nothing about her."

"Are you aware she's missing?"

"I believe Ms. Fontaine mentioned something similar during a meeting, but I really don't remember any specifics."

"To your knowledge, has Beatrice Brooks been a guest of your hotel?"

Delilah snorted. "I don't keep a list of our guests in my head, Detective Orsini."

Frances hummed, nodded and tucked the notebook under her arm. "Of course. Thanks for your time." She took Ruby's wrist and tugged. "C'mon, let's go."

Ruby resisted the pull. "If you don't mind, I'll stay here."

For the second time, Frances glanced between her and Delilah. "Is everything okay? Because if you need me to hang around—"

"No, it's fine." Ruby mustered a reassuring smile. "Really. It's all hunky-dory."

"If you're sure..." Frances's voice trailed off. She bent enough to kiss Ruby's cheek and smiled. "Want me to pick you up for our date? Or meet here?"

Ruby glanced in Delilah's direction and found the woman staring at her. A dark, mean little impulse made her steal another kiss from Frances and murmur, "I'll meet you here for our date. Don't be late. The crawl starts at six o'clock."

"No problem. See you later, Ruby." Frances walked away toward the parking lot, her brown leather coat swinging around her legs with each stride.

Delilah crossed her arms over her chest, her face filled with cold fury. "How long?"

"How long what?" Ruby snapped. The question made no sense.

"How long did it take you to decide to whore yourself out for that notebook's sake? I'm just curious." Delilah continued while Ruby spluttered in outrage, "Must have been a hard decision. Such a terrible ordeal, pretending to like the ice queen, the frigid bitch—yes, I know what people call me when my back's turned. Pretending to enjoy my company. My *intimate* company, no less." She spoke the word like it was a profanity. "Nice performance, sweetheart. Real Academy Award material. You spread your legs for me in bed so fast, I'm surprised you didn't get friction burns."

"It wasn't like that," Ruby protested, loathing this side of Delilah—the horrible, nasty, furious woman lashing out with all the ugliness at her command.

"Don't kid yourself," Delilah sneered. "You used me."

"Stop! I wasn't looking for the notebook. I found it…by accident," Ruby finished weakly. She flushed. "Bee's book *was* in your desk. You lied to the police."

Delilah moved closer until they were separated by a scant inch. Her lips parted. "Prove it," she said, biting off each word with snaps of her teeth.

Ruby flinched at the emotions boiling like molten lead in the gray eyes boring into hers. She took several steps backward, her heart thumping. At once, Delilah's gaze became shuttered, hiding whatever she felt behind an impenetrable shield.

"One more thing," Delilah said in a clipped tone. "You're still under contract to the hotel. From now on, you'll report to

Severin. I won't be involved in your meetings with him and I'll inform Security that your access is restricted to the kitchens. Don't try sneaking into people's offices and pawing through their things, Ms. Fontaine. I'll be watching." She marched down the boardwalk, her head held high, her pumps slamming onto the wooden walkway with each forceful step.

Mouth dry, her chest squeezed tight, Ruby watched Delilah go, abruptly uncertain that she'd done the right thing.

CHAPTER EIGHTEEN

The next day, Ruby had a great time with Kaitlyn at the aquarium, even though the visit was exhausting and somewhat harrowing in parts. Kaitlyn's new tendency to pitch a fit when thwarted alarmed her, but the nanny—a lovely Chinese-British woman named Jennifer, who spoke with the kind of cultured accent she'd heard on TV shows—had explained that the six-year-old's behavior wasn't uncommon. Kaitlyn was acting out in confusion and anger over her mother's continued absence.

Despite the occasional tantrum, Ruby was glad she'd made the effort. Kaitlyn had brightened in the company of someone familiar, an "auntie" who understood exactly how she wanted her peanut butter and grape jelly sandwich prepared—no crusts, or "icky limbs" as she called them, cut into four precise triangles and served with four Granny Smith apple slices.

Kaitlyn had been entranced by the dolphins and octopuses, vaguely horrified by the special exhibit of preserved and dissected sharks and other "sea monsters" and fell in love with the stingrays in the touch tanks. Ruby spent a lot of their time together explaining why Kaitlyn couldn't take a spotted ray home and keep it in the bathtub as a pet.

Returning Kaitlyn to the hotel and saying goodbye left Ruby almost in tears, but Jennifer was warm, affectionate and not shy about looking after the little girl's best interests. The nanny had practically ordered her to join them next week on a trip to the wildlife park in a nearby town and planned to incorporate regular visits into Kaitlyn's schedule.

Ruby departed the hotel suite and headed downstairs to the kitchens for a meeting with Severin Valois in his office. She had come up with a new bonbon she wanted him to try and had brought a sample with her, keeping it safe in a small box tucked into her purse.

After the solemn tasting, the thickset man perched on the edge of his desk, staring down at her and tapping his fingertip against his lower lip. When she started fidgeting in her chair, he sighed. "Ah, *petite*, what am I to do with you?"

She sat up straighter. "What do you mean, Chef? Is the bonbon no good?" Her mind began scrambling to tweak the recipe.

Severin made a disgusted noise and flapped a hand. "The pinot noir bonbon, it is excellent, as you know. A triumph. But what have you done to Delilah?" He overrode her halfhearted squawk. "I have not seen her so...so...*très en colère*. No, not in many months has she shown the temper so violent. This morning, three housemaids and an assistant manager were reduced to tears by her savagery. I ask again, what did you do?"

"Nothing," she blurted hastily.

Perhaps too hastily, judging by the sly grin spreading across Severin's seamed face. "*La querelle de l'amant*, eh? A lover's quarrel."

Ruby felt her cheeks flaming. "Oh, no, Severin. No." Her night with Delilah would remain a secret, not the subject of petty gossip by the hotel's employees. As far as she was concerned, even Severin had no business knowing. Besides, thinking about

Delilah—the contempt, the hurt, the anger—made it difficult to swallow around the knot in her throat.

"You went on a date with her, did you not? Your face is as pink as your hair, *petite*. Don't lie. Be a good girl and tell Uncle Severin the truth," he wheedled.

"We went to dinner together, some charity auction thing," Ruby told him, making her date with Delilah seem more casual. "And nothing happened like you're suggesting." *We didn't quarrel*, she added silently. *Delilah's a liar. She betrayed me first.*

"Hmph." Severin studied her and finally shrugged, the motion of his bulky shoulders straining the buttons on his white chef's jacket. Much to her relief, he went around his desk and sat down. "Eh, *bien*, as you say. Nothing happened."

While he settled in his chair, Ruby recalled how Delilah had run out on her the morning after their date. "I heard there was an emergency at the hotel."

His brows rose. "The merest mishap," he sniffed. "You know the top of the hill, yes? A guest and his wife went to the ruins accompanied by a vodka bottle. It is no surprise they thought they heard ghosts. The phantom nuns—you have perhaps heard the story? *Bon*. Well, in running away, the man fell and broke his leg. His wife, she collapsed in hysterics. Lawsuits were threatened, but I tell you nothing will come of this low comedy. Bah! Let us forget these fools and turn to matters more important, such as your charming bonbon."

For the next hour she and Severin also discussed her input regarding the promotional materials for the brand and brainstormed ideas for the remaining chocolates. She avoided the subject of Delilah, always turning the conversation back to her preferred topics.

When their meeting concluded, Severin printed out notes from his computer for her to study. "Only a few suggestions," he said as she flipped through a dozen sheets.

Ruby lifted her head. "A few?"

He shrugged away her glare. "On presentation and so forth. The flavors are without fault—impeccable! But your presentation, it requires work, *petite*. Too simple."

"I was going for simple elegance. Sophistication." Had she restricted herself too much? She'd wanted to avoid blatant ostentation.

"In some cases, you have succeeded, but not all. These chocolates—when they are looked upon, they must give a sense of immense luxury. Indulgence." Amusement carved deeper lines around his mouth and in his forehead. "One must feel as if one is eating money."

Ruby stifled a chuckle. "Right. I can work on that."

"*Bon.*" Severin stood, reached behind his head and tightened the elastic band holding his longish salt-and-pepper hair in a ponytail. He walked toward the door. "Come with me. Perhaps we will find something useful in my inventory."

Ruby followed him into the kitchen area, a space so large she figured an airplane or two would fit inside without much difficulty. As they went through the pastry department, he paused now and then to issue an instruction to a chef, taste a preparation, or inspect trays of exquisite cakes, tarts and other sweets glistening like jewels. She thought he ran his section very well, giving his people enough leeway to do their jobs while overseeing the results.

Severin showed her multiple pantries filled with supplies. She ended up with her purse rattling with small jars of interesting and experimental ingredients: dehydrated green olive powder, candied angelica, edible gold powder, dried lemon myrtle leaves, dried mulberries, fennel pollen, *urfa biber*—a dried and powdered Turkish chili pepper—dried pomegranate seeds, smoky black cardamom pods, black cumin seeds and a spice called *mahleb.*

"A Greek/Turkish spice," Severin said, tapping a measure of off-white, finely ground powder into a small plastic jar. "*Mahleb* tastes of cherry, almond and roses, with a bitter finish. Beautiful with honey." He screwed on the lid. "We use it to flavor a breakfast *vasilopita*, a kind of Greek brioche. Very tasty. I will have the kitchen save one next time you visit."

"Thanks, Chef. You've given me some great inspiration here," Ruby told him, not minding the weight of her filled purse hanging on her shoulder. She shifted the strap higher, took the jar he held out to her and stuck it in her purse to join the rest. "I should have something new for you to taste in a little while."

He rubbed his hands together in anticipation. "You need no appointment with me, of course. When you are ready, I am waiting." His grin melted to a frown. He closed the short distance between them to say quietly, "Listen to me, *petite*... Delilah is not herself. Not since Josette left her has she behaved as if the world and life itself offends. You do not wish to speak of private matters. *D'accord*, but if there's anything you can tell me that will help—"

Ruby cut him off. She couldn't stand the pleading note in his voice. "I'm sorry. There's really nothing I can say."

His keen glance sliced through her. She held firm under his regard. Finally, he shifted tactics. "*À raconter ses maux, souvent on les soulage*," he murmured coaxingly in French.

She translated the phrase as the equivalent of "A problem shared is a problem halved," and shook her head, repeating, "I'm sorry. I can't talk about it."

Severin sighed. "It was worth a try."

On her way out of the hotel, Ruby saw Councilman Harrison Lovett seated at the circular bar in the lobby talking to Delilah, who perched on a stool next to him. Behind her stood Frank Marion and Eugene Burley, the construction businessmen with alleged mob ties. She recognized them from the photos Frances had shown her.

Light poured down from the glass ceiling dome, picking out the gleaming reddish highlights in the loose chestnut curls tumbling over Delilah's shoulders. Today she wore a severely tailored pinstriped gray business suit. Her mouth was pinched, but she gave Lovett her full attention, although she sat rigid on the stool, her body angled away from him.

Marion and Burley cut similar figures. Their wide-shouldered and solid bodies were unconcealed by the designer suits they wore, and both men had their black hair slicked back. Marion and Burley looked hard and mean, like no one in their right mind would cross them.

Behind Lovett stood another man Ruby recognized from the police photo array: Red Iverson, whom Frances had described as "Lovett's hatchet man." The thin, scruffy-looking man had been seen with Beatrice a little while before she disappeared. Iverson hadn't bothered buttoning his black suit jacket, leaving his shoulder harness and gun in plain sight.

Ruby stopped midstride. Despite her hurt at Delilah's cruel words on the boardwalk last night, the presence of Iverson drove her to make her way to one of the soaring red marble pillars around the bar area. She chose the column closest to Delilah and Lovett, hoping to lurk behind it and overhear their conversation. With any luck, Iverson wouldn't spot her.

Lovett and Delilah spoke too low for her to make out much, just a scattering of words: "path," "beach" and "cooperate" from Lovett, which had Delilah shaking her head. Delilah's reply wasn't intelligible, but Lovett's expression became thunderous.

"I don't need to plant anything on you, you're already involved," he spat. All the personable charm he'd shown at the auction was replaced by irritation and arrogance. "Get this into your pretty little head: you'll do as you're told or I swear I'll—" Noticing the bartender drifting their way, he broke off, leaned closer to Delilah and whispered in her ear.

Whatever he said made Delilah recoil, rearing back to scowl at him balefully. Marion chuckled. Burley merely lifted his highball glass and drank half the contents in a gulp.

Ruby let out an embarrassing squeak when a hand wrapped around her bicep. While she'd been intent on listening, she'd taken her eyes off Iverson and he had snuck around to intercept her. Thwarting her attempt to twist out of his grasp, the wiry man dragged her out from behind the column and marched her over to Lovett.

"Well, if it ain't the prettiest girl with the most flamingo hair I ever did see." Lovett signaled to the bartender for a fresh drink. His otherwise affable tone held a sour note. "If you want to join in, honey, no need to hide." He grunted when the bartender poured a measure of Glenfiddich into the empty tumbler in front of him. Picking up the glass, he tossed back the expensive whiskey with a practiced flick of his wrist.

Marion nodded at Lovett. "See you around, Harry," he said in a baritone rasp.

Burley said nothing. He followed Marion across the lobby.

Ruby yanked her arm out of Iverson's grasp. "Join in what, exactly?"

Delilah gave her a withering glare and said nothing.

"Me and Ms. Kerrigan were discussing employment opportunities," Lovett replied, sliding off his stool and hitching up his pants. Pink scalp gleamed under the thinning hair on top of his head. His pale cream suit attempted to flatter his figure, but his beer belly lapped over his belt, almost hiding the brass buckle shaped like a Cadillac. "You want a job, honey?"

She tried to hide her shudder when the man's gaze crept over her—a near palpable touch lingering on the front of her mehndi printed blouse. When she'd chosen the garment that morning to go with her pants, she hadn't considered how much the viscose material would cling to her breasts, outlining her generous curves. Now she regretted the decision.

"You'd do well with what I have in mind," Lovett went on, flashing her a white-toothed grin she'd bet had cost him a few grand at a dentist's office, "and there's money—"

"Harry," Delilah gritted, the warning coming through with the subtlety of a flung brick. Her hands were fisted at her sides. "There are no jobs available."

Lovett ignored her. "I find I'm late for the next meeting on my busy social calendar and I can't give our discussion the time it deserves. Maybe next time, pretty girl." He chucked Ruby under the chin. "I'll be in touch," he added in an undertone to Delilah and strode away with Iverson trailing behind him like a vicious but loyal dog.

Ruby shook her head, rubbing her upper arm where Iverson's unpleasant phantom touch lingered. "What's Councilman Lovett's problem? I've got a job already," she commented to Delilah without thinking.

Delilah whipped around and snarled at her, "Don't pull that innocent crap on me. I know you're working with him. Get out! Get out of my hotel or I'll have you thrown out!" Leaving Ruby gaping in shock, she made a beeline across the lobby, headed toward the front desk and the security guard talking to a desk clerk.

Upset and confused by the accusation, Ruby exited the hotel.

CHAPTER NINETEEN

After hectic days overseeing the Magic Bean's business and developing new chocolates for the St. Clare Hotel, the day of her date finally arrived. Ruby looked forward to an evening with Frances, hoping to find some respite from her jumbled feelings about Delilah Kerrigan. She had been to the hotel on business a few times lately, but Delilah made herself scarce. The distance gave her plenty of time to think.

The last time they'd crossed paths, the woman had accused her of working with Harrison Lovett, which made no sense. Why would the city councilman employ a chocolatier? Yet Delilah had blasted her as if this nonexistent connection was a fact.

She'd tried to speak to Severin at one of their meetings, but he had warned her to tread lightly where Delilah was concerned. He believed someone higher up in the corporation was pressuring Delilah over a managerial issue and putting her under a lot of stress. He was confident Delilah would work through the problem without interference.

In the bathroom, Ruby picked out a tube of cherry-red lipstick from her makeup bag and ran the tip over her lips, her mind circling around the troublesome topic of Delilah. *Start at the beginning.* Was Delilah involved with Beatrice's disappearance? She'd once believed in the woman's guilt, based mostly—she had come to realize—on that bad first impression.

Beatrice was supposed to pick up Kaitlyn from school that day and drop her off at my apartment because she had a meeting with a source. Ruby returned the lipstick to her bag and leaned forward, gripping the edges of the sink while she ran through the facts. *When I arrived at the parking garage, I saw Delilah, who was furious about something. What was she doing there?* She'd never asked, not wanting to bring up the embarrassing encounter, and now didn't dare.

Frances said she couldn't find any connection between Beatrice and Delilah. The detective's straightforward statement had seemed to prove Ruby's suspicion wrong until she found the notebook. The discovery showed she'd been right—in some way, for some unknown reason, Delilah was implicated in whatever had happened to Beatrice. Or was she?

Ruby sighed and bowed her head. Maybe she'd been too hasty. Weren't there other explanations? Perhaps a guest or someone else found the notebook on Magdalena Island and turned it in to a desk clerk who later gave it to Management. Perhaps Delilah herself had picked up the notebook in the parking garage that day and forgotten about it. She'd given the woman no chance to explain, instead rushing to judgment in her zeal.

I won't make that mistake again, Ruby swore. She couldn't leap to assumptions anymore, especially not when those assumptions caused such pain to everyone involved.

As for what to do about Delilah...she didn't know. Irrevocable actions had been taken, bridges burned, painful things spoken. She frowned. The day she'd found the notebook, and she and Frances had bumped into Delilah on the boardwalk, the word "whore" had been used. She didn't understand where that accusation came from either.

Stepping away from the sink, Ruby decided to ignore Delilah and focus on her date. Tonight, she'd adopted a slightly more glamorous look, sweeping up her pink hair in a twist held by pins sporting little rhinestone stars. Glittering stars also shone on the earrings dangling to the shoulders of her A-line black dress. She'd continued the theme with a silver star-shaped nose stud and a thin silver belt at her waist.

She padded out of the bathroom to check the alarm clock on the nightstand by her bed. Time to leave or she'd be late. After stepping into a pair of black pumps, she grabbed a knitted shrug almost the same color as her lipstick—the temperature was sure to be cooler on the boardwalk and most of the restaurants offered outdoor seating.

Purse in hand, she left her apartment, determined to forget about Lovett and Delilah for a while and simply have a good time with a beautiful woman.

* * *

On arriving at the Grand Strand Promenade and Boardwalk, Ruby spotted Frances outside the first restaurant on the scheduled crawl.

Frances literally stood head and shoulders above most other people in the immediate area. The woman's short-sleeved, dark orange tunic and bronze crêpe de chine trousers accentuated her tall, athletic frame. In a change from the casual ponytail she usually sported, she'd pulled her black hair into a knot at the crown of her head. The stark style brought the classical lines of her face into even greater prominence.

Holy warrior princess! Give her a shield and a spear and she could pose for an Amazon statue, Ruby thought, stepping forward through the crowd.

"There you are," Frances murmured, bending to press their cheeks together. Her warm breath tickled the side of Ruby's throat. "Hello, gorgeous."

"Hi." Ruby shivered a little. She'd always thought of herself as a heavy-duty kind of girl, as compact and sturdy as a Shetland pony, but standing close to Frances made her feel small, dainty and petite, almost delicate—a weird sensation.

Frances straightened and gave her a dazzling smile. "You smell good."

"You too." Ruby glanced at the restaurant sign. "*Sette Pesci*. My Italian's pretty rusty, but doesn't that have something to do with seafood?"

"Seven Fishes," Frances translated. "Like the *Festa dei Sette Pesci*, the traditional Italian feast on Christmas Eve. My uncle Salvatore always goes crazy with the sardines." She gazed down at Ruby and frowned. "You're okay with garlic, right? Because otherwise, we probably won't get much to eat around here."

"Don't worry." Ruby playfully bumped Frances with her hip. "If you can take it, I can take it. We'll just have to stink together."

Frances nodded, setting her gold hoop earrings swinging. "Excellent call."

The event's organizer came around with a clipboard to check in the participants and get everyone seated at the restaurant's outdoor terrace for the appetizer course.

At their table, Ruby let Frances play the gallant suitor and pull out her chair.

A waitress brought over bottles of an American-style wheat ale, pouring them each a glass that foamed to a creamy head at the rim. Recognizing a local brewery's label, Ruby murmured thanks. She tasted the ale—as good as she remembered, well balanced and smooth—but Frances didn't appear pleased.

"What, no wine?" Frances asked, wrinkling her nose.

"It's only the first course. We'll be visiting several other restaurants and they'll serve wine with their courses, I'm sure." Ruby hoped so anyway. The crawl's online description hadn't mentioned a beer-only evening. "Have you had any luck with Bee's notebook?" She steeled herself to focus on Beatrice and Frances. Thoughts of Delilah were banished for the evening. She didn't want to dwell on the wreckage of her love life.

"Ms. Brooks's editor at the paper wasn't much help. We've got a consultant from the college working on the code," Frances replied. She held her glass to the candlelight and changed the subject without pause. "I'm curious…what kind of chocolate goes with ale?"

Ruby nodded, accepting she'd have to be content with a scrap of information. That so little had come of the notebook was disheartening, but she wouldn't lose hope. Nevertheless, she felt uneasy. Why hadn't Frances mentioned Delilah? Was the situation as screwed up as she feared? Had she accused an innocent woman? Surely Frances had investigated where Delilah had gotten the notebook in the first place. She considered asking, but only briefly, deciding she preferred to remain quiet on the subject.

I'm on a date tonight. I can always press my luck tomorrow. "Depends on the ale," she said, tapping the half-empty amber bottle with her fingernail. "This one, I'd probably start with a dark chocolate," she began, "seventy percent cacao or better…"

Frances proved a good listener, asking questions in the right places. Soon, Ruby began to relax into the flow of conversation. *Maybe our date won't be a total disaster.*

The appetizer brought to the table consisted of an amuse-bouche trio: a garlicky, buttery crab sourdough bruscetta, sweet and smoky grilled shrimp in a fire roasted tomato sauce, and warm charred octopus with arugula leaves, diced peaches and aged balsamic drizzle. Ruby enjoyed every morsel and had to stop herself from licking the plate. The delicious flavors awakened her palate. The ale complemented the dishes very well.

Frances sat back when she finished, staring at her empty plate with a mournful expression. "Do you think everybody would consider me a complete Philistine if I asked for a second round? Or maybe about a dozen orders to go?"

Ruby took a sip of ale and admitted, "I could eat a bucket of those shrimp."

"God, you have no idea." Frances patted her midsection. "Working out's a pain, but if I didn't hit the gym three times a week, I'd balloon like my Aunt Mary, who hasn't seen her feet since '79. Being a detective is mostly butt work, you know.

First, you work your butt off chasing down witnesses and leads, then you sit on your butt waiting for paperwork or a break in the case. But I've got nothing against curves," she added, her espresso-dark gaze boldly locking onto Ruby's. "I love the feel of a woman in my arms, all soft and lush and juicy so you just want to hang on and never let her go."

Warmth crept upward from Ruby's chest to burn in her cheeks. She was sure the hunger gleaming in Frances's eyes had little to do with the appetizer. An unexpected memory seized her—Delilah sprawled in the bed, her chestnut hair spilling over the pillow, her naked body pale against the sheets, the only points of color the rosy nipples, the patch of wiry hair between her legs, the kiss-reddened lips and the gray eyes blazing with shameless desire.

To cover her deepening blush, Ruby raised her glass and drank a few swallows of ale. Thank goodness Frances took the hint and turned the conversation to less provocative topics.

Soon, the group walked to the second destination a few yards down the boardwalk. Through the next course—a raw appetizer at an oyster bar—Frances entertained her with anecdotes about police work interspersed with mild flirting. Nothing too heavy-handed, no leering or lewd gestures, just playful banter. Ruby found herself responding in kind.

As the evening progressed from restaurant to restaurant, Ruby relaxed further, truly enjoying Frances's charming, attentive company.

Frances treated her like a lady, always pulling out her chair, collecting her purse and shrug whenever the group moved, offering an arm to escort her to the next destination. Although their interactions weren't overtly sexual, she was aware of a simmering undercurrent of attraction and desire between them.

In spite of her promise to herself, the specter of Delilah hovered. When Frances ate a bite of steak, Ruby recalled Delilah suggestively licking sauce from her fork during their dinner at the charity auction. Frances's story about a "haunted" toy store—the spooky events actually due to mice—reminded her of standing on the balcony at the hotel, watching the moonlight on the ocean and feeling Delilah's body so close to hers while the woman spoke about the ghosts of the two nuns in the cloister ruins on the hill. The recollections didn't quite spoil her experience of tasting food and wine at different restaurants, but the more her mind insisted on comparing Frances to Delilah, the more frustrated she felt.

Why did she keep returning to Delilah? She'd seen the deep, intense passions usually hidden behind Delilah's cool exterior. No doubt the woman was capable of hate. If there had been the potential for anything beyond a strict employer/employee relationship for them, the possibility had died the moment she took Bee's notebook from Delilah's desk drawer.

"Hey, anybody in there?" Frances waved in front of Ruby's face, startling her. "I'm going on about how good your bacon brittle is—my brother-in-law is addicted to the stuff—and you blanked out on me. Are you okay or am I boring you with praise?" she teased.

"I'm sorry." Ruby set down her fork, somewhat surprised to find her plate empty. Apparently, she'd finished the final course, a portion of chocolate marquise with pomegranate gelée, without tasting a single bite. "I didn't mean to get lost in my head." When a hand settled on her knee under the table, she sighed and gave Frances a rueful smile.

"It's fine. You've got stuff on your mind. Me too." Frances kept her hand in place, a welcome patch of warmth on Ruby's knee. Her eyes gleamed with amusement and affection. "But I'd like to forget my problems tonight." Her voice dropped lower. Her tongue crept out, wetting her lower lip until the plump flesh gleamed a suggestive scarlet. "How about you?"

Ruby wasn't naïve. She understood the implied question and how Frances had been testing the waters with her all night, leading up to this moment. This decision.

Her attraction to Frances wasn't as potent or intoxicating as the wildfire between her and Delilah, but that door was closed for good. She swallowed, her heart jerking painfully in her chest. Delilah was out of reach. The loss cut deeper than she expected.

Her mood threatened to dampen the spark with Frances. She couldn't let regrets about the past dominate her present or her future. *Frances is right. We should have a little fun together. Why not?* She could use a distraction.

"My apartment isn't very far," she said with an inviting look, reaching under the white tablecloth to caress Frances's hand where it rested on her leg.

Frances grinned and saluted her with the wineglass. "I've been there. Nice place, but I haven't seen the bedroom."

The statement was made so slyly, Ruby laughed, the cloud lifting from her spirits. "Not yet, but you will tonight," she promised, standing up, pulling on her knitted shrug and collecting her purse. "Come on, we're both done eating and I'm ready to go."

Putting down the wineglass, Frances rose with flattering haste, reaching across the space separating them to interlace her fingers with Ruby's.

They walked together out of the restaurant and into the night.

The wind blowing off the ocean carried a chill edge. Piles of dim clouds skimmed overhead, obscuring the moon. The fresh scent of rain tingled her nose. Ruby glanced at the beach and the waves beyond. A storm must be brewing at sea. As though in confirmation, a jagged, blue-white lick of lightning lit up a patch of sky and water. For a split second, the darkness trembled and broke like the surface of a pond disturbed by a thrown stone. The humped shape of Magdalena Island was clearly visible in the distance. Light faded and disappeared almost in the same instant. The island vanished from view.

Ruby forgot to breathe. *Delilah.* The name blossomed and withered in her mind as quickly as the far-off lightning strike. Why? Why couldn't she let the woman go? She curled her fingers more tightly around Frances's hand and deliberately turned her head away from the ocean. From the island. From Delilah. *Enough. I don't want to think anymore.*

She and Frances reached the municipal parking garage. The smell of exhaust hung in the air, trapped by the humidity. Frances towed her inside, past the rows of parked cars toward a corner where harsh white illumination from the overhead fluorescents didn't quite reach and the angles meant the area was a security camera blind spot. Ruby didn't protest when Frances pressed her against the concrete wall.

She gasped, feeling Frances's strength, the solidness of bone and muscle, the softness of breasts. A hand clenched on her hip, another on her shoulder, pulling her forward the few inches necessary for her head to tip back in surrender.

Frances's mouth suckled at her throat, traveling upward kiss by kiss. Ruby parted her lips to let Frances's tongue inside. Hot. Thick. Perfect. She whimpered, her hands flattening on the wall behind her. Rough concrete scratched her palms. Sweet sensation flared, but didn't consume her entirely. Something held her back.

Memories. Places on her body still remembered how Delilah had touched her. Kissed her with a soft pink mouth that became fierce and demanding, drawing incandescent pleasure pangs from the deepest part of her. Understanding came to her in a rush. Delilah was a fire in her blood devouring her bite by glorious bite. An inferno under her skin, searing her to the marrow of her bones. She would never be free.

A sense of wrongness shuddered through her. Her chest heaving, she shoved Frances away, her eyes so wide, the muscles around the sockets ached. Without the wall supporting her, she would have fallen to her knees. She gasped for breath, a fist pressed hard against her chest where pain radiated from her racing heart.

Frances stared, both hands raised either in surrender or to fend off an attack. Her expression turned watchful. "What's wrong, Ruby?" she asked in an unspeakably gentle tone, the same she might use to soothe a frightened, cornered animal.

Or a victim having a panic attack, Ruby thought, struggling to control her breathing. Her mouth felt swollen. Her neck stung. Had Frances bitten her? It didn't matter. "I'm sorry. Really sorry. I—" Her voice cracked. "I can't do this with you. Not now."

"Okay." Frances straightened, still eying her with concern. "Okay. Not a problem. Just tell me, did I do something or say something that caused you to have a bad reaction?"

"No." Ruby ran a hand over her face, not caring she was smearing her makeup. Nervous sweat had already done its worst. "I know this sounds stupid, but honestly, it's my fault." She averted her gaze. "Blame it on a…a recent breakup. A nasty one."

Frances's sympathy was immediate, though a slight suspicion lingered. To Ruby's relief, Frances didn't push for answers, but walked her to her truck and along the way made casual small talk centered around the dishes they'd eaten earlier, the wines they'd tasted, the other diners—inconsequential chatter that helped calm and ground her.

On arriving where she'd parked her vintage Dodge truck, Ruby tilted her face up to Frances. "Thanks," she said, trying to put her gratitude for everything in the simple word.

Frances slowly and carefully put an arm around her shoulders and hugged her. "If you're sure you're okay—"

"I'm fine." Ruby did not want to talk about the source of her upset. She pulled her keys from her purse and unlocked the truck door.

"From your mouth to God's ears," Frances murmured, releasing her. She paused. "Is there somebody I need to 'talk' to?" The emphasis on the word, her balled fist, the shadow in her face and the edge of violence in her tone made her meaning clear.

Ruby tried to conjure a reassuring smile. From Frances's frown, she failed. "No, it's not like that…look, it's okay. I'm okay. Really. I need time. But thanks anyway."

Frances hesitated before giving Ruby a nod and helping her step into the truck.

She waved goodbye as she drove out of the garage in a pensive mood, wishing the end of the evening had been as pleasant as the beginning.

CHAPTER TWENTY

"This bonbon is very good," Severin said thoughtfully a week and a half after Ruby's aborted date with Frances. "Tangy, yes, and a little bitter from the dark chocolate, but there's an unusual note." His raised eyebrows invited an explanation.

"Wild plum cream with wild plum liqueur and a kick of ginger and bay leaf," Ruby replied, easing back in the chair now that she knew he approved. His office door was closed, shutting out most of the kitchen noises. She appreciated the quiet. "The bay leaf gives the fondant a piney note."

Severin nodded and made a note on a form in front of him on his desk. "*Bon*. The flavors marry well and have depth—just sweet enough without becoming cloying. You show a deft touch. And this next one?"

She watched him taste her second bonbon before answering. "A paste of toasted black and white sesame seeds, almonds, extra virgin olive oil and palmetto honey spiced with the Turkish *mahleb* you gave me plus orange blossom water." She felt quite proud of the combination, a riff on an Egyptian sweet. "The bee embellishment is a chocolate covered organic almond striped with white chocolate and the wings are shaved almonds."

He nodded, licking his lips. "The flavor is almost floral," he decided. "Complex with a perfect balance. Once again, I congratulate you. These bonbons are approved." He made another note and set aside the ballpoint pen, giving her a serious look from beneath his thick black eyebrows. "Tell me, how are you doing in your own business?"

Ruby considered how she ought to answer him. The Magic Bean was busier than ever, which meant she'd been worked off her feet making candies, taking care of orders and dealing with the minutiae of running a business while also experimenting for the hotel's chocolates project. The meeting with Severin seemed like the first time in days she'd had a chance to sit still for five minutes and breathe.

"Lots of work. I often wish I had a third pair of hands around the place," she said, wondering what had provoked his curiosity. He'd never asked about the Magic Bean before.

His steady regard made her apprehension rise. "You will need to do more than wish, *petite*. The deadline for our project has been moved up. *Je suis désolé*, but I am only hearing the news this morning." He passed over an interoffice memo.

Ruby's eyes widened when she read the notice. "A week?" she yelped.

Her panicked thoughts darted here and there, tumbling over one another seeking solutions, alternatives, excuses—any way to stave off disaster. *It's not possible. I can't come up with six more original bonbons so fast. Can't they see that? I'll be in breach of contract. The hotel will sue me and I'll lose everything.* All at once, in the midst of her frantic groping for a solution, the authorizing signature seemed to leap off the bottom of the page straight into her brain, smothering her impending hysteria in its tracks.

"Delilah ordered the change, I see," she observed, grim anger settling over her. Her hand clenched on the memo, crumpling the paper.

"Yes." Severin sighed, his forehead pinched in a frown. "Delilah has refused my calls. I will try again, do not worry. *Alors là*, the bosses above her in the corporation do not understand. They go forward too quickly, thinking an artist creates by pushing a button in the mind instead of working with their blood and tears."

This isn't anybody's fault except Delilah's. Ruby spent a few minutes barely listening to Severin's promises, her hands smoothing the wrinkles out of the crumpled memo while she considered what to do about the deadline change. At last, she made a decision. "I'm going to see Delilah right now," she declared, standing up and making a move to the door before her resolution failed her.

If Severin spoke a word to stop her, Ruby couldn't hear him over the thunderous pounding of her pulse in her ears. Carried on a wave of righteous indignation, she walked through the kitchens, past the busy chefs and into the administrative area, taking a roundabout route through the maze of corridors to avoid Security since Delilah had revoked her privileges and forbidden her access anywhere except the kitchens.

I'm sorry I upset you, she thought to Delilah, *but this is going too far.*

She understood rage. She understood bitterness and hurt and lashing out at the cause of that pain. However, she didn't understand Delilah's actions, not this cold, vindictive crushing of her life, her dreams, her future. The woman wanted her gone. Well, she wouldn't go quietly with her tail tucked between her legs.

Marching past Kyle's desk—paying no attention to the receptionist's protests—she burst into Delilah's office, brandishing the memo like a weapon. "I want to know why," she said, stomping over to slap the paper on the desk. "Why this… this…abomination?"

Delilah glanced at her, the gray eyes holding a flinty shine. "Pardon me, Stephen, something urgent has come up. I need to call you back," she said into the headset microphone Ruby belatedly noticed. "Yes, that would be acceptable."

Robbed of her momentum, Ruby was forced to wait until Delilah ended the call. A headache muttered in her temples.

The moment Delilah removed the headset, she said in a rush, "You can't do this. A week isn't enough and I'm sure Marketing isn't finished with—"

"Marketing has another three months before their first deadline," Delilah said, folding her hands together on top of her desk. She looked calm and unruffled. "*Your* deadline has been changed to seven days." Her cool, disinterested tone cut Ruby more deeply than shouted curses. "If you're unable to fulfill the terms of your contract, we have no choice except to drop our association with you immediately and hire another, more experienced chocolatier who can better meet our expectations and requirements."

Ruby gritted her teeth and struggled not to scream or cry. "That's not fair," she said, each word grinding out painfully past the boulder in her chest and the lump in her throat. "Besides, our contract gives me until next year to complete my end."

"There's a clause which allows the hotel to change your deadline at our discretion." Delilah's slight smile was chilling, a crack in a glacier. "I'm choosing to exercise that discretion." She glanced over Ruby's shoulder. "It's all right, Kyle. We're fine. Security isn't needed. Please shut the door on your way out."

Doesn't anything move her? Ruby was unable to reconcile the warm-blooded, passionate woman she'd made love to in her bedroom with the aloof ice maiden seated behind the desk. She couldn't see a way out, not when Delilah seemed dead set on ruining her.

Behind her, she heard the door close. Kyle didn't slam it shut, but the click sounded louder than a thunderclap in the silent office.

"Why are you being so petty?" Ruby whispered. "The time we spent together, that was personal. What you're doing here is business. An abuse of power."

Delilah's mouth tightened. Her nostrils flared. The mask slipped a little, revealing scorn and a flash of anger. "You made everything personal. I don't know how you managed to worm your way into my hotel—"

"I did not!" Ruby interrupted, outraged. "You invited me!"

"Worm your way into my bed—"

"As I recall, we were in *my* apartment at the time."

"—and you pretended to find that damned notebook in my desk as part of some sordid little plot," Delilah continued, her voice coming out flat and poisonous, as brittle as sugar work. "You can tell Harry that I may have to put up with him and his schemes, but you are out, Ms. Fontaine. Out of my hotel. Out of my sight. Out of my life."

Overwhelmed by indignation and the need to contradict the awful accusations, Ruby flailed for words. She finally managed to squash the impulse to throw something at Delilah and wrestled her emotions into submission. "I found the notebook in your desk by accident. I did not put it there," she said in the calmest manner available to her at the moment.

Delilah scoffed. "Don't bother with denials. The notebook wasn't in my desk that morning, then you conveniently 'found' it when you were alone in my office."

Ruby plopped down in the visitor's chair opposite the desk. How could she convince Delilah of the truth? Her anger drowned in a wave of sadness mingled with resolve. Maybe the task was impossible, but she could start at the beginning and attempt to unravel the threads of what she suspected were mutual misunderstandings. She had nothing to lose by trying.

"I saw you that day," she began.

"What day?" Delilah gazed at her narrowly.

"The day Beatrice Brooks disappeared." Ruby went on to explain about her proposed meeting with Beatrice and her encounter with a swearing, furious Delilah in the parking garage below her apartment building. "I suspected you, of course, after I had to report Beatrice missing when she didn't pick up Kaitlyn from school. You were a stranger, very hostile, very rude. I jumped to conclusions, I guess because you rubbed me the wrong way. I wanted to believe you were involved."

Delilah listened, not a single twitch betraying her thoughts. "Go on."

The whole tale spilled out, piece by halting piece. Ruby was light-headed when she finished. "I don't know what to think at this point," she confessed. "The only thing I know for a fact is that I found Bee's notebook in your desk drawer. I wasn't looking for it and I sometimes wish I'd never seen it, except I really hope the police can use it to find Bee."

"I'll tell you what I told the police in my interview: I have never seen that notebook before," Delilah offered stiffly. "I assumed you told them that to involve me in some scheme cooked up by Lovett."

"Why would you assume a connection between me and Harrison Lovett? You accused me of…well, of being in league with him." Ruby's lip curled. "I would never work for that guy, by the way. He's disgusting."

Delilah made a skeptical sound. "You know Red Iverson. I saw your face. You recognized him in the lobby the other day."

"Only because Frances Orsini showed me a picture of Iverson and told me who he was," Ruby explained.

"Oh." Delilah deflated slightly.

"How could you believe I'd have anything to do with Lovett after the nasty things he said to me—" Ruby almost said "when we had our first date," but changed her mind at the last second to "—at the charity auction."

"You could have staged the encounter. Women have endured worse for the sake of money and Lovett is a rich man." From the tone of Delilah's voice, even she didn't believe it.

Ruby lifted her eyebrows.

"You're right," Delilah admitted. "Lovett's smart, but not that clever. If what you say is true, how did the notebook get in my desk drawer?"

"Ask Kyle, who was in your office that morning."

Delilah pressed a button to call Kyle from his desk. When he didn't appear, she shook her head. "He's probably in the break room. I'll speak to him later." She folded her hands together on the desk blotter. "Let's move on. If my suspicions are wrong and something else is going on, then I'm in the dark. What do you know that I don't?"

"Frances told me a witness saw Iverson and Bee together shortly before she vanished."

The color drained from Delilah's face. Her frozen façade shattered. She bolted up, swayed and collapsed back into her chair.

Alarmed, Ruby started to stand.

"Together?" Delilah said in a harsh undertone, her fingers gripping the edge of the desk. She stared ahead with a haunted look. "My God, they were together."

Uneasiness crept cold fingers down Ruby's spine.

Delilah shook her head. "Impossible," she declared as if she were trying to convince herself more than Ruby. "That can't be right."

"Call Detective Orsini. I have her number," Ruby said, sitting down and hoisting her purse onto her lap with the intention of finding Frances's business card. She froze when Delilah made a sharp negative gesture.

"But it can't be—" Delilah broke off and took a deep breath, frowning. She stayed quiet a while, clearly lost in thought. At last, she glanced at Ruby.

Ruby supposed the woman was torn, fighting to understand what she'd learned versus her perception of events. *Been there, done that.* The strange reaction to the information about Iverson and Beatrice was puzzling, but she knew better than to pry right now. She saw the exact moment Delilah accepted the truth. Her despair lightened. "What about the deadline?" she asked, taking a chance and breaking the silence.

Delilah grimaced. She picked up the memo, tore the paper into three strips and let the pieces flutter into the wastebasket. "I made a mistake. Your original deadline stands." She gave Ruby a remorseful look. "I apologize, Ruby. What I did was wrong. I shouldn't have used my authority to punish you for what I believed was a personal attack and I'm sorry I hurt you. I'm sorry I wasn't a better person. I'm just...I'm sorry for everything."

Ruby felt a warm glow start in her chest, moving through her veins as though filling her with liquid sunshine. She dropped her purse on the floor and stood. "I'm not," she replied, moving around the desk. The things she wanted to say were right there, bubbling up from her heart. "I have regrets, some of the blame falls on me, but I'm not sorry we met. I'm not sorry we clicked the way we did. And I'm not sorry we had sex." Delilah's faint blush emboldened her to continue, "I like you. I like you a lot."

She didn't expect any particular response. Delilah surprised her by standing and, following a moment's hesitation, giving her a hug.

"Me too," Delilah said softly in her ear. "I won't apologize for mixing business and pleasure either, Ruby." She pulled back a little, her gray eyes warm. "We have a special connection. In my world, that's rare. Cherished," she added with a smile, her face alight in remembered pleasure. "We have some work to do, but I'd like to try. If you would, that is."

A fragile hope bloomed inside Ruby. She nodded, a great weight lifting from her heart. Perhaps she and Delilah would be okay after all.

CHAPTER TWENTY-ONE

Over the next several days working in her rented kitchen, Ruby found herself thinking about Delilah more often than not. The papery skin on a hazelnut made her recall the color of Delilah's hair and the way sunshine drew reddish highlights glinting from the brown curls. The delicate pink of a raspberry fondant became the soft curve of Delilah's mouth.

Even today, making a batch of her customers' favorite Sleeping Beauty Bites—a dome of honey and macadamia nougat enrobed in white chocolate and embellished by a tiny, bright red chocolate dot on top to represent the princess's pricked finger—she couldn't help flushing at the memory of Delilah's shapely breasts.

She paused, piping bag in hand, when she heard three loud raps on the door. *I'm not expecting any pickups or deliveries.* Frowning, she wiped her hands on her apron, went across the kitchen and opened the door, revealing an older woman standing at the threshold.

The newcomer was in her late fifties or early sixties, short and squat, almost stumpy—the loose denim shirt and black leggings she wore did nothing to enhance or conceal her barrel-shaped figure. Her graying hair was cropped short and styled in fussy tight curls covering her head, reminding Ruby of poodle fur.

"Ms. Fontaine?" the woman asked in a hoarse, raspy voice redolent of bourbon, cigarettes and juke joints, although she looked more like a grandmother than a barfly.

"Yes," Ruby answered, followed quickly by reeling off her usual spiel, "but I don't sell to the public except through my website. I'm also not making donations right now if you're soliciting for a cause. And if you're selling something, I'm not buying, and I'm not interested in learning more about any religions, thank you. Have a nice day." She started to close the door, stopping when the woman shoved an envelope at her through the crack.

"You might want to read that first, sugar," the woman said with a gap-toothed smile. "And my name's Eileen, by the way. Eileen Eggleston."

Ruby leaned a hip against the doorjamb, tore open the envelope flap and withdrew a letter. St. Clare Hotel and Resort stationery, she noted, and signed by Delilah. Dread fluttered a moment, but she and Delilah were on friendly terms again. More than friendly, in fact, if she was any judge. The last time they spoke at the hotel, Delilah's sidelong glances and touches on her elbow or upper arm were definitely flirty. She smiled to herself and read through the handwritten note in a few moments.

Dear Ruby,

Severin mentioned you're having some trouble juggling the demands of your Magic Bean business with your work for the hotel. If that's the case, I'd like to offer the assistance of Eileen Eggleston, one of our finest administrative specialists.

Eileen isn't a chocolatier or even a cook, but she is very talented at business organization, paperwork, light bookkeeping and other office duties, leaving you free to do what you do best in the kitchen. It's just a temporary loan and you'll be responsible for Eileen's pay while she's working for you, but you won't regret it, I promise.

Having said that, if you find yourself in a pinch, I'm sure we can work something out. Please don't hesitate to contact me.

With warmest regards,

Delilah

Ruby glanced at Eileen. Despite the letter's semiformal tone, a warm, happy feeling spread through her chest and made her heart thump twice. She tucked the letter into the envelope. "Come in," she said to the woman, standing aside to let her bustle into the kitchen.

"Nice place," Eileen said, glancing around before her attention narrowed on the desk. She walked over and sat down on the chair, pulled a pair of bifocals from her purse and perched them on her nose. Gazing at Ruby over the top of the tortoiseshell plastic frames, she continued, "Let's get the awkward stuff out of the way, if you don't mind."

"By all means."

"I want to be paid in cash at the end of the week."

"Cash is fine, provided you're as good as Delilah said."

Eileen's grin broadened. "I'm better. Tell me what needs doing, sugar, and I'll get it done provided the job doesn't require heavy lifting or pole vaulting. And my fee is reasonable given my skills set and years of expertise." She named a sum.

Ruby's eyebrows rose, but business was good and she could afford Eileen's price for a limited time. "I'll pay you on Fridays," she agreed.

"Then I'll get started here. Lunch break at one o'clock. Do you like Italian?" Eileen began sorting through the stack of inventory forms. "There's a hole-in-the-wall place around here, I know the owners, best chicken parmesan in town. And you're buying."

Laughing, Ruby returned to the stove to start a pot of sugar syrup for marshmallows.

By the end of the working day, she could have gotten on her knees and kissed Eileen's sensible shoes. The woman was a miracle of efficiency.

Eileen organized website orders and updated inventory, boxed candies for shipping and delivery, answered customer service emails, dealt with the financials, bills and billing, and didn't hesitate rolling up her sleeves, putting on a spare apron and washing pots as needed. Just like Delilah promised in the letter, a delighted Ruby was able to concentrate on her confectionery work, making it the most productive day she'd enjoyed in a while.

Time flew. When Ruby glanced up from smoothing a pan of goat's milk fudge with a spatula, she realized it was four thirty p.m. and Eileen was getting ready to leave.

"Have a good night," Eileen said at the door, her big black purse under her arm. "By the way, I can only be here until two o'clock on Thursday." She beamed proudly. "My granddaughter's school play. I need to measure her for the costume I'm sewing."

Ruby chuckled and grabbed a dish towel to wipe her hands. "Sounds like fun."

"Sounds like a pain in the patootie to me, sugar, but the kid's seven years old. What's a grandma to do? I can't refuse the brat, my daughter would kill me." Eileen produced a key ring from her purse. "Take care, dear. See you tomorrow, bright and early."

Once Eileen left, Ruby sat on a stool gazing in satisfaction at the neatly stacked boxes of orders to be shipped tomorrow and the trays of sweets she'd made. These last few weeks, she'd really teetered on the verge of cracking under the pressures of increased work and mixed emotions, including guilt over the misunderstandings with Delilah. *But I think it'll be better now I've been given some breathing space.*

Brisk, staccato raps sounded at the door. She slid off the stool and went to answer, thinking Eileen had forgotten something.

Delilah waited on the other side.

Ruby's delighted surprise transformed into a grin. "Hey there. I wasn't expecting you." She whipped off the stained apron, holding it in her hand. A hint of heat strayed into her cheeks. Compared to Delilah's elegant, knee-length burgundy dress with a pleated skirt, she felt like a slob. *Had I known she'd come over, I'd have picked something nicer to wear than a ratty old orange T-shirt and the ripped jeans I dug out of the dirty clothes pile.*

"Should I have called first?" Despite the question, Delilah's easy manner showed she hadn't been worried about her welcome.

"No, it's fine." Ruby motioned for Delilah to come inside, wondering what prompted the visit. Not that she'd complain. The real woman in the flesh was much more alluring than any fantasy image in her head. "I'll start a pot of coffee." She tossed her apron in a laundry basket and went to the coffee machine on the counter.

Delilah glanced around the kitchen and refocused on Ruby with a hint of anxiety. "How did today work out with Eileen? I hope you don't mind. Severin seemed concerned about you, and I...well, I wanted to help."

"You did, thank you. You saved my sanity, if not my life. Eileen is a treasure. If I could afford her, I'd keep her on full-time." Ruby had to turn away from the brilliance of Delilah's grin before she hugged or kissed her. She thought Delilah had been cautiously flirting at their previous meetings, but refused to make assumptions considering how much trouble jumping to conclusions had earned her in the recent past.

"Good. I'm glad." Delilah's calm mask slid into place.

Was there a trace of worry under the placid expression? Ruby wondered. "Is everything all right?" She placed a fresh paper filter in the machine's basket and added scoops of cinnamon-flavored coffee she took from a vintage ceramic canister she'd bought at the weekend street market because she liked the painted rooster on the front.

"With the hotel, you mean?" Delilah sat down on a stool at the worktable. A fold of her dress's pleated skirt flipped over when she crossed her legs, revealing a small run in her pantyhose—an imperfection Ruby found endearing. "I've been busy quelling rumors about the so-called haunted ruins on the hill."

"Did something happen?"

"Overactive imaginations. A couple of the younger housekeepers dared each other to climb the hill up to the cloister last night, even though the site is off-limits after dark because of safety issues. Scared themselves—and some of the other staff—half to death with some wild story. I can't let the situation go on. We'll have canceled reservations next."

"From what you said before, I thought the panic was limited to the staff."

"Employees talk. Word spreads. Guests hear things. Not everyone is willing to stay in or schedule a major convention in a haunted hotel. Usually, the legend of the Magdalena Island nuns is an interesting folktale, nothing more. Lately, it's taken on a life of its own."

Ruby filled the glass carafe with water, poured the liquid into the coffee machine and pressed the start button. "You told me once that these things come in waves," she said, leaning her back against the counter, her arms folded across her chest.

"And we're in the middle of a tsunami." Grimacing, Delilah made an impatient gesture that ended with her tucking a loose chestnut curl into the chignon at the base of her neck. "No, a plague would be more apt. Fear is a sickness, an infection that keeps spreading. Of course, not everyone's susceptible, thank God, but we haven't had this much tension at the St. Clare since a maintenance worker entered the wrong room a few years ago and interrupted a guest dismembering his murdered wife in the bathtub."

"Really? I don't remember reading about that case. When did it happen?" While she spoke, Ruby collected two mugs from a cabinet and a carton of half-and-half from the refrigerator as the rich smells of cinnamon and coffee filled the kitchen.

"A few years ago. For once, the police kept a lid on the gruesome details. To this day, the room has a bad reputation with the staff."

"Another ghost?"

"More like a story told to frighten new employees." Delilah shrugged. "A hazing ritual. Pranks. Harmless, so I don't usually interfere as long as everyone does their jobs."

Neither of them spoke for several minutes. Ruby filled two mugs from the carafe when the coffee was ready and brought them, a bowl of sugar cubes she kept on hand and the carton of half-and-half to the worktable. She sat on the stool next to Delilah, sipping from her cup of milky coffee and trying to think of something to say to break the silence.

Delilah took her coffee with sugar only. At the first sip, she made a little sound of appreciation. Eventually, she set down her mug. "Good coffee. The cinnamon's very nice." She paused and licked her lips. "Ruby, I'd like to try again," she went on, staring across the room at the stove as if she found the view fascinating. "With you."

Ruby was struck anew by the purity of Delilah's profile, the angles of bone and smooth skin emphasized by the smooth cap of hair. "Dating, you mean."

"We ended abruptly, I know."

"You want a re-do."

A wry smile tugged the visible corner of Delilah's mouth. Her gaze flickered sideways to Ruby. "Another chance, yes. If that's possible. If you want to try."

"Before I answer, I have a request." Ruby waited until Delilah shifted around on the stool to face her. "Tell me what's going on between you and Harrison Lovett."

The question clearly made Delilah uncomfortable. With the air of someone taking the Fifth in the witness box on their attorney's advice, she said, "I'd rather not tell you." Cutting through Ruby's objection, she went on, "You're better off not knowing. Trust me. Please accept there are things I must keep private and reasons why I won't tell you."

"He's an abusive, sexist, horrible man and he hurt you," Ruby insisted. "Why do you continue to condone his behavior? Anybody else who put bruises on you in the hotel lobby would've been thrown out on their keister."

Delilah sighed. "Yes, Harry's come very close to crossing a line at times, but unless he does something blatantly illegal, as the hotel's general manager I have to grit my teeth and put an important customer ahead of my feelings. For what it's worth, I don't believe he meant to cause me physical harm. He's frustrated, not stupid."

"Uh-huh, not stupid enough to leave marks where they might be seen." Ruby didn't wait for an answer. She rose and collected the empty coffee mugs, taking them to the sink, then returned to the worktable. "I wish you'd talk to me. I want to help."

"I don't have any answers to give you." Delilah caught Ruby's hand in a firm grip. Her palm was cool, dry and soft—a complete contrast to Frances's calluses. "Forget Lovett. He's a cretin and I can handle him. He's not important. What *is* important is whether or not you'll give us another chance."

Against the hope she read in Delilah's eyes—and a desire, a hunger that mirrored hers—Ruby could do only one thing. She nodded. Just to make sure, she added, "Yes."

Delilah's smile warmed her to her toes.

CHAPTER TWENTY-TWO

With the Magic Bean temporarily running more smoothly because of Eileen, Ruby devoted herself to creating confections and rebuilding her personal relationship with Delilah, whose habitual icy mask had thawed to reveal a lovely, affectionate woman.

She and Delilah ate lunch together twice at the hotel. They also went out on a second date, a riverboat cruise followed by a carriage ride through the oldest part of the city. To her mingled disappointment and relief, the evening didn't end in sex, but she knew the slow burn of attraction still sizzled between them—ready to flare into a bonfire the moment they touched with intent. In the meantime, she enjoyed the flirty, fun, teasing side of Delilah.

Now Ruby stood at the rail on the deck of the ferry gliding toward Magdalena Island, filling her lungs with clean ocean air. The noon sun and a freshening wind turned the sea to a rolling carpet of shimmering disco glitter. She turned her head at the mocking laugh of a gull. The white wings folded and the bird dove, splashing into the water.

As instructed by Delilah, she'd worn casual clothing: a lemon-yellow T-shirt with white stars on the front, comfortable jeans and sneakers, and hadn't bothered with a purse. To keep her pink hair from blowing into her eyes, she'd tied a vintage silk Hermès scarf inherited from her late grandmother around her head. The light blue, magenta and gold abstract pattern—modern in the 1960's—hadn't faded despite the scarf's age.

When the ferry reached the wharf, Ruby saw Delilah holding a woven picnic basket. She grinned and waved before disembarking. Other passengers swarmed around them, but she couldn't care less about being a roadblock when the most beautiful woman in the world stood not an arm's length away, smiling back at her.

"Hi." For some weird reason, Ruby felt suddenly shy.

"Good afternoon." Delilah gave Ruby a hug and a brief brush of lips. She stepped back and turned to lead the way, the picnic basket swinging from her hand. "I hope you don't mind, I planned a little outing for our lunch today."

Ruby fell in step beside Delilah. "Where are we headed?"

"The top of the hill. You've never seen the convent ruins up close and the view from up there is amazing." Delilah gazed at Ruby sidelong, amusement gleaming in her gray eyes. "Maybe we'll hear the ghosts of the nuns. Anyway, we'll be alone. The managers and I have declared the site off-limits to employees and guests, at least until the rumors die off."

While they walked, Ruby studied Delilah, appreciating the boatneck blue-and-white striped shirt with the red embroidered anchors and the white jeans molded to the woman's slender legs. Very much in the style worn by the yacht set, right down to the topsiders that looked brand new. Delilah's chestnut hair was fastened in a loose ponytail at the crown of her head, allowing the curls to bob in time with her steps on the path leading to the hill.

How the heck did I get so lucky? Ruby asked herself at the almost painful jerk of her heart when Delilah glanced at her. *And what the heck am I going to do about it? What if she doesn't want me anymore? What if I lose her again?* But the sun felt warm on her skin. The air smelled like mown grass and the drowsy ocean breeze. There wasn't a place for doubt or speculation on such a lovely day. She set her worries aside.

The climb took several minutes, but the path was well kept and not too steep. Ruby soon found herself looking at the ruins of the old St. Clare convent, mostly broken and scattered masonry pitted and stained by more than two centuries of neglect. A wild muscadine grapevine, heavy with leaves and bunches of dark purple fruit, twisted in knots over something taller than her head, concealing the object from her view.

Delilah approached a knee-high stack of stone slabs about the size of a card table and seated herself, setting the picnic basket next to her. "Under the grapevine is what's left of one of the convent's chimneys. The other collapsed about five years ago."

Ruby joined Delilah on the slabs, sitting on the other side of the basket. The stone beneath her felt cool and rough to the touch. *Huh. Not actual stone*, she thought on sighting pieces of oyster shell on the surface. *Tabby concrete, like they sometimes use for patios nowadays.* Chill seeped through the seat of her jeans, a contrast to the sunlight's heat on her face and shoulders. "What actually destroyed the convent?"

"None of the contemporary accounts agree on the cause. Lightning setting the thatched roof on fire was one possibility." Delilah reached into the basket and withdrew a bottle of Beaujolais Rouge, two glasses and a corkscrew. She continued speaking while uncorking the bottle. "Two nuns were killed— the lovers in the legend, presumably—and a visiting priest injured. He died later. The surviving Poor Clares left the area and never returned." She poured wine into the glasses. "No one knows what happened to the sisters afterward."

Ruby tried the wine, tasting strawberries, raspberries and a dryness hinting at dust. She saluted Delilah with the glass. "This is excellent." She took another glance around the landscape, the well-tended grass and the lack of bushes or shrubs.

Delilah removed a couple of small, wrapped baguettes from the basket and said, correctly interpreting Ruby's unasked question, "The hotel doesn't own the whole island, just a part. The city maintains migratory bird and loggerhead sea turtle sanctuaries on the back half. A few times a year, researchers come out to do studies, but most of the time, the place is deserted except for the wildlife. As for the hill, while the city actually owns the property, we assume responsibility for keeping the site safe and maintained. In return, we get a tax break."

"A good deal?"

"According to our accountants, yes."

Ruby unwrapped her baguette and sniffed, trying to identify the contents. Arugula and thin slices of rare roast beef smeared with a dark red condiment that didn't smell like ketchup were stuffed inside the freshly baked bread.

"Chef Daniels's roasted tomato and currant chutney." From the basket, Delilah produced forks, linen napkins and a wide-mouthed, lidded glass jar filled with watermelon feta salad. "For dessert, I have buttermilk almond cake and caramelized peaches."

Ruby bit into the crusty baguette, chewed and swallowed. "Wow."

"Wait until you try Severin's cake. I had a slice for breakfast and thought I'd gone to heaven." Delilah laughed and unwound the plastic wrap from her baguette.

The throaty sound of Delilah's laugh stirred a longing in Ruby, a desire to topple the woman into the grass and rediscover the smooth flesh beneath those smart clothes. She didn't act on the impulse. Returning her attention to the sandwich in her hands, she tore into the bread and meat in a futile attempt to sate a hunger that had nothing to do with food.

The salad was refreshing, the cake and grilled peaches as tasty as Delilah had claimed. The meal soothed her stomach if not her libido. After she finished eating, Ruby absently poked at a white-flowered chickweed growing from the thin fringe of longer grass at the base of the slabs. "It's really quiet. Peaceful." In the near distance, she heard the hissing of the tide surging on an unseen shore. She sneaked a sidelong glance at Delilah.

"Mmm-hmm. Would you like to see something more interesting than weeds?" Delilah stood, holding a pair of small binoculars she must have taken out of the basket, and brushed off the seat of her white jeans with her free hand.

"Sure." Ruby got up and touched the tip of Delilah's nose. "You're turning pink here." She thought about drawing her thumb along the curve of the full bottom lip, excusing the intimacy with a lie about cake crumbs. Her nerve failed her, then it was too late.

"Oh, a little more sun won't hurt me." Wisps of chestnut hair had escaped the ponytail, framing Delilah's face and softening her cheekbones. "Come on. I want you to see this." She started walking across the debris-strewn field to the other side of the hill.

Ruby followed, wishing she hadn't been so hesitant.

Delilah came to a halt near a place where the hill simply ended, as if some long ago giant had chopped off the land with a knife, shearing away a sizeable portion and leaving an abrupt, ragged edge with only the blue sea and bluer sky beyond. "Go on. Take a look."

"Are you sure it's safe?" Ruby moved a few steps closer to the edge and peered down at the sheer drop. At the bottom, the beach and the dark, almost black craggy ridges of rock stretching out from the island formed a horseshoe-shaped cove. The booming surf sounded loud to her ears, the rhythmic rushing crash of a Leviathan's pulse.

"We're fine. Use these." Delilah handed her the binoculars. "You'll get a better view."

Ruby held the binoculars to her eyes and adjusted the focus.

Waves slapped against a shore covered in creamy, coarse-textured sand and battered the pockmarked ridges extending from the island. Thin spray flew high and ran foaming back into the sea, combing out the long strands of seaweed trailing like hair from the rocks. Further out, she glimpsed the hunched mounds of Little Tsiskwa and St. John, two other islands in the barrier chain that helped protect the coast from Atlantic storms.

Arms twined around Ruby's waist. A chin rested on her shoulder. "There's a path down to the beach, but it's very steep, eroded and considered unsafe," Delilah murmured. "You can get there by boat. The water's deep enough and the beach is private. We'd be alone. We could do what we want. Whatever we want." Ruby felt the woman's smile against her throat. "You know, I'd love to see you in a skimpy bikini with your breasts spilling out of the top, barely restrained and hot as hell. You can strip off the bikini bottom, rub your sweet, juicy pussy on my face and nobody will hear you screaming when you come. And after? I'll lick you clean and do it all over again."

Trembling, Ruby lowered the binoculars and turned her head, tingling with arousal. Her face was very close to Delilah's, their lips almost touching. She willed her heart to stop darting around in her chest like a butterfly on a sugar high. "Oh," she breathed, slippery heat dampening the crotch of her panties. "I…um…I'd like…oh, yes. Yes to everything—"

Delilah kissed her, swallowing the rest of her stupidly inadequate words.

A dozen kisses, a hundred, a thousand. Ruby lost count. Her senses narrowed to this precise moment—to the tongue in her mouth, the slender form pressed to her, the hands gripping her buttocks hard and holding her fast. She could stay in Delilah's arms forever.

A dizzying certainty overwhelmed her: if only she could pry open her ribcage and tuck Delilah inside. Enfold Delilah under her bones, in her flesh, locked deep beneath her skin.

Ruby's body awakened. Every inch ached, on fire with longing. Her breasts felt heavier and fuller. Pleasure drunk and greedy for more of Delilah's touch, she tore her mouth from the kiss and whipped off her shirt over her head. Some urgent thought intruded. She paused, panting. "Are we okay? I mean, will anybody come up here and see us?"

Delilah stood still, her face mottled. Her fingers clenched and unclenched. "I don't give a shit." Her eyes were huge, the gray irises nearly drowned by blown pupils. "But the answer is no. Get over here. Now," she growled, impatiently tearing at her shirt.

Ruby stumbled forward, already unfastening her jeans and pushing them down past her hips. An unfamiliar sound made her stop, clutching her shirt to her chest—a hollow, keening

moan, rising and falling in eerie cadence. She stared at Delilah.
"Do you hear that?"

"It's the wind," Delilah replied, tossing aside her bra. Sunlight
gilded the slopes of her small breasts and the pink nipple furled
tight. She made a coaxing gesture. "No one's there."

The moan returned, this time lower and softer, just audible
above the surf. Ruby yanked up her jeans. Her imagination
supplied an image of a strange man crouching hidden
somewhere, a voyeur getting his kicks watching them. The
third moan, loud and clear, carried to her ears. She shuddered,
goose bumps pebbling her flesh, and moved several steps closer
to Delilah. "I'm not imagining things. You heard that, right?"

Delilah shook her head. "The wind is blowing through the
cracks in the old convent stones. It's not ghosts, I promise." She
rubbed Ruby's back, her smile a bit forced. "Ghosts don't exist.
Those dead nuns are long gone. We're the only ones here."

Ruby wanted to believe she and Delilah were alone on
the hill. Unfortunately, she couldn't shake the conviction that
someone had their eyes on them. She tried to relax, tried to
return Delilah's heated kisses, tried to recapture the passion and
desire that had burned so brightly, but the mood was ruined.
At last, she let her lips cling to Delilah's for another moment
before she drew away. "I'm sorry. I can't. Not right now."

"All right." Delilah didn't appear too upset. She sighed, her
fingertips grazing Ruby's jaw. "I see this isn't the best place or
time. Perhaps later. Dinner in my suite tonight?"

"Love to." Ruby blushed and bent to pick up her shirt from
the grass. "I'm sorry," she repeated in a mumble.

Delilah stopped her. "Don't apologize. Ruby, you're very
special to me. When we make love, you should be comfortable."
She flashed a wider smile. "Believe me, you're worth the wait.
Would you like to go downhill and take a walk by the marina?"

"Don't you need to go back to work?"

"I made time just for you today."

The simple declaration ignited another kind of warmth in
Ruby—a gentle affection for the woman standing next to her.
She felt her expression soften and gave Delilah a return smile.

No longer embarrassed, she went to retrieve Delilah's shirt and bra, her mind and heart singing with such happiness, she almost forgot about the unearthly moans.

Almost.

While she and Delilah walked hand in hand on the downhill path, she glanced over her shoulder, half expecting to hear phantom nuns sobbing for the lives and the love they'd lost. She only caught the sounds of the wind and the sea.

Shrugging at her earlier nervousness, Ruby let Delilah tug her along.

CHAPTER TWENTY-THREE

Ruby managed to forget Greg Brooks was staying in town until she ran into him on the boardwalk on her way to the ferry wharf, three days after her picnic on the hill with Delilah. "Oh, um…hi, Greg."

The man slanted a brittle green glance at her. He slouched elegantly in a tailored designer suit so fitted to his lean body that the garment might have been painted on. "I wanted to talk to you, but didn't have your number," he said with a pointed frown, as if his ignorance was her fault.

Ruby ignored the complaint. "How's Katie?"

He huffed. "Fine, I guess. Do we need to talk about the kid?"

"If I didn't know any better, I'd say yes." Ruby pinched the bridge of her nose and counted to ten. She'd been looking forward to meeting Delilah for breakfast. Losing her temper with Greg would only make her late. "What do you want?"

The wind tried to ruffle Greg's platinum blond faux-hawk. His hair product withstood the assault. "I got a letter in the mail. *In the mail*," he emphasized with a finger stabbed at a blue

US Postal Service mailbox standing near a lamppost. "In an envelope with a stamp. Do people still do that? Anyway, this asshole wanted me to give him a lot of money."

Ruby waited, but the rest of the story failed to materialize. "And?" she prompted.

"And I'll give them the money," he groused. "That's not the problem. They want you to deliver the ransom before they release Beatrice."

The word *ransom* caused her brain to stutter. She stood locked in place, gaping at Greg while people moved around them. Recalling the hoax ransom demand she'd received in the recent past, she told herself to relax. "I'm sure it's fake, Greg. What did the police say?"

He shrugged. "I haven't told the police."

"What? You need to call the cops!"

"I can't. They'll hurt her. The letter said they're watching me."

Ruby fell silent, aware of the curious glances she and Greg received from passing pedestrians. She grabbed his arm, paying no attention to his squawk about wrinkling his suit, and pulled him into the nearest shop. Once inside, the shelves of boxed candy and the aroma of cheap chocolate made her realize her thoughtlessness had landed them in Miss Vanita's Finest Chocolates Seaside Emporium. *Oh, please give me strength.*

She shuddered at a wooden barrel filled with pieces of pastel-colored, sugar-free saltwater taffy and wrenched her attention back to Greg. "Do you have the letter with you?"

"No. Obviously." Greg rolled his eyes. "Why would I carry that around with me? Anyway, I still don't get it. Why you? Am I not good enough?" he asked petulantly.

Ruby bit her tongue as a familiar and unwelcome figure glided toward them.

Vanita McNair, the owner of the shop, was almost as thin as Greg and just as blond. She styled her long, thick, peroxide-blasted hair with feathered bangs and waves flipped over the sides and stiffened by hairspray á la Farrah Fawcett. The elaborate tresses didn't suit her horsey face. "You look plenty good to me, stud," she cooed to Greg, who ignored her. She eyed Ruby and bared her teeth. "Come to apologize about my divinity, Fontaine? The nasty things you said on that review site were uncalled for and you know it."

"Genuine divinity is never made with marshmallow cream, McNair," Ruby snapped automatically, drawn into the old argument. "Neither is fudge. But that doesn't matter because you don't cook anything on site. You buy your inventory from a discount warehouse."

Vanita drew back, hissing, "Lies!"

"Excuse me," Greg broke in, making a point of checking his watch, "but I'm late for a bee venom facial and I can't stand here all day listening to two women squabbling over something stupid like...like...whatever the hell divinity is. Christ, do people still eat sugar? Actual cane sugar? That shit's poison. No wonder you're fat," he said to Ruby while Vanita smirked. "Well? Are you going to help me or what? I mean, somebody has to pay the ran—"

Lunging at him, Ruby managed to slap a hand over his mouth before he said anything revealing in front of Vanita. "Yes, I will help you," she told him. "I'll meet you at the hotel in a little while, when you're finished with your facial, and we'll talk." She lifted her hand. "Don't speak to anybody else, okay?"

He nodded, fidgeting and paying more attention to his watch than to her.

"I'm warning you, if you mess this up in any way, if Bee gets hurt, I won't kill you," Ruby said, making an effort to catch and hold his gaze so he knew she was serious. "I'll tie you down and tattoo a Groucho Marx mustache, eyebrows and eyeglasses on your face."

"Don't do anything hasty," Greg breathed, his green eyes wide. She had his full attention now. "Give me a couple of hours and I'll be back at the hotel. We'll talk." He spun around and left the shop, murmuring about his ex-wife and her crazy lesbo friend.

"My, my, my," Vanita purred, pursing her lips as she watched Greg walk off. "He's hot. Like, hot times infinity plus infinity. Is he married? Can I get his number?"

"I couldn't be that cruel to either of you," Ruby replied on her way out of the shop.

She managed to catch the next ferry to Magdalena Island. During the trip, she stayed in the almost empty passenger lounge area on the upper deck, her thoughts preoccupied with what Greg had told her.

If a kidnapper had really sent Greg a letter demanding ransom for Beatrice and if the demand wasn't another fake... she had too many unanswered questions. She wanted to call Frances, but Greg could be mulish when he had an idea in his pretty head. He'd probably refuse to cooperate. *I'm sure it's just another hoax*, she told herself. *Nothing to worry about.*

On the island, she walked quickly to the hotel and went to Delilah's office, intending to say a quick "Good morning." When she entered the reception area, Kyle—talking on a headset as usual—smiled and waved her through without a word.

Ruby entered the room and halted, blinking at the scene. A table had been set up between a pair of leather chairs. On the pristine white cloth stood a few covered dishes, plates, tableware, a coffee service and a small crystal vase holding pink tea roses. She hadn't expected an elaborate breakfast, maybe a croissant and coffee. Her stomach growled.

Delilah sat in one of the chairs, the dusky amethyst dress she wore lightening her gray eyes to a clear shade approaching blue.

"Good morning." Ruby gestured at the table. "You didn't have to go to such trouble."

"Good morning to you too," Delilah said, rising with her arms open in invitation. "I asked the chef to put together something I know you'll like. Will you join me?"

Ruby didn't hesitate. "Love to." She stepped forward into Delilah's welcoming arms and gave her a kiss. *Like coming home*, she thought as she melted against the woman's body. *A home I didn't know I needed until now.*

Delilah finally broke the kiss. "Our food will get cold," she whispered.

Ruby willed her quivering stomach to behave and sank into a chair.

Delilah sat down, smiled and removed the covers from the dishes to reveal French toast with blueberry preserves, fresh blueberries, toasted almond slivers and slices of crispy bacon. "Our first night together, I had to run out because of an emergency at the hotel. You said I owed you breakfast and you were partial to French toast with blueberries."

"You remember that?" Surprised and pleased, Ruby almost fumbled her fork.

"When it comes to you, I remember everything," Delilah stated matter-of-factly, snapping open her linen napkin and draping it across her lap.

Ruby stammered her appreciation, flushing to the roots of her pink hair at Delilah's fondly indulgent look.

The French toast was fluffy and moist, spiced with cinnamon and vanilla. Blueberries and preserves added tang and sweetness. Ruby felt grateful for the company and the food to take her mind off her upcoming meeting with Greg. She and Delilah spoke about chocolate, traveling, food and wine, their favorite movies. Just when it seemed they'd run out of topics, another mutual experience or interesting tidbit popped up to fuel the discussion.

When did we start getting so comfortable around each other? Ruby wondered, looking at the smooth column of Delilah's throat when the woman threw back her head to laugh at a joke. Another thought came out of the blue: *when did I start wanting more from her than just friendship with benefits?* The realization left her quiet for several moments, poking at a blueberry with her fork. A little more consideration informed her that she had enough problems. Her crush on Delilah—or maybe not just a crush—could wait.

At the end of the meal, Ruby picked up her big leather purse and rose to leave. "I'm really sorry to eat and run. I'm meeting Greg in a bit."

"Greg Brooks? I thought you two didn't get along very well." Delilah stood, hope blossoming on her face. "Has your friend been found?"

"Bee's still missing. I need to talk to Greg about Kaitlyn." To hide any possibly betraying expression, Ruby made a show of tugging the hem of her sleeveless poppy-figured shirt while she spoke the lie, but deceiving Delilah didn't bother her that much. They'd enjoyed a pleasant morning and she'd been able to briefly forget her troubles. Now Beatrice took precedent and she had to go meet Greg.

Ruby said goodbye, exchanged a quick kiss with Delilah and left the office. On her way to Greg's suite, her cell phone buzzed. She stopped in the corridor to answer the call, first stepping out of the way of a uniformed bellhop pushing a wheeled cart piled with Gucci luggage, garment bags and expensive-looking golf bags.

"Sorry I haven't called you. I had to travel out of town on a case." Frances sounded rushed. In the background, Ruby heard ringing phones and a man's voice raised in an incoherent shout. "How are you doing? I was worried about you after our date."

"I'm good," Ruby replied, leaning against the wall and closing her eyes, the better to picture Frances. Part of her still found the tall woman alluring, but her attraction had dwindled compared to the more powerful pull toward Delilah. "I'm sorry I flipped out on you."

"Hey, I'm the one who moved things too far, too fast. I'm just glad you're okay. Again, I'm sorry I didn't check up on you. If you're in the mood, there's a dinner and wine tasting at the Atalee Vineyard on Saturday night. No expectations, I promise. Are you free or…?" Frances left the sentence tantalizingly incomplete.

"Sorry, I'm seeing somebody."

"The same somebody who made you so upset?"

"Yes."

"I see. Well, if this woman breaks your heart again, you call me."

"Why, so you can arrest her for assaulting my feelings?"

"No, because when it comes to really good revenge sex, I'm your girl."

Ruby chuckled. After pushing aside the urge to tell Frances about the recent ransom demand—*not until you talk to Greg—*

she asked, "Is something new with Bee's case? Did you find anything in her notebook yet? Did your expert crack the code?"

"We have some good leads," Frances replied without actually answering any questions. "Did Ms. Brooks ever speak to you about Councilman Harrison Lovett?"

Ruby straightened and opened her eyes. The man was an offensive blowhard and she didn't like his attitude, or his treatment of her or Delilah. "No, but I've met him. He's not a nice person. And I met Red Iverson too. Sort of," she added, recalling their encounter in the hotel lobby, which she'd rather not repeat.

"Stay away from Lovett and Iverson," Frances warned. "I'm serious. Those guys are bad news and they run with a bad crowd."

"Is there a reason I should avoid an elected official and his employee?"

"If I say, 'Because I told you so,' would you listen?"

"That didn't work for my mother, so probably not."

Frances sighed. "I can't tell you why. I'm asking you as…I guess as a friend."

Ruby smiled, though she knew Frances couldn't see her. "I can do that for a friend."

"Good." The word was muffled, like Frances had covered the phone's mouthpiece with her hand. Her voice returned more clearly. "Sorry, I've got to take another call. I'll get back in touch with you tomorrow, okay?"

Ruby agreed, ended the call and put her phone away, her thoughts circling back to her upcoming meeting with Greg. Squaring her shoulders, she continued down the corridor toward his suite, every other consideration buried under a weight of worry and hope.

CHAPTER TWENTY-FOUR

"I still don't get it," Greg said while she examined the ransom note. "Why you?"

"Hush," Ruby said, turning the letter more toward the light from the window. She handled the sheet of paper gingerly, mindful of fingerprints thanks to TV shows, though she knew Greg hadn't been as careful. The note was printed from a computer.

Two million cash, nothing larger than $20, all used, no sequential bills, delivered by Ruby Fontaine only. No cops. No feds. Will contact with proof of life and time/date.

Greg snorted. His green eyes narrowed to slits. "Look, I called my financial manager already. Getting the money isn't a problem; I've got a line of credit at Summerland First Federal. But this idiot doesn't realize two million dollars in twenties weighs a couple of hundred pounds, and you're supposed to carry the whole thing by yourself?" His contemptuous gaze raked over her. "I mean, that's like lifting your own body weight, right?"

Ruby set her jaw, her dislike of the man flaring into absolute loathing. "Shut up, Greg. If that's supposed to be a joke, I'm not laughing. You don't need to worry about me. Whatever needs doing, I'll do it."

He turned away from her with a dismissive sniff and went to the small bar, a very modern design made of rosewood, oak and steel. An ice bucket, cocktail shaker, glasses and various bottles of liquor stood on one side of the thick, green-tinted Plexiglas top. Ruby recognized a few of the labels as very pricey brands.

"Suit yourself," Greg said.

"I will," Ruby muttered, moving across the room to sit on the black leather sofa. Her hands trembled. She laid the note on the coffee table. "We should call the police."

"No." Greg scooped a handful of ice cubes from the bucket, dropped them in a chunky glass and added Grey Goose vodka. "The kidnapper said not to and I won't risk Beatrice's life. I can't be saddled with the kid for much longer. Jesus Christ." He took a gulp of vodka, his slender throat working. The glass slammed back on the bar. Liquid slopped over the rim. He didn't appear to notice the wetness on his hand and shirt cuff. "I've got to get out of this podunk 'burg and go home. I already missed the opening of Sid's new club. Do you know who was there?" He rattled off the names of several A-list celebrities while splashing more vodka in his glass. "I'm missing everything because I'm stuck here with the kid."

Ruby held her tongue with difficulty. He could have ignored Kaitlyn and let his undesired daughter stay in foster care, but he'd flown across the country to take custody and was willing— granted, for selfish reasons—to pay ransom to save his ex-wife. For Beatrice and Kaitlyn's sakes, she would swallow his insults and put up with his lousy attitude.

Greg continued to sip vodka and brood. He didn't offer her a drink. She sat on the sofa, waffling between reporting the development to Frances or waiting to see what happened next. She didn't want to waste time filing a report if the ransom demand proved false.

The perky, cheerful, inane strains of a popular song—not her ringtone—shattered the silence. Greg answered his cell phone, his tone clipped. He listened a moment, then pulled the device away from his ear, tapped the screen and stared for several seconds with his lips compressed into a tight line.

"What is it?" Ruby's mouth went dry as the unnerving silence stretched.

Still silent, Greg turned the phone around so she could see the screen where a video played, a nightmare in miniature.

Beatrice was tied to a metal chair. Her hair hung around her bruised face in dark, greasy strings. A gag in her mouth. A blindfold covered her eyes. Ruby struggled to distinguish details from the horrifying image. The room was dark, but a circle of harsh white light illuminated Beatrice. She couldn't see the source. Behind the bound woman, she could just make out what appeared to be regular rows of bricks forming a wall.

A copy of that morning's *Central Ledger* newspaper was propped up against Beatrice's chest to keep the masthead with the date visible. A tablet PC poked into the side of the frame to one side of Beatrice, obviously held midair by someone out of camera range. The device played a television program Ruby recognized as a popular morning talk show on a local station. She glanced at her watch. The show was broadcasting now.

The video and the call ended abruptly.

"Hey!" Ruby made an instinctive grab for the phone, but Greg held the device out of her reach. She recalled him watching the screen before he showed her the video. "Was there a message or something at the beginning? Where do we drop the ransom?"

Greg tucked his phone in his pocket. "I'm sure we'll find out eventually. I'll get in touch with the bank." He walked toward the bedroom, giving her no opportunity to comment.

The second he disappeared from view, Ruby snatched up her purse and retrieved her cell phone. Thank goodness she'd put Frances's number on speed dial.

Her stomach sank when the call went to voice mail. She left a message to contact her, praying Frances would receive it in time. After ending the call, she bit her lower lip until the fragile skin threatened to burst, agonizing over whether to make a report to the regular police, try to contact Detective Anderson, who'd investigated the previous bogus ransom demand, or wait for Frances to reply. Greg's return took the decision out of her hands.

He eyed the cell phone she clutched and shrugged. "The money will be ready when we're ready," he said, moving to the bar. He picked up his glass, downed the rest of the vodka and immediately poured another full glass. "I think you should go."

"I'm not going anywhere except with you." Ruby rested her head on the sofa cushion behind her, wishing she were home so she could wrap herself in Meemaw's soothing quilt. Nervous energy jittered through her body. Her mind chased its own tail, back and forth, around and around. Call the police. Call Anderson. Wait for Frances. Which was the right thing to do? A decision seemed impossible to make, so she watched Greg from beneath her lashes while he drank.

Greg gave her a flat stare and put down the almost empty glass. "I'm headed to the mainland. Don't follow me. I'll contact you when I have the money." His long, lean legs ate up the little distance between the bar and the door of the suite. He paused, his hand on the knob, when she sat up with a shout of alarm.

"You can't leave me here! What about Bee? What if the kidnapper calls you with the ransom location while you're on the mainland?" she cried, jumping up from the sofa and taking a half step forward. "Promise you'll come back for me."

"I can pay the ransom, but I can't deliver it," he said, speaking slowly and deliberately, as if explaining a difficult concept to a child. "God knows why, but they want your lard ass to haul the cash, remember? When I hear from the kidnapper and know when and where, I'll call you. Stay here or go away—whatever butters your muffin—but I intend to pick up the money and then get another drink. Christ, I can't believe this is happening to me," he whined under his breath. He yanked open the door and exited, leaving Ruby to gather her purse, leave the empty suite and find the elevator at the end of the hall.

In the lobby on the ground floor, she forced a smile and gave a little wave to the desk clerks before pushing through the Employees Only door. She'd decided to ask Severin Valois for advice since she couldn't trust herself. Her mind wasn't working properly, like her thoughts had been put in a blender and whirled around at high speed, making it impossible for her to choose which course of action would lead to Beatrice's safe return. She needed to talk to someone more clearheaded.

Moving on autopilot, Ruby walked down a corridor in the direction of the kitchens, turned a corner and almost bumped into Delilah. Her heart sank. *I really, really don't want to talk to Delilah about Beatrice. She's got enough on her plate with the staff spooked over the ghost nuns on the hill and whatever secret thing she's got going on with Harrison Lovett. She doesn't need me blubbering on her too.*

"How'd your talk go with Greg Brooks?" Delilah stood close, stunning in her amethyst dress. The silver moonstone cuff circled her wrist, matched by a silver necklace with a big moonstone pendant. She stared at Ruby with concern. "Was he particularly offensive today? You look queasy."

"I'm fine," Ruby replied, realizing her answer had been too glib when Delilah gazed at her narrowly. "I'm looking for Severin. Have you seen him this morning?"

"He's probably in the pastry kitchen or his office." Delilah frowned. "Ruby, are you sure you're okay? If Brooks has done or said anything to upset you—"

"No, no, I'm fine. Greg was his usual obnoxious self, nothing out of the ordinary." Ruby tried to breathe normally and keep the frustration out of her tone and expression, a hard task when the tension cranking her nerves to the humming point might shatter her to pieces and she'd fly apart like an over-wound clockwork doll. She felt her control slipping under Delilah's scrutiny. "I just...well, I'm sure you're busy and I'm on a schedule today, so I guess I'll see you later."

Delilah pursed her lips. "I have a few minutes before a phone conference with a client in Berlin. We could go to my office for a cup of coffee if you have time."

Please, just leave me alone! Ruby begged the woman silently. She shook her head and repeated, "I'm on a schedule today and I really need to get with Severin before I'm late." *Let her think I have an appointment with him, that's enough of an excuse.*

"Are we still on for dinner tonight?"

"Uh, yeah, sure."

"All right. I'll call you later."

Relieved, Ruby managed a genuine if shaky smile. "Looking forward to it."

"You should be. Want a sample of the menu?" Delilah moved in closer to give Ruby a sweet kiss. No exotic perfume today, just the fresh citron, honey and coriander scent of the Crabtree & Evelyn soap she often used. "Come by my office when you have a few minutes. I want to talk to you about our project," she murmured.

Ruby wished she could fall into Delilah's loving embrace and cry out her woes. If she lingered here any longer, the unshed tears burning her eyes would fall and destroy any illusion that she wasn't floundering and desperate. She pulled away and headed down the corridor, leaving Delilah and terrible temptation behind.

She found Severin in his office, pecking at the computer keyboard. He glanced up when she entered. "Bah! This device, it is the devil. But *petite*, what has happened?" He stood, coming around the desk. "Sit down. You are white, like death."

Ruby stumbled to the chair and sat heavily. "I need your help."

Severin perched on the edge of the desk, his bushy black brows drawn together in a worried grimace. "First, do you need water? *Un médecin?*"

"I don't need a doctor. I need advice." Ruby shut her eyes. Her head throbbed. Kitchen noises drifted through the open door: clattering pots and pans, hissing steam, spluttering fat, the rise and fall of voices. She heard Severin move to close the door and almost wept in gratitude at the sudden quiet.

"*Bien.* You want no doctor. What then, *petite*, do you need from me?" he asked, his voice unbearably gentle.

She opened her eyes and focused on the Frenchman, taking in the familiar sight of his salt-and-pepper ponytail, the chef's white jacket covering his stocky frame and the seamed face dominated by an impressive nose. He'd always been kind to her. "It's about my friend, Beatrice Brooks, the one who's missing. You must not tell anyone else, not even Delilah. This is between you and me only."

"I am as discreet as the priest in his confessional," Severin promised without a trace of humor. Like Delilah, he looked concerned for her. Rather than ask questions, he waited for her to speak, his hands clasped together loosely in front of him.

Ruby told him everything, starting at Beatrice's disappearance, her suspicion of Delilah, the scanty details of the police investigation and the false ransom demand. She went on to talk about finding Beatrice's notebook in Delilah's desk drawer, how the discovery had ruined their budding relationship and how the misunderstandings had been resolved. The confession took several minutes. Any second, she expected to hear from Greg. The longer her cell phone remained silent, the more anxiety gnawed at her.

"Today, Greg Brooks—Beatrice's ex-husband—told me he'd gotten a ransom demand from kidnappers claiming to have her," Ruby concluded wearily, rubbing her aching head. "I thought it was another fake, but the kidnappers sent proof: a video of Bee with a copy of today's newspaper and a tablet playing a TV show airing at the time. Oh, Severin…my poor Bee looked bad. She was tied to a chair, blindfolded—" She stopped, choking on fear, and had to find the strength to finish. "Gagged. Bruised. They haven't been taking care of her and I'm just so afraid, so afraid that—" Again, she couldn't find her voice. She touched the wetness on her cheeks. Had she been crying?

Severin handed her a tissue from a box on his desk.

Ruby mopped up her tears and blew her nose.

"Very well, you have called the police, yes?" Severin's frown deepened when she shook her head. "Why not?"

"I can't get hold of the detective in charge of Bee's case. I left a voice mail message."

"Then you must call another policeman. It is the only sensible way left to you."

He sounded so sure of himself, Ruby put her hand in her purse and took out her cell phone. She hesitated.

Severin bent to look at her directly and touched her wrist. "Make the call, *petite*."

With a few taps, Ruby connected her phone to the hotel's Wi-Fi and did a search of the city's online White Pages. She glanced at Severin, who gave her an encouraging nod, and dialed the local police station.

When the operator answered the call, she shored up her eroding calm and said, "This is an emergency. I want to report a kidnapping. I've seen a video the kidnapper sent. This isn't a hoax. I need to speak to Detective Anderson."

CHAPTER TWENTY-FIVE

An hour after her call, Ruby stood on the dock at the hotel's marina, watching a police launch grow bigger as the vessel approached Magdalena Island, traveling fast. A light breeze stirred her hair, blowing pink strands across her eyes.

The ocean resembled a sheet of hand-blown glass, blue-green and almost flat, hardly disturbed by waves. To avoid a rowboat carrying a couple of fishermen, the launch carved a curve through the water, throwing back a rooster tail of spray in a rainbow arc that sparkled in the sun like a handful of tossed brilliants.

Detective Anderson stood braced at the bow, she noted half in relief, half in worry. The wind of the launch's passage had blown open his black jacket to expose a white button-down shirtfront stretched over a broad chest. His red tie flapped over his shoulder. He grabbed the rail when the launch skidded sideways and throttled down, gliding in and kissing the end of the dock as it came to a gently bobbing halt. A crew member tied off the launch.

Ruby came forward to greet Anderson when he stepped onto the dock. His polished black leather shoes were marred by water droplets. "Thank you for coming," she said over the rumble of the launch's idling engine, glancing at two other men carrying plastic cases—one chubby and blond, the other average except for the acne scars pitting his cheeks, and both wearing T-shirts and jeans—who jumped from the launch to the dock and hustled away. She raised an eyebrow at Anderson. "Who'd you bring with you?"

"Technicians who can set up a phone trace. I've got more backup on the way and another team on standby. Tell me, Ms. Fontaine," Anderson said, his squashed nose adding a nasal quality to his speech, "where's Greg Brooks?" His mirrored aviator sunglasses hid his eyes, but she had a feeling he was dissecting her with his gaze.

"I haven't seen or heard from Greg since he left his suite about—" Ruby checked her watch "—two hours ago, give or take."

"Is he still on the island?"

"I have no idea. He said he was going to the bank and then getting a drink. There's a cocktail bar in the lobby, but I didn't see him there, so I guess he's at a bar on the mainland."

Anderson grunted and began walking to the hotel.

Ruby scurried behind him, wishing she'd been able to contact Frances. The man's brusque manner really got under her skin.

In the lobby, Anderson removed his sunglasses and glanced around at the guests and employees, his sharp gaze taking in the restaurants, golf pro shop, sundries shop, reception desk and bar and seating area. He refocused on her. "Do you see Brooks now?"

"No." Ruby lifted her cell phone. "I have his number. Want me to call him?"

"Please," Anderson grated as if the word hurt coming out of his throat. He radiated impatience while he waited.

Ruby turned her back on the bull-necked man, pressed the right speed dial button and put the phone to her ear. "No answer," she reported at last.

"Do you know the name of Brooks's bank?"

Ruby had to think a moment before she recalled the detail from her conversation with Greg. She told Anderson, who whipped an absurdly small cell phone from his inner jacket pocket and stabbed a speed dial button.

"Linda, head over to First Federal Bank on Bayard Street," he said, holding the phone close to his mouth. "Talk to the manager. They have the cash for the ransom. I need to know if Greg Brooks picked up the money himself or if the bank sent a courier to the island. Yeah. Soon as." He ended the call and strode across the lobby to the massive reception desk, where he flashed his badge and spoke to a clerk who picked up the house telephone and made a call.

Ruby was dismayed but not surprised to see Delilah come through the Employees Only door a few minutes later wearing her cool and confident hotel manager's veneer.

Delilah talked to Anderson and shot a glance across the lobby at Ruby. She said something to the clerk that caused the man to grab the house telephone again. The clerk shook his head after a minute. Delilah left Anderson at the desk and walked over to join her.

"Why didn't you tell me about the ransom demand?" Delilah asked as soon as she came close enough, her mask gone and replaced by genuine concern and some confusion. "Of course I'd have helped—"

"I don't want your help," Ruby blurted. At Delilah's hurt look, she added, "I mean, I don't want to involve you. You're already dealing with so much here at the hotel and Lovett and… and…" She swept her hand through the air in a helpless gesture. "Whatever we're creating here together. I didn't want to add to your burdens."

"I see." Delilah's pained expression melted to a tenderness that gripped Ruby's heart and stole her breath. "You can always come to me," she said. "Always. Don't ever hesitate. There will never be a time when I'll turn you away." She paused, her gray eyes as luminous as the moonstones she wore. "I care for you, Ruby. I care for you so much."

Something came loose inside Ruby, a sweetly sparking pain behind her breastbone that seemed to swell, growing bigger and brighter until she felt the incandescent glow must make her shine like a star. "I care for you too," she said, smiling when Delilah's palm settled soft and warm on her cheek. The touch lasted a few seconds, but felt as intimate as a kiss.

Delilah returned Ruby's smile, withdrawing her hand when Anderson's return interrupted their privacy.

"Got a response from a housekeeper on the fifth floor," the detective said. "Greg Brooks was seen an hour ago entering room five thirty-two with an unidentified female."

"Room five thirty-two is Mrs. Lily Courtland, one of our frequent and very valued guests," Delilah supplied. "The wife of William Courtland."

Anderson grimaced. "Sounds familiar. Courtland Technology, yeah?"

"Yes."

"I'd better go talk to the lovebirds."

"Be discreet, Detective, and be careful. If I'm not happy with the way you treat Mrs. Courtland and Mr. Brooks, I'll contact the mayor. Mr. Courtland is a generous campaign contributor and I'm sure His Honor would want to know if his friend's wife suffered unnecessary harassment." Undaunted, Delilah confronted the glaring Anderson, giving as good as she got. "I'll go with you to ensure our other guests aren't disturbed."

"No," Anderson said flatly.

Delilah crossed her arms over her chest. "The hotel has a law firm on retainer. Should I deem it necessary, they're on my call list too, and you won't be interviewing any of our guests until the attorneys arrive."

Anderson inhaled, a sour twist to his mouth, and finally shrugged. "Fine. Come on." He started toward the elevator.

Delilah said to Ruby, "You're invited too. Mr. Brooks knows you and I won't let you be left in the dark anymore," before she marched off behind Anderson.

For the second time that day, Ruby found herself hurrying to catch up. She used the brief time in the elevator to gather

her thoughts. That amazing moment with Delilah in the lobby when everything had clicked between them in perfect understanding—the glow still lingered, settling to a steady, comfortable warmth. She glanced at Delilah's blurred reflection in the steel elevator doors and felt slender fingers brush against hers, then catch and cling, squeezing for a heartbeat before they were gone, leaving the impression of silent support.

The doors opened. Anderson exited first, Delilah not much more than a breath behind and maneuvering to precede him down the corridor. Ruby took her time.

Room 532 was about three-quarters of the way down the corridor. Anderson stood back with Ruby while Delilah knocked and called loudly, "Mrs. Courtland, it's Delilah Kerrigan, the general manager. May I speak with you, please?"

When no one answered, Anderson muttered, "Open it."

Delilah reached into her dress pocket and produced a master keycard, which she inserted into the lock to open the door. Anderson pushed past her into the room.

Ruby and Delilah entered together.

Dim gray light leaked through the curtains drawn at the windows. An old Japanese movie with the volume muted played on the flat-screen TV, some giant lizard monster stomping Tokyo flat. Empty miniature liquor bottles, presumably from the minifridge, were scattered across the nightstand. A used condom leaked on the floor. Ruby wrinkled her nose at the reek of strong perfume.

A middle-aged woman lay sprawled on the bed covered by the rumpled white sheet, her black hair splayed over the pillow. Her heavy makeup had smeared to a clownish caricature, especially the vivid scarlet lipstick smudges around her collagen-swollen lips.

When Anderson cleared his throat, Lily Courtland opened her eyes and sat up, a manicured hand reaching for the pack of cigarettes on the nightstand. She didn't appear to notice or care that the sheet fell to her waist, exposing cantaloupe-sized breasts far too big for her scrawny frame and far too perfectly round and perky for her age. "Who the hell are you?" she rasped, lighting a cigarette with a chunky gold lighter set with diamonds. A diamond ring at least eighteen carats weighed down her right third finger.

Ruby hung back. She didn't have a right to be there. Embarrassed, she tried to keep her gaze on Lily's face, not the breast implants on display. *Looks like the lady's putting some lucky plastic surgeon's kid through college.*

"Mrs. Courtland, we tried to contact you from the front desk, but the room's phone seems to be engaged." Delilah glanced at the telephone on the nightstand. The receiver hung off the hook. "I'm sorry for the interruption," she continued without indicating she found the woman's nudity distasteful. "Detective Anderson insisted he speak to you at once." Having thrown Anderson under the bus, she gave Lily an apologetic smile and a small shrug.

Lily also shrugged and took a drag from her cigarette, the smoke trickling out of her nostrils while she examined Anderson with obvious appreciation. "That's fine, Ms. Kerrigan. I don't mind waking up to find such a handsome hunk of a man in my bedroom."

Stone-faced, Anderson didn't react to Lily's leer or let his gaze wander. "Mrs. Courtland, I understand you and Greg Brooks were together today?"

"Goddamn, honey, we were more than just together. He fucked me through the mattress like a champ. That reminds me, Dr. Silverstein needs to tighten up my pussy again or it'll be hot dog down a hallway time down there." Lily tapped ash from the end of her cigarette into an ashtray on the bed next to her thigh. "Listen, Greg may be skinny and look queer, but he's hung like a stallion and an absolute beast in bed. Even better than my Pilates coach at home and that guy's so flexible, you'd think he was made of rubber bands and—"

"When did Brooks leave your room?" Anderson interrupted. "Any idea where he was going or what he planned to do?"

Lily picked up a diamond-studded wristwatch from the nightstand and squinted at the dial. "A little more than an hour ago and no, he didn't say a mumbling word. He got a call, pulled on his clothes and ran out of here. Suits me. I hate saying goodbye to a lover." She glanced at the stoic Anderson and fluttered her eyelashes. "Say, handsome, when you're off duty, why don't you give me a ring? I'll throw you a party like no other, cross my heart."

Anderson demurred politely, thanked Lily for the information and led the way out of the room. In the corridor, he removed his cell phone from his jacket pocket and made a call. "This is Anderson. What's your ETA? Uh-huh. Once you get to the island, have the team spread out and start a search of the hotel's grounds. Brooks is in the wind." As soon as he ended the call, his phone rang. "Anderson. Yeah, Linda, what have you got?" He listened for several minutes, grunted and went on, "The money's still at the bank? Okay. Lock down the wharf on the boardwalk and screen all passengers. Thanks." He turned to Delilah. "My team will be here in ten minutes. We're going to look for Brooks. If any of your staff see him, they're to report to the front desk and the clerks will report to me."

Delilah nodded. "Of course, you have our full cooperation."

Anderson spun around on his heel and walked to the elevator.

Ruby stepped closer to Delilah and waited until Anderson was gone before she spoke. "Greg told me when he left his suite, he was going to the mainland and then to get a drink. I guess he reversed the order if he hasn't been to the bank yet." She suspected he'd received instructions from the kidnapper when the proof of life video came through and he'd kept the information from her—the sort of petty, immature act typical of the man. "Where do you think he met Mrs. Courtland?"

"At the cocktail bar downstairs," Delilah replied instantly, huffing a laugh.

"How do you know?"

"Mrs. Courtland comes to the St. Clare several times a year for three things: young men, good-looking men and our head bartender's specialty martini made with Navy-strength gin and legal moonshine. She's at the bar when she's not in her room entertaining."

"Good heavens." *I'm surprised her liver isn't worn out, let alone other parts of her anatomy,* Ruby thought, recalling Lily's remark about hot dogs and hallways. *No, let's not go there. That's a mental image I don't need.* "What about Mr. Courtland?"

"Ah…the gentleman enjoys the same pleasures as his wife."

"Okay." Ruby didn't need details. "Well, Greg probably met Mrs. Courtland at the bar and they went to her room. When they…uh…finished—" she tried not to stammer at the memory of Lily's language "—he got a phone call and left. I don't know for sure who called him, but it was probably the kidnapper." She sniffed. "Greg's so childish. He knows I'm supposed to deliver the ransom."

Delilah blanched and grabbed Ruby's shoulders. "*You?* Why?"

Ruby winced. "The kidnapper used my name in the letter sent to Greg, said I had to deliver the ransom. Greg was supposed to come and get me when he was given the time and place. Looks like he decided to leave me out." Her conscience prickled. "To be fair, I'm just guessing about Greg's actions. For all I know, the phone call was from his stylist with exciting news about the latest Italian fashions."

"Brooks was going to let you do this, put you in harm's way?" Delilah's lips thinned. Anger shimmered like steel in the depths of her eyes.

"Greg wasn't going to *let* me do anything," Ruby protested. "It's my choice." She pried herself free from Delilah's grip, but kept the woman's hands loosely clasped in hers. "Besides, I didn't keep it a secret. I called in the police, didn't I? Which means I'm not stupid enough to try and rescue Bee by myself. Having said that, if the kidnapper still wants me to make the drop, I'll do it. I'll do anything to rescue Bee."

Delilah studied Ruby a few moments before some of the tension drained from her body. "No, I wouldn't say you're stupid. Too loyal and too brave for your own good, perhaps, but never stupid." She pulled away, only to take a step forward.

Ruby closed her eyes when Delilah sealed their mouths together in a searing, demanding kiss. A tongue touched her lower lip and pushed inside, mapping her teeth. She shuddered, every nerve blossoming into fire at the touch. A current of eager heat ran under her skin, igniting her blood. Despite the urgent situation with Beatrice, she was helpless, unable to prevent her body's response.

Whimpering, Ruby tried to press herself closer to Delilah, devouring the woman's soft lips. Delilah's lipstick was flavored with chemicals, but her mouth was delicious—a candy-coated treat sweeter than sugar and more addictive than the finest chocolate.

Desire pulsed in her veins. She lost all sense of time and place. Her existence became the arms around her, the heat of another woman's breath on her face and the urgent tongue driving the flames higher. She craved warm skin. Her fingers scrabbled at the zipper on the back of Delilah's dress.

Delilah broke the kiss. "Hush. Not here and not now. Later." Her features seemed sharper, her expression fierce and possessive. She stepped back, straightening her hair and dress, but her hot, passion-filled gaze remained fixed on Ruby.

With an effort, Ruby stopped herself from whining. She panted and stared at the gold-and-cream striped wallpaper. "I want you in my home and in my bed. I want to make love to you, touch you everywhere. I want to kiss you everywhere too," she said in a low rasp through a throat gone tight. "I want to hold you until morning and make love to you again." She lifted her gaze. Delilah's hungry look threatened to buckle her knees, forcing her to glance at the dark brown carpet stretching along the corridor. "Do you...do you feel the same?" she asked, her breath catching on the last word.

"Yes," Delilah replied without hesitation. "Oh God, yes, I want you. There's nothing I want more, not even air or sunlight. But I think right now—" She took a deep breath and squared her shoulders. "Now you should concentrate on your friend, Beatrice."

Ruby couldn't argue. "When it's over, when Bee's safe, we'll be together, I swear."

Delilah's face was wreathed in a brilliant smile that made Ruby's heart seize, too full of yearning to beat. "I'll hold you to that promise."

A muffled ringing startled Ruby. The source of the noise was her purse, lying on the floor a foot away. The strap must have slid off her shoulder when she and Delilah kissed. She had a vague recollection of feeling something drop on her foot and kicking it off, too preoccupied with Delilah's luscious mouth to care.

She went to her purse and retrieved her cell phone. "Hello? Oh, Detective Anderson." She motioned for Delilah to come nearer. "What can I—what? Greg. I see. No, I'll be right there." The call cut off on Anderson's end. She dropped the phone inside her purse.

"What's wrong?" Delilah stroked a lock of pink hair out of Ruby's eyes.

"The police found Greg unconscious at the foot of the hill. They think he might have a skull fracture and internal injuries from a fall. They've called for a medical helicopter to take him to the hospital. I need to go see him." Realization dawned. "Oh, fudge, I have to tell Kaitlyn's nanny and try to notify his lawyer too. I'm sorry. I wish—"

"Go to him," Delilah said firmly, turning her around and giving her a small push toward the elevator. "I'm coming with you," she added, "so if you need anything, tell me and I'll make sure you get it."

Glad for the company and the support, Ruby didn't need any further encouragement.

CHAPTER TWENTY-SIX

When Ruby glimpsed the knot of uniformed police officers, hotel employees and guests standing in a huddle near the foot of the hill, she walked faster. The hard crunches of Delilah's high-heeled shoes on the path hurried right behind her. She'd never heard a more welcome sound.

Spotting Detective Anderson's head rising above the crowd, she pushed her way straight to him. "What happened?"

He turned around, his expression grim, his eyes hidden by the same aviator sunglasses he'd worn on the police launch. Ruby saw her weirdly distorted reflection in the mirrored lenses, a carnival funhouse image. "We're not sure," he said. "We think he fell up there or was pushed and rolled down to the bottom. Medivac's on the way."

"Is Greg still unconscious?"

"Hasn't moved, spoken, or opened his eyes."

Ruby bit the inside of her cheek to keep from crying out at the sight of Greg Brooks sprawled on the grass to the left of the path leading up to the hill's crown and the cloister ruins. Only the movement of his chest showed he still breathed. *He looks so fragile and awkward with his arms and legs crooked like that. He'd hate people gawking at him when he's so messed up.*

His face was dark with rising bruises where his skin wasn't bloody, likely from a head wound. More blood stained his shirt collar and the grass beneath his head. With his eyes closed and his battered features relaxed as though he were asleep, Greg resembled an angel who'd fought against an iron-fisted attacker and lost.

"Oh, Greg," Ruby whispered. She had no liking for the man, but she didn't wish him harm. How Kaitlyn would react to the news, she wasn't sure. Did the little girl even know her father as anything but a name and a photograph? She'd have to ask the nanny if Greg ever visited his daughter or spoke to her.

She sensed rather than saw Delilah stepping beside her. "Should Mr. Brooks be made more comfortable while we wait?" she heard the woman ask Anderson. "I can send for pillows, a blanket, a first aid kit. Anything he needs."

"No, Ms. Kerrigan. He shouldn't be moved, he might have spinal or neck injuries." Anderson lifted the absurdly small cell phone in his hand to his ear. "Linda, we found Brooks, he's been injured. Yeah, it's pretty bad. No idea if the kidnapper made contact. I'll call you back when we have something to go on." He stuck the phone into his jacket pocket.

Spinal injuries? Ruby didn't want to imagine Greg in a wheelchair. She felt an arm settle across her lower back, a hand curve over her ribs. Delilah, giving silent comfort. She leaned gratefully into the touch.

The staccato thump-thump-thump of rotor blades slicing the air caught her ear. She glanced at the sky over the water to see a bright red and white air ambulance helicopter rushing to the island, skimming above the waves like a gaudy dragonfly.

"Ms. Fontaine, do you remember anything else Mr. Brooks might have told you? Did he mention another call from the kidnapper?" Anderson asked, bending over a little and raising his voice to be heard above the noise.

Ruby held her ground as the bystanders milling around her were pushed back to a safe distance by police officers. "No, he didn't say anything," she shouted, hugging Delilah to her side to ensure they wouldn't be separated.

Anderson used his bulk to chivvy her and Delilah toward the rest of the crowd.

The helicopter landed with a bump in a clearing on the opposite side of the hill, its rotors still spinning. Wind flattened a nearby stand of tall, ornamental pampas grass, bowing the white feathery tops almost to the ground.

A door slid open on the helicopter's side and a paramedic hopped out. The red jump-suited figure wearing a white helmet ran bent at the waist to Greg. What looked like a large, blue nylon case was slung by a strap over his shoulder. When he reached Greg, he knelt, opened the case and began checking the unconscious man's vital signs. A second paramedic came out of the helicopter towing a gurney.

Ruby hung on to Delilah while she watched the paramedics attach a cervical collar to Greg's neck, carefully roll his body and strap him onto a backboard, and insert an IV needle in his inner elbow. The fluid in the IV bag held up by a paramedic was as clear as the vodka Greg had been guzzling in his suite.

Faster than she'd thought possible, the paramedics had Greg on the gurney, across the path and in the helicopter. The door slid shut. The rotors spun faster. The helicopter lifted, its snub nose swinging to point at the city before it sped away.

"He'll be fine," Delilah murmured. "Come with me back to the hotel."

"Just a minute." Ruby tapped Anderson on the shoulder. Beneath the stretched fabric of his jacket, the muscles seemed as hard as tiles. When the detective tilted his head to look at her, she asked, "Can you check the contact list on Greg's phone? I need his lawyer's number. I don't know the name, but I'm pretty sure the practice is in Santa Monica."

"We'll notify Mr. Brooks's next of kin," Anderson replied.

"Greg doesn't have any relatives except Bee and she's not here," Ruby persisted. "I just need his lawyer's office number, that's it." She was tempted to explain to Anderson about Greg's temporary custody of Kaitlyn, but feared interference from Child and Family Services. Better to alert Greg's legal representatives and let them preemptively take care of any issues in family court before social workers stepped in. She had to secure Kaitlyn's welfare first. That's what Beatrice would have wanted.

Anderson let out a put-upon sigh. "Sure, Ms. Fontaine. As soon as the techs pull some info out of Brooks's cell phone, I'll make sure you get the lawyer's number. Anything else?" he asked, the question laced with forced patience.

Ruby shook her head. "Thank you." She started walking to the hotel with Delilah. Fat, fluffy clouds the color of iron had blown in from the south, bringing a damp chill and the threat of rain. She rubbed her bare arms, glad when they entered the lobby.

"You look like you could use a drink." Delilah steered Ruby over to the cocktail bar and sat her on a stool. Ignoring a sign proclaiming the bar opened at one o'clock, she called, "Two planter's punches, please," to the Indian bartender, who put down the knife she'd been using to cut oranges.

"Just finished a batch," the bartender replied, wiping her hands on a towel.

Ruby noticed the name tag pinned to the bartender's white T-shirt—a stark contrast to the woman's dark bronze skin, brown eyes and straight black hair—read *Amrita*.

Amrita retrieved a metal jug and put ice cubes in a pair of sturdy old-fashioned glasses. The aromas of fruit and alcohol rose from the pink liquid she poured out of the jug.

Ruby's eyebrows rose. The glasses were garnished with cherries and a pineapple slice and placed on the bar in front of her and Delilah. "Thank you." She wasn't sure she ought to drink something that smelled like it might knock her off the stool by the fumes alone. "You know," she said to Delilah when Amrita returned to the other end of the bar to cut more oranges, "it's too early to get drunk."

"Try it. I think you'll like the flavor. We use fresh orange, pomegranate and pineapple juices and Myer's dark rum." Delilah saluted Ruby with the glass, took a delicate sip and licked her lips. "Besides, the sun's over the yardarm somewhere in the world."

Ruby chuckled. She raised her glass and tasted the punch, finding it strong with a citrus bite and a smooth burn. "S'good," she said, setting the glass on the bar. "But if I drink too much it'll go to my head and I need all my brain cells functioning today."

She turned around on the stool as rain began pattering on the glass dome set in the roof so far above her head. A sudden storm wasn't unusual for the time of year. Her gaze fell on the hotel entrance, where she could glimpse the outside through the doors. Wet, gray drizzle. Leaden clouds. A palm tree's spiky fronds whipped by the wind. She could picture the churning ocean waves and the sailboats and fishermen scuttling to safe harbor.

Within the next ten minutes, men and women carrying golf bags or tennis racquets scurried inside the lobby making loud complaints about the weather.

Delilah said something, but Ruby paid scant attention, arrested by a familiar figure entering the lobby, scattering raindrops when he slammed through the doors. Lean, wiry, dark-haired Red Iverson, his heavy beard scruff giving him a rough appearance at odds with his suit and tie. *What's he doing here? Is Councilman Lovett with him?* She didn't see the tubby politician/used car salesman. She started when Delilah's fingers caressed her cheek.

"Where'd you go? You were far away for a minute." Delilah shifted on her stool and crossed her legs. "Thinking about your friend's little girl?"

"Something like that." Ruby drank from her glass of planter's punch while she continued watching Iverson walk to and fro, talking on a cell phone.

His footsteps left muddy tracks on the pale stone floor. Rain had plastered down his hair and darkened the shoulders of his blue pinstripe jacket. His tie hung askew. Ruby couldn't figure out what he was doing on the island, much less in the hotel without his boss. She swiveled on the stool to face Delilah and asked, "Is Red Iverson a guest here?"

Delilah followed Ruby's gaze, glancing across the lobby. "No, he's not."

"Any clue why he's here now?"

"Not one."

Ruby made a discontented sound. "I wonder what he wants."

"Whatever he's here for, he won't get it." Delilah shot Iverson a dark look and returned her attention to picking through a bowl of crunchy, fried, Jamaican spiced hominy mixed with dry roasted edamame the bartender put in front of her. Her silver cuff bracelet slid up her arm a few inches when she lifted a small handful of edamame to her mouth.

Ruby recalled the woman's bruised wrist. "I asked you before and you didn't really answer—just what's the deal with you and Councilman Lovett? He's such a nasty piece of work. I can't imagine why you put up with him."

"My dealings with Harry Lovett are complicated." Delilah pushed aside the bowl of bar mix. "I'd rather not bother you with the details."

Ruby split her attention between Iverson, still talking into the cell phone pressed to his ear, and Delilah, whose good mood had evaporated. "Please. Tell me."

"There's nothing you can do," Delilah snapped. She inhaled and let the breath out through her nose. "I'm sorry I was sharp. I'd rather not discuss Lovett. All right?"

"Fine." Ruby reached for the bowl and ate a handful of hominy and edamame. The Caribbean spices set the back of her throat on fire. A gulp of planter's punch didn't help. Glancing sidelong at Delilah watching her cautiously, she added, "Apology accepted. I won't bring it up again." *Not for a while, anyway, but I'm nothing if not mule-brained. Sooner or later, I'll get to the truth.*

"You'll be going to talk to Mr. Brooks's daughter soon?" Delilah asked in a more reasonable tone, clearly trying to salvage the moment.

Ruby nodded. She noticed Iverson's pacing had slowed and decided to coax Delilah into talking more about Lovett another time. Now she wanted to continue observing Iverson, who had ended the call and started walking purposefully across the lobby toward the front doors. Where was the man going? Recalling Lovett's ill treatment of Delilah, she wanted to find out what his employee was up to. Until Anderson contacted her, she had nothing else to do except fret or go break the news about Greg to Kaitlyn, an unpleasant task she'd rather put off. *And if I hang out with Delilah, she's sure to notice when Anderson calls.*

"That was my plan. I guess I'd better hop to it." Ruby slid off the stool.

"Let's meet later for dinner." Delilah stood, gathered Ruby close and whispered in her ear, "Don't do anything dangerous." She pulled back, her expression solemn. "Promise me?"

Ruby nodded, but she'd already made up her mind. Beatrice needed her, period. If she could save her best friend and sister of choice, she would, even if it meant lying to her lover. Ignoring the guilty twinge, she crossed her fingers behind her back and said, "I promise."

After a final sip of planter's punch to fortify herself, Ruby walked to the elevator, pausing at the gleaming steel doors to glance behind her at Delilah, still at the cocktail bar chatting with the bartender, Amrita. The women appeared intent on their conversation, neither looking her way. She left the elevator and hurried across the lobby to the front doors.

On the way, she glimpsed Severin Valois coming through the Employees Only door. Her stomach turned inside-out. She pretended not to see the pastry chef's raised hand and walked outside uncaring about the rainstorm, her mind intent on pursuing Iverson.

CHAPTER TWENTY-SEVEN

Ruby grimaced. A steady curtain of rain fell, turning the day brooding, somber and bleak. Masses of storm clouds piled overhead, refusing to be budged by the wind that blew stinging drops in her face. Cold water trickled down the back of her neck. *Wish I had an umbrella.* She was already soaked. *The last thing I need is a summer cold.*

Seeing Iverson some distance ahead of her, she bent her head to keep the rain out of her eyes and followed him, not walking too quickly since she had no intention of catching up. Soon, he veered onto the path to the hill. She continued trailing him.

She lost sight of Iverson when he disappeared over the top of the hill. Cautiously approaching the summit, she stepped into the open and dashed behind a large piece of fallen masonry, probably the remnants of a wall, standing taller than her head. She huddled against the hard surface, fear gnawing at her confidence. The situation seemed too much like the time in the lobby when she'd tried to eavesdrop on Lovett and Delilah and been caught by Iverson. *Did he see me? Please, don't let him see me.*

The rain softened to a drizzle. The wind died down. Although the clouds began to shift, the sky stayed dreary and overcast. She blinked raindrops from her lashes, her breath coming a little faster. What was she doing out here? Was she crazy? What if Iverson caught her? Anxiety gripped her guts. She gathered her courage, smoothed her sopping pink hair from her face and peeked around the corner.

No sign of Iverson at all.

His absence meant nothing. He might not be in her line of sight. Ruby ducked behind her cover. She stayed rooted in place, her hands pressed to the damaged wall and her ears straining for any hint of Iverson coming toward her.

Several minutes passed. Her muscles stiffened and complained. Other discomforts broke her concentration. A spot between her shoulder blades itched. A chill seeped through the soaked clothes clinging to her skin. She gritted her teeth and clutched at the wall, almost cracking her short fingernails on the shell-studded old concrete.

Where's Iverson? There's nowhere to go except the path on the other side of the hill that goes down the cliff to the beach, and Delilah said it was unsafe.

She risked another peek and saw Iverson standing next to the wild muscadine grapevine, talking on his cell phone. Suppressing a gasp, she moved back to her hiding place.

Hadn't Delilah told her the huge old grapevine concealed what was left of the cloister's chimney? From the shape and size of the vine-covered mass, the chimney must be mostly intact under the greenery. *There may be space for a grown man to hide if there's a way inside the chimney, but why would he do that if he believes he's alone?*

Ruby tried to think of a reason for Iverson's disappearance and reappearance. Had he seen her following him? No, or he'd have confronted her already. Her mind ticked over the possibilities before seizing on the most likely. What if Iverson had hidden something in the chimney? Something he—or Harrison Lovett—didn't want found.

Both Frances and Delilah had warned her, without giving specifics, that she should avoid Lovett. While she had no idea if the councilman indulged in shady practices, he *was* a used car salesman and a politician. Wasn't that almost the same as a con man? And the ugly way he'd treated her and Delilah…well, she wouldn't call him one of the good guys. If Lovett was an awful human being, his "hatchet man" Iverson must be worse. The man looked like a criminal, for heaven's sake, and he carried a gun.

Abruptly, Ruby recalled Frances mentioning Iverson and Beatrice had been seen together shortly before she vanished. The information didn't have to mean anything—she'd learned a lesson about jumping to conclusions based on flimsy evidence and avoided thinking too closely about the mysterious meeting. Now she wondered…why would Iverson want to meet with Beatrice in the first place? He didn't strike her as a whistle-blower, so she doubted he'd wanted to disclose information on his employer.

Had Iverson kidnapped Beatrice? He seemed capable. The idea was plausible, but lacked a clear motive. She felt certain he'd never act on his own, so the question became: why would Lovett want Beatrice out of the way? Was her exposé about him? But it seemed ridiculous to suggest a seasoned politician would go to such lengths. Furthermore, asking for ransom was also asking to be caught. Lovett wouldn't be that foolish.

She looked around the corner. Iverson was still talking on his cell phone. He turned around so his back was to her. She sucked in air. Did she dare go closer? She firmed her resolve. She'd seen another shattered wall much nearer to Iverson that seemed large enough for her to hide behind and eavesdrop on his phone conversation.

Ruby took a few breaths and ran over the slippery grass, her gaze fixed on her goal. Halfway there, the toe of her shoe struck something solid—a rock or another piece of masonry half-buried in the dirt. She fell forward, her startled scream turning into a grunt when her hands struck the sharp edge of a stone slab. Despite the fiery pain lancing across her palms, she managed to land on the ground without otherwise hurting herself.

She rolled over to find a gun pointed at her, the muzzle a black hole capturing her horrified fascination and sucking her in. Slowly, she managed to tear her focus from the gun to the person holding it—Iverson, his cell phone pressed to his ear with his free hand.

Expressionless, the wiry man gazed down at her, his dark eyes filled with ruthless calculation. His mouth twitched into a frown. "Don't worry. I'll take care of it," he said into the phone. He listened a moment longer and finally put the device in his jacket pocket. "Get up," he said, gesturing with the gun.

"What are you going to do to me?" Ruby sat on the grass with her throbbing hands wrapped around her knees. She gazed up at Iverson, her mouth dry. Her pulse fluttered.

"You can get up on your own or I can make you. Your choice." Iverson's disinterested gaze was worse than outright gloating. "Be quiet. Don't scream. Don't try to run."

Tremors ran through Ruby's muscles, but she managed to get her feet under her and stand. The moment she was upright, Iverson gave her a little push toward the muscadine grapevine. She obeyed, keenly aware of the gun behind her. Even if she yelled for help, no one would hear her. She doubted anyone would hear a gunshot either. The storm had driven guests into the hotel, too far from the hill to do her any good.

Iverson lifted a grapevine almost as thick as his wrist. Rain droplets dripped from the broad leaves, pattering on his shoes. He didn't appear to notice. "Inside."

Ruby suppressed an objection. The lightless space beyond seemed like a yawning mouth eager to devour her. The cold metal of a gun muzzle prodding between her shoulder blades guaranteed her reluctant obedience. She turned sideways, ducking so she'd fit through the gap in the vines. Iverson followed.

In the dim light under the vines, she couldn't see much. Roughness caught at her sleeve—bricks, she realized. A breath of air tickled her face. A darker patch of shadow lay directly in front of her. The gun poked harder. She flinched.

"Don't move," Iverson warned.

She heard him step away, but the knowledge he'd kill her if she tried to run stilled any thoughts of escape. A moment passed. Suddenly, blazing light flooded the area, searing her eyes. She almost cried out. Recalling her captor's threat, she bit her tongue and kept her eyelids tightly closed, waiting for her sight to adjust.

When she felt ready, she opened her eyes and immediately gasped. "Bee!"

Beatrice sat blindfolded and gagged, her hands and legs tied to the folding chair. The scene was illuminated by a large, powerful, box-shaped flashlight sitting on the dirt and looked nearly the same as in the video sent to Greg.

Ruby stumbled toward her friend. "Oh, Bee..." she whispered.

Iverson's tight grip on her arm halted her. "I told you not to move." He resisted her efforts to twist out of his grasp.

"Let go!" Ruby needed to make sure Beatrice was all right. The woman's head drooped, a curtain of lank hair hiding her face. Was she even breathing?

Iverson snarled, "Shut up!"

The gun barrel struck the side of her head, but the blow wasn't really hard, more of a warning than a punishment. "I'm sorry," she blurted, "it's just...please, you have to let me make sure Bee's okay." Sudden inspiration made her add, "If anything happens to Bee, Greg won't pay the ransom."

Across the small space, Beatrice lifted her head and whimpered around the gag.

"She's fine. Keep your trap shut." Iverson's cell phone rang. "Stay here." He gave her another painful jab with the gun.

Ruby cringed, anticipating a second blow. To her relief, Iverson turned and left. She waited only a few seconds before hurrying over to Beatrice. As soon as she reached the bound woman, she reached out to remove the blindfold and hesitated when a horrible thought occurred to her. "Bee, can you understand me? Just nod."

An agonizing moment passed. Finally, Beatrice nodded.

"Do you know who kidnapped you? Can you identify him to the police?"

Beatrice shook her head and made a muffled sound.

"Then I'm leaving your blindfold on," Ruby decided aloud. "We don't want Iverson thinking you can ID him or he might do something drastic. Hang on, I'll take the gag out."

A red bandana had been rolled and tied to hold in the piece of wadded cloth stuffed inside Beatrice's mouth. Ruby picked apart the knot on the bandana, removed the soggy cloth, dropped both on the ground and wiped her fingers on her pants, belatedly realizing the dark stains on the fabric were blood from the shallow cuts on her palms. "We have to be quick and quiet, Bee. He's right outside."

"Ru...by?" Beatrice croaked, her dry tongue creeping out to touch cracked lips.

"I'm here, Bee." Ruby laid the back of her hand against the woman's cheek, choking back tears. She kept her voice steady. "I'm here."

Beatrice leaned against the touch. "Katie?"

"Katie's fine. Greg came all the way from California to take care of her." Ruby kept the news of Greg's accident to herself. No need to distress Beatrice when neither of them was in a position to do anything except be upset about the situation.

She glanced at their surroundings. The space bordered by tall chimney walls had barely room to contain them. Eight feet or so above her head, a near solid mass of leafless grapevines had grown unchecked into a twisted, spiraling, Gordian knot of a canopy anchored by tendrils rooted in the crumbling mortar between the bricks. No other exit as far as she could tell. Iverson guarded the only way in and out. She returned her attention to Beatrice.

"Your ransom's going to be paid," she said under her breath, hoping Iverson wouldn't return too soon. "You're going home to Katie, I swear."

"Ruby, promise me—" Beatrice broke off to cough, a hacking sound that hurt Ruby to hear. "Promise you'll take care of Katie. Not Greg."

"Yes, absolutely," Ruby soothed, brushing Beatrice's oily hair from her forehead. "You know I love her."

Beatrice fell silent when Iverson returned.

"Get up," he commanded Ruby.

Ruby stood, feeling as though all the air had rushed out of her body. His glance had nothing human in it, just cold-blooded detachment. Her death or Beatrice's death would mean nothing to him. *Business as usual.*

"Let's go," he said shortly, gesturing at the opening.

Ruby leaned over to hug Beatrice. She only had time to put her arms around the woman and whisper, "You'll be okay," when Iverson tore her away and shoved her ahead of him, his gun digging into the small of her back.

She walked toward the weak sunlight, unsure if she'd ever see Beatrice again.

CHAPTER TWENTY-EIGHT

At Iverson's snapped command, Ruby stopped walking a few feet from the edge of the cliff. The wind blowing from the ocean tangled her hair and cut through her wet clothes, chilling her skin and raising goose bumps. She turned to face Iverson, raised her chin and stared at him, unwilling to weep or beg for mercy. The man had none.

Iverson's expression didn't change. If anything, he seemed bored. "Jump."

"No," Ruby told him, her words muffled by the hollow rushing in her ears. "You'll have to shoot me." Maybe the sound would attract attention now that the rainstorm was over. With any luck, Beatrice might be rescued. And Delilah...

She found herself thinking about Delilah in the hotel talking to Severin, doing paperwork, taking a phone conference, or any of a dozen other management tasks. A sharp pang caused her to press a fist against her chest. Delilah might never know what happened. She'd never see the beautiful woman again, touch her, kiss her. Would Delilah even remember her? Would she become a vague memory taken out now and then, fading into the past with each year until only a vague recollection of a particular summer remained? She wrenched her maudlin thoughts back to the present.

Iverson's short, dark hair had already dried, although his suit jacket remained damp from the earlier rain. "That reporter's your friend, yeah? Either you jump or I go in there and shoot her dead. Makes no difference to me. Now jump," he ordered a second time, the words ringing through the air like a slap.

Ruby tried to buy time. For what, she wasn't sure, but every second of life was precious. "I thought Lovett pulled your strings. Does he know you're trying to kill me? Does he know you're threatening to kill Beatrice?"

Iverson ignored her question. "Do I shoot your friend or not?"

"Better think about what you're doing," Ruby persisted. "What's your boss going to say if you shoot Beatrice and lose him a two-million-dollar ransom?"

"Don't you worry about Mr. Lovett." Iverson gave her a death's-head grin. "He's got everything figured out. That reporter's headed for the landfill anyway, money or no money. So quit stalling, sweetheart, or I'll shoot her first while you watch and then it'll be your turn."

All hope for herself withered. Whether she took those final steps or not, she wouldn't live long. At least this way, she might give Beatrice a chance to survive a few more hours.

Glancing down at the drop-off, Ruby realized she stood inches from death. Filled with a strange calm, she wondered if she'd feel any pain when she hit the beach far below. Would she die on impact, or break her neck or spine? Would she lie paralyzed on the sand while the tide trickled in to settle deeper and deeper on the shore until she drowned?

Low moans carried on the wind came to her ears, the same she'd heard during the picnic with Delilah. *The nuns, the lovers long dead... Will I haunt the hill after I'm gone?* An image of screeching, terrified housekeepers in black uniforms and white aprons falling over each other in their haste to get away popped into her head. From somewhere deep inside, fueled by hysteria, an irresistible wave of laughter bubbled up.

She laughed and laughed, helpless to stop. Tears poured down her cheeks and dripped into her widely stretched mouth. The liquid tasted like bitter salt—impossible to distinguish from the regret clawing at her heart. *Delilah.*

The annoyance on Iverson's face made her wheeze a breath into her spasming lungs only for the air to explode out in more laughter. "You…" she gasped, swaying on rubbery knees. "You…" She couldn't finish the sentence. Whatever she meant to say was lost.

Iverson pressed the gun's muzzle in the dip between her collarbones. "Shut up, you stupid bitch. Jump or—"

At the touch of metal, Ruby stilled, her laughter abruptly cutting off. The muzzle dug into her soft flesh, urging her to step backward. Behind her, she envisioned the crumbling edge of land, the long fall, the hungry sea. In her soul, she said goodbye to her family and to Delilah. If only they'd had more time…

Her eyes widened when Iverson grunted loudly and collapsed on his knees, his weapon slipping to the ground.

Delilah stood behind him, her face filled with a fierce, protective fury. Her gray gaze was as stark and chilling as a drawn dagger. "Get away from him," she ordered, dropping the stone she'd used on Iverson and snatching at Ruby's hand to pull her to safety.

Ruby practically fell into the woman's embrace. She couldn't speak, just make incoherent noises that sounded too much like crying. She trembled, relief warring with a jarring sense of unreality. Was she already dead? Was her dying brain trying to comfort her with a final illusion? But Delilah's arms were around her. Delilah's possessive hands in her hair. Warm breath on the side of her neck. A familiar body molded tightly to hers. Everything told her the moment was real. Delilah was here. She clutched the woman with desperate strength, almost overwhelmed by relief.

"We need to go." Delilah pulled away.

Ruby glanced over her shoulder at Iverson, still on his knees. The hair above his right ear was matted and glistening. The dark strands brushing his shirt collar left bright red bloodstains. Delilah's blow with the rock must have opened his scalp, she thought. Judging from his uncoordinated movements, he probably had a concussion.

Iverson pawed at the dropped gun and started lumbering heavily to his feet.

An electric wave of panic surged through her. "Come on!" She grabbed Delilah's arm and ran in the direction of the vine-covered chimney, only to skid off-balance and land on her hip in the grass when the woman stopped moving.

"What are you doing?" Delilah helped haul Ruby to her feet. "We should—"

"Bee's in there." Ruby gestured at the muscadine grapevine. "I can't leave her. Don't ask me to." She willed Delilah to understand. Common sense told her Iverson would likely trap them in the chimney with no way out, but she couldn't abandon Beatrice. "What if Iverson hurts Bee? Takes her somewhere else? I'd never forgive myself."

Delilah hesitated, frowning. Her gaze flicked to the grapevines, to Iverson—staggering in their direction at a slow pace, but gaining speed through sheer momentum—and back to Ruby. Her mouth thinned. "Go," she said, giving Ruby a push. "Get out of here. Detective Anderson's in the hotel. Get him."

Ruby balked. "Are you crazy? I won't leave you here."

"Red won't hurt me. I'm too valuable to Harry Lovett." Delilah shoved her shoulder. "Get out of here. Just go! I'll make sure your friend stays safe."

Delilah was right, Ruby reluctantly admitted to herself. Iverson wouldn't lay a finger on someone important to his boss, but she couldn't bear the thought of leaving Delilah behind either. She hesitated.

"Go, Ruby! I'll be fine." Delilah made a stiff little smile, an obvious attempt at reassurance that failed miserably. "We'll be fine."

So many words wanted to be spoken, but they turned to ashes in Ruby's mouth. There wasn't time to speak about her fears, her desires, her dreams. Not enough time to show how much she felt or how deep she suspected those feelings ran.

After a last look at Delilah, she turned away before she lost her courage.

Praying she wouldn't regret her decision, Ruby took off through the ruins.

A gunshot cracked behind her. Terror gripped her by the throat. Despite the fear, she couldn't look back. If she did, if she saw Delilah fallen…she deliberately blanked her mind and kept going, her side burning with the effort. Getting help was their only hope.

The flight down the hill proved gravity wasn't her friend. She stayed upright more by accident than by design as she ran, slipping and sliding her way to the bottom with her legs on fire and her heart threatening to burst. Sweat stuck her shirt to her back and stung her eyes. She hurried in an awkward jog while trying to suck in humid air around the knife in her ribs. When she finally reached the hotel, she could have wept in relief.

In the lobby, Ruby found Detective Anderson talking to several hotel employees and uniformed police officers. She hurried over and gasped out an explanation while pressing a hand against the searing pain in her side.

"Ms. Fontaine, you're bleeding," Anderson interrupted when she began repeating herself. He frowned. "Where are you hurt?"

Ruby became aware of wet warmth. She raised her hand, staring at the blood on her palm. *The gunshot*…Iverson must have been aiming for her, not Delilah. She hadn't heard a second shot, thank goodness. "Just send your people to the hill," she croaked.

Exhaustion swept over her in a black tide. She collapsed on the floor to alarmed shouting and a flurry of activity, but raised her head to see Anderson disappear with a handful of officers. Someone put pressure on her side, sending her pain roaring up the scale. Dark spots swam in and out of her vision.

Before unconsciousness took her, she imagined Delilah and Beatrice smiling, her loved ones safe and unharmed.

CHAPTER TWENTY-NINE

After being transported off Magdalena Island by boat and into a waiting ambulance at the ferry wharf, Ruby spent a few frustrating hours stuck in the Emergency Room at the hospital without a cell phone or any way to contact the hotel. Between the initial examination—Iverson's bullet had grazed her side and left minor tissue damage—and the cleaning and bandaging of her wound, she fretted about Delilah and Beatrice until her blood pressure soared, earning her a scolding from a nurse.

When the doctor finally released her, Ruby's anxiety continued to simmer like a pot of sugar syrup on the verge of boiling over.

The uniformed police officer assigned to take her home just stared in stoic silence while she peppered him with questions. When she ran out of things to ask, he put her in the backseat of a patrol car and drove to the pharmacy to fill her prescriptions for antibiotics and pain medication. Later at her apartment, he opened his mouth for the first time to say she should stay put until Detective Anderson contacted her.

Fat chance. As soon as the officer left, she sat on the living room sofa and called the hotel, but neither Delilah nor Severin were available to talk. The front desk clerk politely refused to answer her questions, transferring her instead to the Public Relations Department. She hung up after listening to a prerecorded message containing no real information and a lot of corporate double-speak. A call to Mike Michelson at the *Central Ledger* went to voice mail. Out of other options, she dialed Anderson's office number and left a message.

Ruby pressed the heels of her palms into her eyes and tried to think. What if she drove to the police station? She grimaced, recalling her truck was parked in the municipal garage at the boardwalk. A taxi? Sure, but she doubted anyone at the station, including Anderson, would give her the time of day if she dropped by.

She picked up the remote and turned on the television to find the local news running an update on Beatrice's kidnapping. According to the news anchor, Beatrice had been found by the police on Magdalena Island and taken to the hospital on the mainland, where her condition was listed as serious but stable. Red Iverson, the suspected kidnapper, had been arrested and taken to the hospital for treatment, no details given. Nothing about Delilah, which could be good or bad. She tossed the remote on the coffee table.

The doorbell rang.

Ruby dragged herself off the sofa, went to the door and opened it, hoping to find Anderson. Instead, Delilah stood in the corridor.

For the longest moment, Ruby couldn't move or speak.

Delilah looked disheveled, unlike her usual polished self. She'd scraped her chestnut hair into a ponytail, leaving wispy curls framing her pale face. Her pantyhose were laddered and her pumps muddy. The left sleeve of her amethyst dress was ripped at the shoulder. Her mascara and eyeliner were smeared, but Ruby had never seen anyone more beautiful.

"Oh!" Her eyes wet with relief, Ruby lunged forward and wrapped her arms around Delilah, holding on with every bit of strength in her body. "You're okay," she murmured into the woman's neck.

"I'm a little battered, but I'm fine." Delilah kissed Ruby's forehead, pressing her lips hard to the spot as though she wanted to permanently brand the skin with her touch. "Nobody would tell me anything and when I tried your number, my call went to voice mail."

Ruby's face went hot when she considered how she'd burned up the telephone lines desperately seeking news. She took Delilah's hands and led her into the apartment to the living room. Were it possible, she'd crawl into Delilah's lap and wear the woman like a coat, but she had to content herself with sitting together on the sofa so closely, their thighs touched. "What happened with Iverson?"

"First things first. How are you?" Delilah's gaze searched Ruby's face. A worry line deepened between her brows. "I heard the gunshot, but you kept running."

"I didn't know I'd been hurt until I got to the hotel. The bullet grazed my side, nothing serious," Ruby explained hurriedly when Delilah swore and reached for her, "and the doctor in the ER said I didn't even need stitches."

Delilah yanked up Ruby's shirt and stared wide-eyed at the white bandage taped to her side. "Christ! You could've been killed."

Ruby shook her head. "You knocked Iverson cross-eyed with that rock. I doubt he could've hit me at point-blank range. He got lucky, that's all, and I'm not really hurt." She pulled down her shirt and settled back against Delilah, snuggling into the curve of the woman's arm. "Now tell me what happened after I went to get help."

"Red couldn't see very well. Your 'cross-eyed' comment really hit the mark. I'm surprised he didn't shoot himself in the foot. I just wish I'd hit him a bit harder."

"Maybe next time."

Delilah glared. "Next time?"

Ruby giggled.

"He threatened me, but I reminded him Lovett wouldn't be very happy if I died," Delilah went on. "After he chewed on that fact a while, he started to go to the chimney where he'd stashed Ms. Brooks. I distracted him because I knew when the police showed up, he'd be cornered in there and we know how cornered rats panic." She fingered the tear in her sleeve. "He didn't take kindly to my interference."

"Did he hit you?" Ruby bolted upright, ready to run to the kitchen for ice or, alternatively, to the police station to fillet Iverson with her Tuscan chocolate knife.

"He smacked me around, but I'm a big girl. I can hold my own." Delilah made a savage grin. "Besides, every slap added to the criminal charges. Just for the kidnapping, he's looking at a life sentence in Hays State Prison."

Slowly, Ruby subsided to the temptation of Delilah's embrace, though she still wanted to gut Iverson. "Go ahead, tell me the rest."

"Anderson and his officers finally showed up and arrested Iverson, then brought out Beatrice Brooks. She's in pretty rough shape, but I overheard at the police station that the doctors expect her to make a full recovery." Delilah paused. "Do you recall the alleged ghost nuns on the hill? All the trouble I've been having with the hotel staff?"

"I heard the moans today too, and in broad daylight," Ruby confessed.

"Beatrice was responsible for the noises everyone heard. Apparently, the old chimney has weird acoustics." Delilah chuckled.

Ruby felt a little disappointed. She liked the tragic story of the nuns burned at the stake as punishment for their love and doomed to haunt the ruined cloister, whether or not the events actually happened. "Now will you tell me what's going on between you and Councilman Lovett?" she asked, changing the subject. "You've never given me a straight answer and I think at this point I have some right to know."

Delilah sighed. "I suppose since he's been arrested for conspiracy in the kidnapping of Beatrice Brooks, I can tell you the truth."

"About time."

"Do you want to hear the story or not?"

Ruby nodded.

"Harry Lovett is in bed with a construction company owned by a couple of mobsters, Frank Marion and Eugene Burley," Delilah said in the iciest tone Ruby had ever heard. "The construction company funds illegal moonshine smuggling. The alcohol is produced on a few of the other islands in the barrier chain and shipped by boat to the mainland. Lovett wanted to use Magdalena Island as a central clearinghouse for the operation. To that end, he needed to build a new pathway up the cliff from the beach behind the hill where his boats will land. He had enough votes on the city council to get the protected status lifted on the bird and turtle sanctuaries, but unless our company agreed to give him permission to extend his pathway onto our property, specifically to the marina, his plan couldn't proceed." Her expression turned smug. "The head office left the final decision to me."

"Why'd he pick Magdalena Island? Wouldn't an unoccupied island be better?"

"The waters off the coast are patrolled by the police, so the shorter the distance the smugglers need to go, the less chance they'll be caught. Magdalena Island is ideally situated, and as a bonus, the hotel ferry works a regular schedule to the mainland day and night. The mayor and the Summerland police chief don't want rich tourists hassled by official boarding parties searching for contraband, so the ferry isn't searched. If Lovett moved his product using the ferry, he and his partners would be sitting pretty."

Ruby touched Delilah's wrist where Lovett had once left a bruise on the delicate skin. "You've been refusing Lovett, which is why he's so angry with you."

"Yes." Delilah's fingers sought the same spot. Judging from her cold fury, she, too, recalled the incident. "Until I signed the paperwork, he couldn't deliver what he promised to Burley and Marion. His partners were putting pressure on him and in turn, he put pressure on me. Since he really was a VIP customer, I had to stomach his abuse and threats. I couldn't have him thrown out of the hotel or my bosses would've had my head."

"Why didn't you say anything to me?" Ruby asked, a little hurt. She'd given Delilah plenty of opportunities to tell her what was going on.

"Not because I didn't learn to trust you," Delilah replied quickly enough to salve Ruby's feelings, "but Lovett was getting desperate, which made him more dangerous. I didn't put it past him to hurt you to get to me. And to complicate matters, the reporter I contacted with the story disappeared."

The penny dropped after a moment. "You knew?" Ruby yelped. "You knew Lovett had Bee kidnapped?"

Delilah made a negative gesture. "No, I knew Beatrice Brooks promised to investigate the story and disappeared one day. It wasn't until you told me she'd been seen with Red Iverson that I began to suspect Lovett, but I had no evidence and I wasn't sure. For all I knew, Ms. Brooks was one of his allies."

"Never," Ruby said indignantly. "Bee would never stoop so low."

"I didn't really know her well. We'd only talked on the phone. We were supposed to meet, but she didn't show."

"Is that why you were mad that day in the parking garage?"

"That's right, you were there." A rosy blush stained Delilah's cheeks. "I never apologized for swearing at you."

"You owe my swear jar at least five dollars." At Delilah's puzzled look, Ruby added, "I'll show you later. Tell me why you were upset."

"I'd taken a big chance agreeing to meet Ms. Brooks in public. I went to the garage early, afraid the location might be a trap. Iverson turned up—he'd been following me—and made threats courtesy of his boss. When Ms. Brooks didn't make our appointment, I assumed the worst and thought I'd been a fool. Then you were in the garage giving me attitude and I lost my temper. I'm sorry."

"We both made assumptions. I'm glad we worked things out." Ruby snuggled into Delilah's side. She let a few moments pass in contented silence before she asked, "Why did Lovett kidnap Bee and ask for ransom? He went to an awful lot of trouble and ran a terrible risk of being caught. Does he have a lot of debts or something?"

"If I had to guess, I'd say Lovett probably intended to keep Ms. Brooks under wraps a couple of days, only until he could bully me into approving his construction plan, but I wouldn't cooperate and more time passed while he tried to force me. I doubt he had anything to do with the ransom demand. That boneheaded scheme sounds like Iverson. Lovett just wanted to prevent a damaging story from publication for as long as possible. I'm sure he intended to release Ms. Brooks once he had what he wanted from me."

"Lovett's as much an idiot as his goon," Ruby declared. "Did he think Bee wouldn't go to the police about her kidnapping the minute she was free?"

Delilah shrugged a shoulder. "If Iverson threatened her daughter, would Ms. Brooks still want to take her story to the police? It's the sort of thing Lovett excels at—figuring out a person's weak points and taking advantage. He's been playing dirty politics for years."

Ruby knew Delilah was right. Beatrice wouldn't do anything to endanger Kaitlyn.

"And now Ms. Brooks is safe and she'll be okay," Delilah concluded. "Happy?"

"Once I can visit her, yes." Ruby smiled.

They sat in silence for several more minutes while Ruby attempted to work up the courage to tell Delilah how she felt.

"I can't do this anymore," Delilah abruptly announced.

Ruby's stomach sank. She sat up, bracing herself for the painful words she knew were coming. Building a new relationship with Delilah had taken time and effort on both their parts, but she'd believed they were on the way to becoming more serious than the occasional date and sexual encounter. *Seems Delilah doesn't feel the same.* She hunched her shoulders, anticipating the blow. In her experience, breakups made no mark on the body, but left the heart shattered. Losing Delilah would be like losing the ability to breathe.

"I gave a statement at the police station and I'll have to talk to the District Attorney later. That's what I *need* to do," Delilah said, shifting to face her. "But Ruby...oh, sweetheart, what I really *want* to do is this..." She moved, bringing their lips together.

Ruby's surprised grunt was muffled by the warm mouth on hers. Delilah's hands slid into her hair, fingers tangling the pink strands while an urgent tongue pressed inside to claim her. Every light touch, every teasing stroke was perfect. She fell headlong into the kiss, addicted to the soft deliciousness of Delilah's mouth.

Not a breakup. Something else. Something more.

At last, Delilah gentled the kiss. The hands in Ruby's hair slid around to cup her face with unexpected tenderness. "Stay with me tonight?" She appeared somewhat nervous but determined. "Or you could stay with me for good."

Ruby smiled and leaned forward to give Delilah her answer in another kiss.

Life was sweet, but love was sweeter.

Bella Books, Inc.

Women. Books. Even Better Together.

P.O. Box 10543
Tallahassee, FL 32302

Phone: 800-729-4992
www.bellabooks.com